Soulvision

Seeing the end is only the beginning

H.Paine

instant
apostle

First published in Great Britain in 2017.

Instant Apostle

The Barn

1 Watford House Lane

Watford

Herts

WD17 1BJ

British Library Cataloguing-in-Publication Data

A catalogue record for this book is available from the British Library.

This book and all other Instant Apostle books are available from
Instant Apostle:

Website: www.instantapostle.com

E-mail: info@instantapostle.com

ISBN 978-1-909728-62-2

Printed in Great Britain

Chapter 1

Their shoulders barely touched but the collision knocked the grey-cloaked Unseen off balance.

'Hey, careful!' Silas cried, as the figure stumbled against the wall. 'Are you all right?' He proffered a steadying hand, but with a shake of the head the Unseen mutely cowered away, glancing up at the glinting sphere protruding from the street corner above them.

'It was an accident,' Silas said. 'Neither of us was looking where we were going. It's as much my fault as yours. You didn't attack me.' He gave an apologetic half-laugh. 'I'm sure the Citizen Safety Monitor can tell the difference.' He leaned back to look up into the monitor. 'I take full responsibility. I wasn't paying attention. No harm done.' He grinned, to reinforce his point, then, leaning forward, he spoke under his breath. 'Before you go, do you know about any recently classified Unseen? They would have been moved here last summer, from a place called the Community?'

A sound somewhere between a groan and a curse escaped from beneath the grey hood as the Unseen pushed away from the wall, sidestepped around Silas and, with a peculiar lurching gait, hurried away through the dark streets.

'OK, you're in a rush. I get it,' Silas muttered.

Every time he saw an Unseen he hoped it was someone from the Community and that they might just recognise him. After all, 200 new Unseen couldn't simply disappear; they must have been relocated somewhere.

Glancing once more at the monitor, he gave another 'I'm fine' smile before straightening his shoulders and striding away.

At least the encounter had done one useful thing. It had interrupted the familiar spiral of melancholy produced by another fruitless visit to Zoe's old house. He should probably stop going there. Nana's message had been clear: 'Zoe needs time away from clinic and away from Prima. She will return when she has fully recovered.'

Silas had understood – if Zoe needed space to grieve and to heal then he wouldn't interfere – but that had been six months ago. What if she no longer wanted to return? Perhaps she couldn't bear to be reminded of the Community, of what they had found there... and of what they had lost.

He looked around to get his bearings, trying to recall the meandering route that had led him to this part of the city.

Most of the surrounding houses were abandoned, and wild tangles of shrubs and weeds spilled from the property boundaries to swallow the pavement. The few remaining residents tried to enforce order on their small patch of land, but they were losing the battle. Soon this street would be added to Prima's ever-growing Uninhabited district.

Somewhere new for me to explore properly tomorrow, he thought, finally shaking off the worst of his lingering gloom. Perhaps after clinic. Maybe Kesiah will want to come.

That reminded him. It was getting late and Kes had said she would drop by for an early morning pre-clinic workout. She had made it her mission to keep him on target and she wouldn't cut him any slack for being tired.

As he turned to retrace his steps, something caught his eye. He peered through the tangled foliage of an overgrown garden. Was that flashes of light from a sunstorer?

It must be another Unseen. He looked over his shoulder. The street corner with its watchful Citizen Safety Monitor was now some distance away, so if he were to ask about the Community, perhaps he would get an answer.

He took another step before realising his mistake. It wasn't a light glinting in the dark. Something white was reflecting the feeble night lamps... something bright white. It was a uniform.

Instinctively, he ducked into the shelter of the tangle undergrowth. He knew he had no reason to hide, but the only people who wore such blinding white uniforms were the Health Advisors, and of all the different authorities, he trusted *them* the least.

It had been the Health Advisors who had sought out and destroyed the Community, taking every man, woman and child for classification. And one Advisor had followed Flawless Leader Helen Steele's orders to do the unthinkable and the unforgivable: Taylor Price. Once she had been Vitality Clinic's Gold Standard, now she was Helen Steele's favourite, and it had been Taylor who had killed Jono.

Keeping low to conceal his own pale blue Vitality uniform, he crawled under the shelter of a prickly conifer. The thick winter fabric protected his back against the worst of the sharp pine needles. Peering upwards between the branches, he could make out four Health Advisors standing in a tight semicircle outside the neighbouring property.

They all seemed tense as they peered into the surrounding gloom. The nearest Advisor kept his hand resting on the solid black disruptor that hung at his side, and his thumb hovered nervously over the blue 'target acquired' button.

They hadn't noticed Silas, and he thought it best to stay hidden. It was unusual for a Seen to be out at night, and he didn't want to be questioned. They would undoubtedly check the Safety Monitors, and that could only mean trouble for the Unseen he had bumped into.

'Wait. Where are you taking him?' A woman's shrill voice spilled from the house, and Silas crouched even lower, the flat boughs suddenly seeming an inadequate shield.

With his face at ground level, he could now only see feet. There were four pairs of spotless white boots of the Health Advisors, and then, drifting into Silas' eye line, the grey edge of an Unseen covering, grazing the path and completely concealing the feet underneath it. Two more pairs of white boots followed

l, and, forming a six-strong escort, the Health
n to lead the Unseen away.

answer me, where are you taking him?' the woman
out in distress. A different pair of feet emerged from the
house. Shoeless, bare and totally misshapen, the toes twisted
over one another into a swollen jumble of skin and nails. Two
puffy, discoloured lumps of purple flesh hobbling forward.

A single pair of white boots halted and turned as the others
moved away.

'Why are you uncovered? Go inside immediately!'

The woman shuffled back but didn't fully retreat. 'Why
won't you tell me where you are taking him?'

'You do not have permission to speak!' Outraged by the
woman's inappropriate behaviour, the Health Advisor moved
closer to the woman.

'No! I'm going in. I'm sorry!' The terror in her voice caused
Silas to lift his head and risk glancing up through the branches.
Fear gripped him as the Health Advisor unclipped the disruptor
from his belt.

With a dismayed cry, the woman stumbled and fell, hitting
the ground with a sickening thud. Whimpering, she curled into
a foetal position, drawing her arms over her head.

Silas tensed, digging his fingers into the earth, ready to rush
at the Advisor the moment he raised the weapon.

As the woman lay trembling on the ground, the Advisor
stepped closer. 'You Unseen are a waste of resources. I'd be
doing you a favour by putting you out of your misery,' he
growled, stepping around her to get to the house. He returned
to drop a grey swathe of fabric over her cowering form.

'There,' he said, with an unpleasant laugh. 'Now that you
have your covering, you are permitted to remain outside.'

His booted footsteps faded into the night, and Silas slowly
exhaled. Perhaps the Health Advisor had been making an empty
threat, but the readiness with which he had reached for his
disruptor was worrying.

With a muffled groan, the woman under the grey covering began to move.

Squeezing through the last clawing branches of his shelter, Silas emerged from his hiding place and, crouching down, gently uncovered her face.

She was younger than he had expected, and amidst a full head of brown hair there were only a few strands of glinting grey to reflect the dim night lamps. Her arms remained shielding her face, but as the fabric moved she peered warily past her bent wrists to regard him with frightened pale blue eyes.

'Let me help you,' Silas whispered.

She looked him up and down. 'You're a Seen,' she murmured back, her voice weakened by pain and fear.

'The overgrowth blocks the view of the monitor,' he said, uncomfortably aware of his Seen status. 'My name's Silas.'

She managed a feeble smile and reached out with a warped hand, 'And I'm Mags.'

Every movement seemed agonising, and she struggled to suppress her cries as Silas helped her to stand.

'Just through there,' she gasped. Leaning heavily on him, she managed to get through the front door into a small, sparsely furnished room. A sleek, top-of-the-range Biocubicle filled one corner.

'It's new,' Mags said, following his gaze.

'Do you need the HE-LP?' Silas asked, seeing a modified Health Emergency key on the side of the machine.

'No!' She looked alarmed and pointed to a chair instead. 'Just help me to sit, and then could you get me some water? I do not want any more Health Authorities getting involved.' Her voice grew stronger as the shock of her encounter wore off.

Silas filled a glass from the dispenser and handed it to Mags. She took it carefully, gripping the glass between her twisted wrists, rather than with her fingers.

'Thank you,' she murmured.

'You don't need to thank me,' Silas responded. 'I'm just glad you weren't harmed. The way that Advisor spoke to you… and the disruptor! What did they want with you and the other Unseen? Had you missed an assessment?' he asked, glancing at the shiny new Biocubicle.

'Far from it. We follow the recommendations and, thanks to the Flawless Leader, we have our own personal cubicle so it's even easier to do our bit for Future Health. But tonight the Biocubicle scanned for something new. My brother's results showed a problem. The Health Advisor said it was a contagion… they insisted on taking him away.'

Silas frowned. 'What sort of contagion? Was your brother sick?'

'No, he wasn't ill.' She shook her head. 'I mean, we both have the same condition.' She held out her twisted hands for inspection. 'But his is further progressed than mine.'

'So what did the Biocubicle find, then?' Silas asked, trying not to imagine how grotesque Mags' brother's hands and feet must be.

A knock at the door interrupted them. Silas looked fearfully at Mags. Perhaps they had returned for her.

'Don't worry,' she said with a grim smile. 'Health Advisors don't knock. Come in!'

With a rustle of fabric, two cloaked Unseen entered, flinging back their hoods as they stepped over the threshold. The first was an old woman with dark-brown skin and iron-grey hair, and behind her was a young, pale-faced man who looked a similar age to Silas.

'Mags, what's wrong? Derry told me that the Health Advisors were here. I came as quickly as I could.' The older Unseen barely noticed Silas as she rushed to Mags' side. However, the man lingered in the doorway and eyed him suspiciously.

'Oh, Felesa,' sobbed Mags when she saw her friend, 'the Biocubicle found a problem. They came and took Torin away.'

As Mags began to recount what had happened, the Unseen man took a limping step closer to Silas, and it occurred to him that this was the Unseen he had collided with at the street corner.

"oo are yoo? Wha' yoo wan'?' His mouth moved awkwardly, and it was as if words and sounds were trapped behind his stiff, puckered lips. His eyes communicated volumes though, and Silas could almost feel the open hostility searing through him. How was he going to make this Unseen understand that he may be a Seen but he wasn't like the Advisors?

'I was just passing,' Silas explained. 'We bumped into each other on the street... before...' The Unseen man continued to glower at him. 'I saw your friend Mags when the Advisors came. I helped her into the house. I'm Silas.'

'Thileth?' A dribble of saliva fell out of the crooked mouth and the man narrowed his eyes in frustration as if Silas had deliberately given him a difficult name to pronounce, 'yoo oh!'

Silas looked at him in confusion. He couldn't understand what this Unseen was saying.

'Derry,' Mags intervened, 'he doesn't need to go. He helped me,' she reprimanded gently. 'Silas, please excuse Derry. It's almost unheard of for someone like you to help someone like us.'

'It's not a problem,' Silas said, feeling embarrassed by her gratitude and Derry's steely glare. 'It's the least I could do.'

Mags began to stand, but her face paled and a hiss of pain escaped through her gritted teeth.

'Are you very hurt?' Felesa asked with concern.

'It's my joints...' she grimaced.

'Maybe you should stay here tonight. Don't go to work. I'll explain to the supervisor. Let me help you upstairs.'

Mags looked like she wanted to disagree, but as another movement caused her to groan in agony, she relented.

'I had better go home. My dad will be expecting me,' Silas said. It wasn't the truth: his father paid very little attention to his whereabouts. He just felt nervous to be left alone with Derry.

'Goodbye, Silas,' Mags smiled. Derry, however, gave Silas a suspicious stare as he edged past him. His look was far more expressive than his incoherent speech, and it clearly meant, 'Go, Seen, and do not come back!'

Chapter 2

It was only as he neared home he remembered that he had wanted to ask about the Community. He groaned inwardly. That would have been the perfect opportunity. Admittedly, Derry may not have been much help, but he could at least have asked Mags.

I'll go tomorrow evening, he thought. I could check how Mags is, and find out if she has heard about her brother. Hopefully Derry won't be there.

The faint sound of a HE-LP Transport caused him to look up. He could make out a dark shape high in the sky, and then his eye was drawn to another distant transport. Yet another flew a bit closer to the ground, and the familiar whine of the flight system sent a shiver down Silas' spine.

There seems to be a lot of traffic out tonight, he mused. Then a more alarming thought occurred to him. Mags had not fully explained the nature of her brother's contagion.

Silas tried to recall his Biology lesson. They'd covered contagious illness a few seasons back. He racked his brains to remember some of the facts. Words such as 'epidemic' and 'pandemic' sprung to mind, along with some frightening death statistics.

What if this contagion was something like that? What if he had caught an illness from going into that Unseen house? What if he had been infected?

He started running, suddenly desperate to get to his own Biocubicle. Why had he got involved with that Unseen? If only he had stayed hidden. Derry and Felesa had been moments away. Mags hadn't really needed him.

'Muscle... 40 per cent. Fat... 9 per cent. Blood pressure... 123 over 59. Heart rate... 64 beats per minute. Weight... 57 kilograms.' The machine went through its recitation of numbers and measurements as the criss-crossing red beams assessed his body.

Peering intently in the reflective Biocubicle wall, Silas performed an assessment of his own, inspecting his face, arms and chest, carefully looking for rashes or other marks of disease. He couldn't see anything unusual, just the same dark hair, pale skin and wiry body.

As the Biocubicle was completing its cycle, Silas spoke: 'Blood test.' His voice wobbled a little. He was scared. Even on the short run home he had seen at least ten more Health Emergency Transports.

'You are not due a blood test,' the Biocubicle responded.

'Override command. Silas Corelle. Confirm routine blood test; add infection screen.'

A small compartment opened in the stainless steel wall and he placed his hand inside, resting his palm on the anaesthetic pad.

Seconds later the machine chirruped, 'Test complete. Await results.' Silas withdrew his hand. He could barely make out the tiny pinpricks where the Biocubicle had taken blood.

'Silas?' His father's voice accompanied a knock at the door.

'Come in,' he said, hurriedly pulling on a black vest and shorts.

'You're home... good.' His father sounded worried as he hesitantly stepped into Silas' room.

They stared at each other for an uncomfortable moment.

'What's the matter?' Silas asked.

His father pursed his lips and glanced towards Silas' window and the impenetrable darkness beyond. He looked exhausted. 'There's been an outbreak of some kind among the Unseen,' he said, rubbing his eyes. 'The Flawless Leader has declared a national emergency. There's an update in ten minutes.'

Heat flooded Silas' face. 'An outbreak? Of what?' His voice sounded strained as he asked the question that he already knew the answer to.

'An infection.' His father frowned. 'It seems to be limited to the Unseen at the moment. That's all anyone knows. But until I find out more, I want you home by sunset. And make sure Kesiah is safe indoors too. Both of you are to stay far away from any Unseen. Do you understand?'

Silas nodded mutely, knowing that he would have to say something. He had already been exposed. By simply going near Mags, Silas had put them all at risk.

'Dad…' he began, but at that moment the Biocubicle burbled into life. 'Silas, your blood test results are ready.'

Silas looked at his father, whose frown deepened as the Biocubicle continued. 'Normal range for all levels. Retest set for four months. Infection screen negative.'

'I didn't know you were due a blood test?' Anton Corelle said, when the machine had finished. 'I thought we all tested at the same time.'

'Oh?' Silas said, trying to sound casual, but inside he was shouting with relief. He was fine! He wasn't sick. 'I think I got out of sync when I went away last season-break.'

Silas hated lying. He knew from his time in the Community and use of Soulsight that lies fed the dark, shadowy, fear-filled parts of the soul. He had promised himself that he would only ever tell the truth. However, his father would ground him for the rest of his time at clinic if he knew how close Silas had come to getting ill.

'What made you add an infection screen?' Anton asked suspiciously.

Silas looked out of the window to avoid his father's searching gaze and spotted the lights of another HE-LP transport high in the sky.

'Maybe it was all the transports. They made me feel nervous,' he said eventually, which seemed to partially satisfy his father.

'I'll see you downstairs for the update, then,' he said, giving Silas one last long look before leaving the room.

For the first time that Silas could remember, the three of them stood together in the Image room. It was such an unusual occurrence. His father was usually at work; Marc had joined their father at Bio-health and seemed equally as busy, and Silas would rather be at Kesiah's or at the tree house than endure the confines of his empty home.

A repeat of last month's Prima City celebration marathon filled the room, and runners were streaming past him. It was on low resolution so the faces were indistinct, but Silas had seen it before. Helen Steele led the race, flanked by the Viva party senior officials. Each of them was symbolically holding a replica of the Viva emblem, the golden blazing torch.

Further back, his father and Marc were proudly leading the Bio-health team. Vitality, as the top clinic, wasn't far behind, and Kesiah, as Female Gold Standard, was heading up the students. Silas knew he was somewhere among the crowd of jostling blue uniforms, but he had looked at the parade from all angles and any view of him always seemed to be blocked by another, taller runner.

The brightly burning flames of the Viva party emblem shone briefly into the room, interrupting the marathon, which rapidly faded away.

'Increase resolution and add sound,' Anton instructed.

The logo disappeared and was replaced by a projection of the Flawless Leader. She walked steadily towards them, scanned the room and made eye contact with each of them before starting to speak.

Silas used to love how special it felt when the Flawless Leader made a personal address. She always made it seem as if the message was for you only. He glanced at his father, who was smiling at the image of Helen Steele.

Her beautiful face was unusually serious, and Silas resisted the urge to feel concerned. He had seen her – the real her – last season-break. His view of her may have been exaggerated by a Soulsight overdose, but Helen Steele's true heart had been shown for what it was: a dark, rotten and foul place. Lies, hate and fear had twisted her and made her into something monstrous.

As she spoke, he forced himself to look past the healthy glowing brown skin and the perfect physique and tried to imagine that he was seeing her with Soulsight.

'Friends, there is no need to be concerned,' she began. That's probably a lie, Silas thought, trying to ignore the desire to trust her. I guess it's time to start worrying.

'I will not let any harm come to you,' she continued, taking another step closer and reaching forward with her hands as if the mere image of her could offer them protection. 'However, I have to confirm that the reports regarding a contagious disease are true.'

Silas raised his eyebrows at her use of the word 'true'. If she only spoke in lies, did that mean a disease wasn't true at all? However, he had seen Mags' brother being escorted away, and the night sky still buzzed with Health transports. There must be some truth in what she was saying.

'Health Emergency-Life Preservation officials describe the illness as targeting fragile genes. Only Unseen citizens are at risk of infection. The new Biocubicle models are able to detect even pre-symptomatic carriage of what the HE-LP have named "Fragile Gene Specific Virus", or "FGSV", and newly diagnosed individuals are being transferred to a special quarantine facility. Health Advisors are already working alongside the HE-LP to ensure that the utmost care is taken of our Unseen brothers and sisters.'

Silas' expression turned grim as he thought of the 'utmost care' that Mags and her brother had received at the hands of the Advisors.

'Even though FGSV infection is impossible among the Seen, for your safety a temporary curfew has been initiated. There will be a 30-minute buffer zone at sunset and sunrise, ensuring ample time for Seen citizens to be indoors and to avoid any Seen–Unseen contact. This will guarantee that the contagion will remain contained and be more quickly eradicated. Rest assured, we will be working ceaselessly to discover a cure, and until a treatment is found, Biocubicle scans will be performed twice daily.'

Silas had heard enough. He left the room as the Flawless Leader was wrapping up her address with a series of clichéd statements about staying calm and pulling together as a nation.

He returned to his room and lay on his bed, watching through the window as the distant lights of the transports darted overhead like shooting stars. The contagion must be spreading like wildfire.

'Please present yourself for assessment.' The Biocubicle burbled to life, making him jump.

'I've just had one,' Silas complained, not moving from his bed. 'I'm sleeping now.'

'Government recommendations are in force. A new regime is effective immediately. Please present yourself for assessment,' the Biocubicle persisted.

'Check your data bank. I had an assessment less than an hour ago,' he argued, then sighed and stood up anyway. There was no point trying to persuade a machine to see reason, and the Biocubicle wouldn't shut up until he had been assessed.

He scowled at the silver box as the door gently hissed closed. 'Muscle...' the cubicle began.

Chapter 3

Silas washed his carboflakes down with another mouthful of protein shake and wandered, bleary-eyed, into the health suite.

He hadn't slept well. The whine of overhead transports had persisted through the night, and then, when he had finally managed to drift off, his dreams had been plagued with visions of his hands and feet becoming as twisted as Mags'.

A flash of movement and a blur of pale blue was his only warning of an ambush as a figure sprang from behind the weights machine to launch itself onto his back. He staggered sideways and dropped the remains of his drink across the dark, spongy floor.

'Kesiah!' Silas shouted, immediately recognising his attacker. 'What are you doing? Get off! Did Marc let you in?' He tried to loosen her grip as she giggled and held on tighter. 'Let go!' he insisted grumpily. 'You are too heavy.'

She laughed in delight at his exasperation. 'Your dad let me in, and no, I won't let go,' she declared. 'You'll have to carry me all morning. That can be your workout.'

He caught sight of their reflection in the mirrored wall. Her slender arms and legs were wrapped tightly around his chest and waist, like a long-limbed baby monkey around its mother.

'You... have... too... much... energy,' he grunted, punctuating each word with sharp pinches to her legs, making her squeal and wriggle. Then, reaching behind his back, he started jabbing her sides, until weakened by laughter she abruptly relinquished her hold and fell to the floor. Now it was Silas' turn to laugh as Kesiah landed in the wet mess of spilled shake. She howled with disgust and jumped to her feet.

'You horrible boy!' She tried to wipe the worst of the brown sloppy liquid off her pale uniform and went to smear it on Silas instead, but he dodged her slimy outstretched hands. 'What am I going to do about my clothes?' She chased after him and just managed to spread a handful down his arm.

'You brought it on yourself, you pest.' Silas was still laughing at her as he pointed the way upstairs. 'Borrow some of my stuff while the house cleans your uniform.'

Moments later she was back in the health suite wearing a pair of his red shorts and a clashing green top.

'Cute!' Silas said to irritate her a bit more. 'Baggy...'

She pulled a face and threw the soiled uniform at his head. 'Catch.'

Raising a hand, he easily intercepted the sticky clothes. 'House, clean the floor in the health suite, and fast clean a winter Vitality uniform.'

'Yes, Silas,' the house acknowledged as he deposited the clothing into a laundry chute.

'It had better be ready in time,' Kes grumbled. 'I am not going to clinic in this.'

He chuckled at her grumpy expression. 'It'll be ready.'

They ran on the treadmills while the sanitiser washed and dried the floor.

'Did you see Helen Steele on the update?' Kes asked, her good humour returning as they kept pace with each other. 'What do you think about this virus? Will it spread to us?'

Silas shrugged. 'I don't know what to think. You know how I feel about her,' he said, dropping his voice to a whisper in case his father was still around. Recently he had caused a huge row when he had suggested that the Flawless Leader may not be as perfect as she looked. Furious at Silas, his father had defended her. 'Without Helen Steele, the Biocubicle upgrades would never have happened. Her Future Health project is the mark of a truly visionary leader.'

Silas had tried to argue. 'But Dad, if that's true, then why are there Health Advisors everywhere, carrying disruptors? How do you *know* you can trust her?' He'd had been sent to his room. End of argument. He was still toying with the idea of using the last few powdered flecks of Soulsight to show his father the truth about the Flawless Leader.

'And how will you cope with a curfew?' Kesiah said sympathetically. 'No sneaking out to check on your imaginary girlfriend and your favourite empty building, or hanging out in the tree house,' she added.

'Zoe's not my girlfriend,' he said automatically, then frowned as he caught sight of Kesiah's teasing expression. 'And she's not imaginary. I honestly wish I hadn't told you about her.'

Kesiah chuckled and winked. 'Your many secrets are safe with me. Don't worry.'

Silas blushed and pushed the speed up on his treadmill. Perhaps he had been too open, but then, who else was he going to talk to? Certainly not his father, and his relationship with his brother was far too strained. There had been a short and precious time after Marc's expulsion from the Health Advisor squad when they had seemed to connect, to understand one another, but that was long past. Marc kept himself busy, and Silas wondered if he was trying to forget his brief stint as an Advisor.

For Silas there had been no one else but Kesiah.

He had checked her out with Soulsight first, and had watched with interest as her true nature was revealed. Her soul burned with an intense transparency. It was like looking into a deep pool of clean water. Open, whole, straightforward and, most of all, safe. And so, over time he had told her everything.

He had started by describing Zoe and how special she was. That had led on to explaining about Soulsight, and they chewed on fragments of the crisp green leaf strands that he had kept hidden under his summer uniform. Kesiah's clear, pure heart drew him from the dark and lonely place that his own soul had drifted to, and he had finally felt able to grieve.

'But there is something odd about this whole contagion thing, isn't there?' Kes mused, drawing Silas' attention back to her. 'How can a disease spread only among the Unseen?'

'Exactly.' Silas looked thoughtful. 'What does this contagious disease do to them, anyway? I met this woman called Mags yesterday. She was an Unseen. It was after I had been out to…'

'Zoe's house?' Kesiah rolled her eyes. 'On the same night that a terrible contagion is announced and strict segregation enforced, Silas is hanging out with the Unseen.'

'I did an infection screen, and the Biocubicle gave me the all-clear,' he said sheepishly.

'You can do a hill as punishment,' Kesiah said with a mock scowl, and leaned over to press a button on his machine. The treadmill added a positive gradient and Silas concentrated on his running.

'So what did this "Mags" have to say?' Kesiah asked, adjusting her machine to match his.

Silas was breathing much faster now. 'Her brother was… found to have the contagion. He was taken… but he wasn't ill.'

'Are you sure?' Kesiah asked, also breathing a little more heavily. 'That's weird.'

'I'm sure…' Silas panted. The gradient flattened out as the treadmill reached the crest of the 'hill'.

'Again,' Kesiah commanded, and forced the running machine to take Silas up another incline. He was struggling to maintain the pace set for him as Kesiah effortlessly bounded onwards.

'Silas, the uniform is ready,' the house chimed.

'Great!' Kesiah slowed her treadmill. 'I'm going to get showered and changed. This *look*,' she pirouetted in Silas' baggy clothes, 'just isn't my style.'

'Sure,' Silas laughed breathlessly as she left the room, then, once he was sure she had gone, he stopped his treadmill. Hills were one of Kesiah's favourite warm-up programs, but Silas would rather be on the weights machine.

He adjusted the weight settings to his normal routine and had just lain down on the bench when the house spoke. 'There is a visitor for you, Silas.'

He sat bolt upright and his chest tightened with anxiety. A visitor? Kes was already here and he had no other friends. It must be something to do with his encounter with Derry or Mags. The Citizen Safety Monitors must have identified him. What if the HE-LP or the Health Advisors had come to take him away?

'I'm not going anywhere with them. House, tell them I'm not here,' he instructed in a whisper as he looked around, wide-eyed in panic. He should hide, or maybe escape out the back, through the nutrition room and across the gardens. He could head for the old cottage in the Uninhabited district and hide out in the tree house. Kesiah knew where it was. She would come and find him when the Advisors had gone...

'Your visitor has left a message. Would you like to hear your message?' the house announced.

'A message?' Silas queried uncertainly. That didn't sound like something the Health Authorities would do. Silas was fairly sure that if they had come for him they would already be in the hallway and have started searching the house.

'OK.' Silas took a deep breath, trying to steady his nerves. Perhaps he didn't need to run yet. 'House, play message.'

'Hi, it's me, Zoe. I wanted to catch you before clinic...' The achingly familiar sound of Zoe's voice filled the health suite. It took a few seconds to process what he was hearing, then, leaping to his feet, Silas sprinted to the front door.

'Zoe!' he cried, banging the door wide open in his enthusiasm.

She was almost at the gate and spun round at his shout.

'Silas...' she responded with evident surprise.

Hearing her say his name was all it took to unlock a whole cascade of memories and emotions. He was transported back to the long weeks in the summer when they had spent every waking moment together. Each time he had looked at her with

Soulsight, it wasn't the plain outside he saw but rather the perfect blend of love, generosity, honesty and kindness, which had combined to make Zoe the most breathtakingly beautiful person that he had ever seen.

He had grown to love her, so completely, so utterly. Now she was standing before him he knew that six months apart had done nothing to lessen the intensity of his feelings.

'Zoe! I can't believe you are actually here.' His amazement at finally seeing her again turned to a giddy rush of happiness, and he bounded down the path towards her.

He would have hugged her. He desperately wanted to. However, there was something in the way she smiled – a reserve, a hesitancy – that caused Silas to falter and stop a few paces short. She seemed different, almost wary.

Physically she looked much the same. A little more tired perhaps, and her broad face was a shade thinner, which would have suited her, except her brown freckled skin was puffy and lacklustre. However, the difference that was of most concern to Silas was not an external one. It ran far deeper than mere looks. Even without Soulsight, Silas knew that Zoe had changed, and he was suddenly unsure of how to approach her.

He had always known that the intensity of feelings he had for her was not fully reciprocated. She had been kind to him, a good friend, but Jono had been the one that she had loved.

Understandably, that would have an effect, Silas thought, trying to steady his racing heart. She must still be grieving for Jono, and for what she had lost when the Community had been destroyed.

An unpleasant jolt of what he recognised as envy coursed through him.

'Er... why don't you come in? I didn't mean to make you leave a message. I thought you were, um, someone else,' he blustered, ashamed of his jealousy.

'Haven't you got to get ready for Vitality?' she asked following him into the house.

'We can be late together,' Silas grinned, turning to gaze at her again. He could hardly believe she was here, at his house. They had so much to talk about. However, his smile wavered as he noticed that she wasn't wearing her clinic uniform. 'Aren't you coming?' he asked.

Zoe shook her head.

'Tomorrow, then?' Silas persevered.

'I'm not going back to clinic,' Zoe said with a tremor in her voice.

'But I checked not long ago, and the manager is still holding a place open for you,' Silas coaxed. 'It won't be so bad. I'll look after you.'

'No, Silas. That's not why I'm in Prima. I…'

'Silas?' A shout from upstairs startled them.

In his excitement at seeing Zoe, he had forgotten that Kesiah was in the house.

'Yes?' Silas called back, giving Zoe an apologetic smile.

'I've finished in the shower, but where has the house put my clean clothes?'

'Who's upstairs?' Zoe asked calmly, but Silas was sure he heard an edge to her voice. Her eyes, which had widened with surprise at hearing Kes' shout, were now narrowed, and she was staring at Silas in a way which made him uncomfortable.

'It's just Kesiah. She's a friend from Vitality,' he said, trying not to sound defensive. Wasn't he allowed to make friends? 'She's just getting changed. She made me spill some protein shake. It was actually quite funny…'

Zoe's unsmiling face caused his explanation to fizzle out.

'Silas?' Kes shouted again.

'Hang on,' he muttered to Zoe before shouting back up to Kesiah. 'Try the rack in the closet in my room.'

'You have a friend?' Zoe said with a sharp nod of her head. 'And she's a girl…' she added frostily, compressing her lips into a thin line.

'Kesiah Lightman,' Silas nodded in agreement, trying to sound positive in the face of Zoe's coldness. 'She started at clinic after… well, after last season-break, and already she's Female Gold Standard, but she's not like you'd expect. She's nice. You'd like her.'

Zoe's eyes narrowed even further. She looked angry. 'And this friend keeps her clothes in your room?'

'That's where the house put them,' Silas said, beginning to feel cross at the accusing way Zoe was speaking. This wasn't how it was supposed to go. He had longed for her to come back to the city. She had been continually on his mind, and now she was being so… so difficult. 'Zoe?'

There was the sound of movement at the top of the stairs.

'I've got to go,' Zoe said abruptly, turning to leave. 'It was nice to see you, Silas, and I'm glad you've been able to move on.'

Without giving Silas a chance to respond, she forcefully closed the front door, leaving him standing in the hallway, his mouth hanging open in shock. What was that all about? Where was the sweet, kind Zoe from last season? She hadn't even bothered to meet Kes. And, how dare she think I've 'moved on'! He glared furiously at the closed door. This season has been hell without her. She left me in Prima and now she wants to make *me* feel guilty about going to clinic and actually having a new friend!

'Did I hear someone? Has Anton forgotten something?' Kesiah asked, as she ran lightly down the stairs, looking around for Silas' father. She was dressed in her clean Vitality uniform.

'It wasn't Dad,' Silas said, then shook his head in confusion. What had just happened? Somehow he had messed up with Zoe and made her angry, but he didn't even know what he had done wrong. 'It was…' he let out an impatient sigh, 'I don't know what it was.'

'OK.' Kes looked at him curiously for a moment, and when he didn't elaborate she snapped her fingers in front of him. 'Come on, Silas,' she pushed him towards the stairs. 'Get changed, and we'll go in five minutes. That should give you plenty of time to plod to clinic.'

Chapter 4

Silas wandered at his usual pace with Kesiah flitting around him, chatting and bouncing with limitless energy, oblivious to his monosyllabic answers.

All he could think about was Zoe's peculiar behaviour. Why would she turn up at his house like that, just to slam the door in his face? Hadn't he made it clear how glad he had been to see her?

Uncomfortable, unresolved emotions swirled through his mind, making him anxious. He wanted to rush to her house straight away and get things sorted out between them. Had he done something to upset her? He had tried to get in touch but Nana's message had made it clear that Zoe needed time. She could have called me, he thought indignantly. Friendships are meant to be give and take. He would go round tonight, he decided, after clinic, and before this stupid new curfew began.

As they turned on to the path leading up to Vitality Clinic, Kesiah paused mid-spin. The change in her pace caused Silas to look up.

At the end of the road, the vast white edifice of the clinic's main building gleamed in the cold morning sun. It was a beautiful sight; an inspirational beacon of health and hope.

'Doesn't it seem unusually quiet to you?' Kesiah asked, turning in a slow circle.

Silas shrugged, his head still filled with conflicting thoughts about Zoe. 'It's because we're so early,' he muttered.

'You've walked even slower than usual, Silas,' she said drily. 'We aren't early. There's something else going on.' She pointed up the road to where a cluster of students had gathered by the crystalline railings. 'The gates are closed. Come on!' Kesiah grabbed Silas' hand and, pulling him along behind her, ran towards the huddle of blue-suited students.

'Excuse me.' She pushed through the students with her hand still firmly gripping Silas' wrist.

'Hi, Kesiah.'

'Hey, Gold Standard.'

The greetings rolled over Kesiah as she nodded and smiled at her fellow students, and they readily parted to let her through to the front of the group. Dragged in her wake, Silas got none of the warm welcome, just a few tuts and scowls as they reluctantly let him pass.

A projection had just started running the other side of the gate, and was rapidly replicated the entire length of the clinic perimeter.

The manager strode into view; his image had been enhanced to seem taller so even the students at the back of the crowd could see him. It wasn't really necessary. Manager Gilroy was already an impressive figure. Just a shade under two metres tall, he embodied everything the clinic stood for: health, strength and perfection. Vitality.

'Good morning.' His deep voice carried across the still morning air and his unsmiling expression seemed even sterner as he towered over them.

There was a small pause, and a few of the students mumbled a half-hearted 'good morning' in return, causing the others to laugh at their stupidity.

'It's a recording,' someone at the back of the group explained with a sneer.

'Shut up, we know,' came another voice, accompanied by more laughter.

'Be quiet and listen,' Kesiah said to the group, and Silas marvelled at the way everyone obeyed her. Without any grumbling they simply did as she said.

Manager Gilroy began his announcement and Silas shifted his attention back to the overlarge projection. 'Owing to the recent outbreak of the contagion FGSV in Prima, and the concern shared by the staff and parents at Vitality Clinic, we have decided, for your protection, to temporarily close clinic for one week...' At this point his words were drowned out by cheers and whistles from most of the students, and Silas strained to hear the last of his message: '... allow the thorough screening of the many Unseen who are employed to maintain the cleanliness and upkeep of our clinic buildings. I expect you to use the time as training leave in preparation for upcoming assessments.'

'Yeah... right.' Silas muttered, and by the hoots of cynical laughter, most of the others were of the same mind, and without the constraints of a gruelling day in clinic the students rapidly dispersed.

Kesiah faced Silas, grinning excitedly. 'Let's go to the tree. We can work on it all day and get the rest of the walls up and maybe start on the roof,' she suggested.

He laughed. 'Are you sure you're Gold Standard?' he whispered, raising an eyebrow conspiratorially. 'No genuine Gold should ever be so keen to miss clinic.'

'Don't worry, Silver-boy,' she winked back at him, 'I'm going to make you work all day. Your own personal coach.' She pulled back her shoulders and tried to broaden her slender form by puffing out her chest. 'Silas Corelle,' she barked in an imitation of Coach Regan, 'I expect better results from you. You are a disgrace to this clinic. Jump to. Training leave starts now.'

He chuckled. Why hadn't Zoe waited around to meet Kes? He was sure they would have got on well. Especially if they had seen each other with Soulsight. As if a light had switched on in his brain, he suddenly recognised the perfect opportunity. 'I've got a better idea,' he said impulsively. 'I've just got to go home first.'

'Seriously?' Kes asked with an impatient sigh, as they stood outside Nana's house. 'Weren't you here only yesterday?'

'Trust me,' Silas said as he steeled himself to knock on the door. He was incredibly nervous. What if she really had changed for the worse, and wasn't *his* Zoe any more? Not, of course, that she ever had been his, but what if Jono's death had pushed her to breaking point? Silas knew how close he himself had come to the edge, and that was despite having Kes to talk to.

He slipped his hand into his pocket and felt for the fold of paper containing the last fragments of Soulsight. It was little more than a fine dark-green powder now, and Silas hoped it had retained enough of its incredible properties.

'Come on, open up,' he muttered impatiently to the door. Surely she hadn't disappeared on him again.

At last he saw a movement through the thick glass pane. A figure was moving down the dim hallway.

Silas turned to grin at Kes.

'No way!' Kes laughed and bounded to the top of the steps as the front door began to open.

The smile on Silas' face became fixed as Zoe greeted them with a wary frown.

'Hi again,' Silas said with a nervous laugh. 'We thought we'd come and see you. Clinic was cancelled…'

For an awful moment Silas thought Zoe was going to close the door in their faces, but Kes stepped forward, pushing Silas to one side, a look of pure delight on her face.

'You must be Zoe. Let me look at you,' Kes gushed. 'Silas has told me all about you.'

Silas winced. 'Not *all* about you. Just some things.' He laughed to cover his embarrassment as the tell-tale heat of a blush begin to creep up his neck. Zoe had never known the full depth of his feelings towards her, and he didn't want Kes blurting out all his secrets.

'Did he?' Zoe's response was cold and indifferent.

'Yes,' Kesiah affirmed, seemingly unaware of Zoe's frosty demeanour as she looked her up and down. 'I thought he had made you up.' She laughed, and her small, dainty features lit up with amusement. 'But here you are, and just as lovely as he described you.'

Silas nearly choked on his own tongue. Kes sounded so sarcastic! He looked at Zoe in panic and saw her frown deepen. The contrast between the two girls was marked – dumpy, plain Zoe wearing an ill-fitting dull green shirt and sagging black leggings – compared to Kesiah, the Female Gold Standard, with her perfectly proportioned gymnast's body displayed to the best advantage in her Vitality uniform. No one in their right mind would call Zoe lovely.

'I told her about Soulsight,' Silas blurted out, in an attempt to put the comment into context, 'and the Community. I had to.'

Zoe didn't respond.

Silas had never seen her look so closed, so distant. 'I had hoped, if it's OK, to talk to you.' He spoke hurriedly, as if trying to break down the barrier between them with his words. 'I don't know why you rushed away this morning. I'm sorry if I said something wrong. Please, can we just come in?'

There was a long moment of silence while Zoe looked from Silas to Kes and back again. Then she nodded once, sharply, and pushed the front door wide open.

Chapter 5

Zoe sat down on one of the old cushioned chairs. A book lay open on the tattered armrest and she carefully marked her place before closing it.

Silas stood in the doorway, taking in every detail of the familiar room.

The chair opposite Zoe's was the one he had sat in when he had first unwittingly used Soulsight. They had been listening to some old-fashioned music and Silas could clearly remember how Zoe had transformed before his eyes. She had become breathtaking, and he had been smitten. It was only later he learned that the beauty he had seen was the true person that made up Zoe: her kindness, her love, her radiant heart.

But that was then, and this was now. This was the new Zoe, and he felt he didn't know her at all. An uneasy silence hung between them while Kesiah busily explored the unusual room.

The whole of Nana's house was intriguing, and the room they were in was full of ancient knick-knacks; mouldering stacks of books, a dusty piano, and shelves lined with pointless old trinkets and ornaments.

'What's this?' Kesiah asked, picking up a short wooden object and thrusting it in front of Zoe.

'It's called a pipe. For smoking. In the olden times,' Zoe began to explain, but Kes had already put it back and was picking up something else.

'Look at all this funny stuff.' She turned a miniature figure upside down and poked her finger into a hole on the base. 'No offence,' she added, glancing at Zoe and smiling an apology.

'None taken,' Zoe answered warily, giving Silas a questioning look.

'I'm so glad to see you,' Silas said eventually.

'Likewise.' Zoe seemed distracted by Kesiah's odd behaviour. Silas had forgotten what a whirlwind Kes could be when she was excited about something, and he and Zoe had the dubious privilege of witnessing Kesiah at her most animated.

'How have...? Why? I mean... I missed you. Where were you?' Silas tried again. He was making a mess of things. He shouldn't have brought Kes with him. She wasn't helping the situation.

Zoe's eyes followed Kes around the room, not answering Silas' question.

This was too difficult, he decided. Zoe wasn't going to tell him anything until she could trust him *and* Kesiah. And she wouldn't do that unless she was seeing properly.

He had been intending to tell her about his last portion of Soulsight, but she was behaving so unpredictably. First she had been angry and now she was cold and distant. He didn't want to risk her next outburst without being able to see what was truly going on.

'Can I make a drink? A hot drink like Nana used to?' Silas asked suddenly, backing into the hallway. 'You can stay here, with Kes,' he said to Zoe who, surprised at his request, had begun to get up. 'I'll be back in a minute.'

He stepped quickly through the door into the nutrition area before Zoe could object, and as the door closed he heard Kes ask, 'What's this for?'

An empty pan sat on the old stove. Silas filled it with water and set it on the heat. He pulled the slip of paper out of his pocket and carefully tipped the remaining Soulsight dust into the pan. He stirred it with a spoon as the fine fragments absorbed water and settled to the bottom of the pan.

Nana had always added things to her hot drinks to make them taste delicious, and Silas began opening cupboards at random. There was an array of pots and jars containing a range of multicoloured substances. He sniffed a few experimentally. None smelt particularly appealing and one was so spicy it burnt his sinuses and caused him to sneeze furiously. At last he spotted a few faded dry sprigs of green on the windowsill. Perfect, he thought, breaking off a couple of stems and dropping them in to the mix. The hot water gave life to the crisp leaves and a sweetly pungent aroma filled the air.

'You found what you needed, then?' Zoe asked, causing Silas to look over his shoulder in surprise. He hadn't heard her move through the house.

'Yes, I think so,' he said with a tentative smile. 'I just need cups.'

'Here.' She collected three cups from one of the tall cupboards and placed them on the table. Silas gave the mixture a final vigorous stir and poured the heated drink out, making sure the flecks of Soulsight were evenly distributed.

He watched Zoe as he sipped from his own cup.

'Mint,' she sighed appreciatively, letting the warm vapour roll over her face before drinking.. 'Shall I get your friend?'

'Kes will be fine. She's able to entertain herself for a moment.' He wanted it to be only him and Zoe for a while longer, just until the Soulsight took effect.

'Where has Nana been? I called around and left com-links but she was never here,' Silas asked when Zoe seemed unwilling to start a conversation.

Zoe shrugged. 'While I was away, Nana chose to stay with Bonnie. Do you remember Bonnie?'

Silas raised his eyebrows, uncertain if Zoe was being serious. Did he remember Bonnie? Of course he did! The woman who had chosen to risk her own life for the sake of her unborn babies. She had been a provocation to him during his stay at the Community. Her heart was full of a golden love that he had heard Nana describe as self-sacrificial. Yet now Silas felt guilty. He had been so caught up in himself and his own pain and loss that he had hardly spared her a thought since his return to the city.

'How could I forget her?' he said, wondering if Zoe could hear the shame in his voice. 'How is she?'

'Not good.' Zoe said bluntly.

Silas frowned when Zoe didn't elaborate. 'The twins... the little boy?'

Zoe gave a terse nod. 'The last I heard, Nana was still trying to help Bonnie come to terms with the loss of her son.'

Silas made a choking noise. 'He died? After all she went through, the risks...'

'He's still alive, or at least Nana thinks he is,' she added hastily, seeing Silas' stricken expression, 'but the Health Authorities have denied all knowledge of his existence. He must be in one of the orphanages for the Unseen. Poor Bonnie. It's broken her heart.'

'That's terrible,' Silas gasped. He had held that baby and had witnessed the incredible potential encompassed in its tiny frame, and yet one defect on his spine meant that his life was destined to be that of an Unseen. His own problems paled into insignificance when he thought of what Bonnie must be going through. No wonder Nana had not been at home all this time.

Zoe sighed and swallowed the rest of her drink. Silas copied her.

'What about Kesiah?' Zoe asked, pointing at the rapidly cooling cup of green speckled tea.

'Oh, yes, in a minute.' From the other room came the sound of discordant piano notes. Silas grimaced. 'Let's leave her for a little longer, shall we?'

He stalled for time by washing his cup out and carefully putting it back into the cupboard. How long did Soulsight take to work, again? he wondered. Maybe it had lost its potency, maybe it was too old and dry and damaged. He looked carefully at Zoe again, and as she returned his gaze she frowned and then gasped.

'Silas,' she breathed out his name in surprise, and stepped towards him.

At last!

'Zoe…' he smiled in relief. The Soulsight was taking effect. She was incredible. Time had dimmed his memory of the vibrancy of her soul, and she was far more wonderful than he remembered. Her beautiful heart became increasingly visible as his perception altered.

Soon the mundane outer shell that was Zoe's exterior was almost fully extinguished, and he watched her transform. Her true nature unfolded before him, like a flower to the sun. The suffering and grief she had endured following Jono's death had left their mark; there was a seriousness to her, a gravity. However, it in no way diminished her. Richer, deeper, wiser, but still utterly stunning. However, there was something else developing as well. Like a storm cloud rolling in from nowhere, the brightness of her beauty was swallowed by what Silas realised too late was pure anger.

Crack! Her hand came round in one strong, fluid movement, her palm flat and open. The sound of the impact was loud and almost more shocking than the pain of the blow, as she struck him hard around the face.

'Zoe!' he shouted in shock, lifting his hand to his stinging cheek. 'What are you doing? Why did you slap me? What did I do wrong?'

'What are you playing at, Silas? Did you just come here to remind me of what I've lost? Hot drink? Ha! You should have asked my permission. I've longed to see properly again, to see *you*. I've been so alone. Why didn't you tell me you had Soulsight? But no. Instead you come here with your "friend" to do what? To show me how happy you are? Well, congratulations!' Her angry tirade was accompanied by a heartbreaking display of emotions that skittered from her.

A few of them Silas instantly recognised. Fear shadows flittered from her eyes, temporarily darkening them, and a twist of mistrust briefly contorted her features.

'Zoe?' Silas said again, stunned by her outburst. He held on to her shoulders, forcing her to look at him. 'Please, I've not come here to trick you. I should have told you what I was doing, but I was afraid you wouldn't let me. You've been so distant and I was desperate to see you properly again. This was the only way I could think of.'

Her expression softened at his words and the stain of fear and mistrust began to recede. He felt her shoulders relax under his grasp as if the fight had gone out of her, and suddenly it seemed the most natural thing in the world to wrap his arms around her and hold her close.

'I just wanted you to see me and remember,' he murmured into her hair. 'You can trust me. I won't harm you. We are friends, aren't we? I need you, and you need me. Like old times.'

'Friends,' she said in agreement, stepping back from his embrace to look up into his face once more. 'But... probably not like old times,' she added softly. 'You've changed,' she admitted. 'You've not had it easy either. I can see that.'

'We've both changed, Zoe,' he said softly. It was like seeing her for the first time. She filled his senses, and blinded him to everything else.

'I've missed this.' She lifted her hand and touched her eyes before brushing her fingertips over Silas' eyes. 'I see you, Silas.'

'I see you, Zoe,' he smiled down at her, and watched the fear retreat a little more. Their faces were just inches apart.

'Is this for me?' Kesiah asked loudly. They had been so wrapped up in each other that neither had heard her come into the nutrition area.

Zoe suddenly stepped away from Silas, widening the space between them. 'It's not what it seems!' she gabbled, and a peculiar stain of guilt crossed her face.

'What isn't what it seems?' Kes asked blithely, picking up the full cup and looking at the bits of leaf floating around in the drink. 'This seems like hot water with plants in it,' she smiled and started to drink.

'This. Us...' Zoe said. 'Silas and I...' she carried on as ripples of embarrassment and confusion spread across her countenance.

'What are the green slimy bits?' Kes asked as she jabbed her finger into the bottom of her cup, still appearing to be far more interested in her drink than in Zoe's clumsy explanations.

'Soulsight,' Silas said.

'Oh? I thought you'd used it all up.' She noisily sucked the last dregs off of her finger.

'I was saving a bit,' Silas said, looking sideways at Zoe. She had just about recovered her composure, and Silas was torn between feeling annoyed with Kes for interrupting them and ecstatic because he knew without a doubt that he and Zoe had nearly kissed.

Chapter 6

As Kesiah's Soulsight took effect, her enthusiasm for Zoe overflowed with unrestrained delight. 'Silas said you were beautiful but he didn't do you justice,' she gushed, adding, 'Look at how much love she has, Silas!'

'Kesiah, please! You don't have to say everything you see,' he said pointedly.

'But Silas' embarrassment is kind of cute, don't you think, Zoe?' she teased, glancing his way.

'Kes, enough!'

'All right,' she giggled. 'I won't say *everything*.'

'It's OK,' Zoe said, as her last traces of mistrust faded. 'I see you, Kesiah. And I can see that you are very honest.'

'Too honest,' Silas muttered crossly.

'And you are kind,' Zoe added. 'I can see why Silas likes you and I am glad to meet you.'

At Zoe's approval, Silas felt the warm glow of success. He knew that the two of them would get on. Soulsight always made everything so much easier.

At last, with the final barriers between them removed, Zoe began to share openly.

Kesiah listened but, being virtually unable to sit still, wandered around the room, opening cupboards and looking in jars. Silas, however, was engrossed. Every word, every expression, each ripple and flare of emotion was riveting. With Soulsight it wasn't that he was simply hearing her speak; he was reliving it with her.

'The fever I had was cured in a few days, but it was like I had a sickness in my mind. Nana thought that if I were to spend some time working on the research ship with my mother's old friends, that may be the answer. A clean break, you know? Something to keep my brain occupied and let my emotions heal… but nothing seemed to help. Do you understand?'

Silas nodded. Oh, yes, he understood. In the weeks following his return from the Community, there had been times when his grief had overwhelmed him. The everyday routines of exercise and eating and going to clinic had felt like insurmountable obstacles.

Zoe gazed into his eyes. 'I think you coped better than I did,' she stated sadly. 'I got lost…'

He could see it. The lingering despair that still left a fracture line deep in her heart, like an old troubling wound. 'I had Kesiah to help me,' Silas said, 'or I don't think I could have carried on.'

'You are lucky,' Zoe said.

'Hello, I am in the room, you two,' Kesiah interrupted, suddenly dropping into an empty chair, her exploration of the nutrition area finally complete. 'I was just thinking, Silas, why don't we take Zoe with us to the tree? An extra pair of hands would be really useful if we are going to sort out the roof.'

Silas frowned at Kesiah's interruption. 'We *could* go out,' he said. At least it would be something to keep Kes occupied. Perhaps she would leave him and Zoe alone. 'I know heights aren't great for you, Zoe, but you can take a look at what we've built. There's a platform now.'

'You told her about the tree?' Zoe sounded faintly surprised, and there was a hint of something else. He frowned, trying to work it out. It was a faint stain, almost like she had an unpleasant taste in her mouth. She looked so tired and her eyes were bloodshot…

'Oh no! My Soulsight is fading already,' he cried. 'That was the last of it. I don't have any more.'

Zoe sighed. 'It was good while it lasted, and actually it was just what I needed, almost a confirmation, if you like.'

'What do you mean?' Silas asked.

Zoe looked at them both and gave a tiny shrug. 'I'm going back,' she said, 'and nothing you can say will persuade me otherwise.'

'Back where?' he asked, with a sinking heart. 'Not back to the ship, not now you are in Prima. I thought you were in the city for good. I know you aren't coming to clinic, but there must be some kind of work. You're really clever. I'm sure my dad could sort something out. Perhaps you could work with your mum.'

'You don't understand,' Zoe said hesitantly. 'I'm going back to the Community. Or at least, what's left of the Community.'

Silas thought he couldn't have heard correctly. 'You're going where?'

'I need to do this. I don't expect you to understand why, but the whole time I've been away I've been thinking about it, and about Jono.' Her voice wobbled as she mentioned Jono's name. Once again the old sensation of envy began to rear up.

'You can't go,' he objected. 'Your mum, and Nana... surely they wouldn't allow you to.'

She raised her eyebrows at Silas, making him immediately regret his choice of words. 'I *can* go,' she said frostily. 'Nana isn't expecting me back in Prima for a few more days yet so this is my chance. I can't explain it clearly but I feel I can't move on. I need to see the Community again, to see what remains, to grieve properly. Does that make sense?'

Not at all! Silas was screaming inside his head. How will going back help you to move forward? What is lost is lost!

'Perfect sense!' Kesiah cut across his thoughts before he had a chance to voice them. 'You should definitely go. You know best what will be able to help you. However, you shouldn't go alone, should she, Silas?' Kesiah announced without looking at him for confirmation. 'We will come with you.'

Grinning with satisfaction, she finally turned to Silas and, completely undeterred by his horrified look, carried on talking. 'Clinic is shut for a week, so this is the perfect opportunity. Let's get out of the city while we can. The crater and the Community sound incredible. I want to see the waterfall and maybe the cavern.'

Zoe gave Silas a sideways glance, which without Soulsight he found difficult to interpret.

'You really did tell her everything, didn't you?' she muttered.

'Only because you weren't here to talk to,' he complained in a mumbled undertone.

Kes was still talking while she bounded around the nutrition area like an overexcited child. 'And to be honest, Silas, I think you still need to work through some stuff; maybe going back is exactly what you need too.'

'But, Kes… no! You don't know what you're saying.' Silas stared at her furiously. Why had he brought her with him? She was making everything so much more complicated.

'It's too risky for you,' Zoe said, shaking her head. 'There are twice-daily Biocubicle assessments now, and there's the curfew.'

'That's right,' Silas agreed, latching on to the first sensible thing he had heard. 'We cannot just disappear for a week. We'd get in serious trouble. We can't be away from the Biocubicle network, and the crater is in the middle of the Outerlands. It's cut off from everywhere.'

However, the light of adventure was in Kesiah's eyes. This was an opportunity far more exciting than building a tree house or exercising in the health suite, and Silas knew that if he didn't put a stop to this, she would go with Zoe, regardless of the consequences. Kes knew no fear of reprisals. It was as if she thought that the rules that bound the rest of society didn't apply to her.

'Oh, that's not a problem. Biocubicles can be tricked,' Kes said blithely, confirming Silas' worst fears. He had to stop this before it escalated.

'No.' He shook his head vehemently.

'They can,' Zoe interjected, and Silas was disappointingly unsurprised that she had sided against him. 'It's simple, really. All you need is a replay square aligned over the data processor and it forms an information loop, recycling previous bio-assessments.'

'Great, that's sorted then,' Kes exclaimed. 'When are we going?'

'Stop!' Silas cried, and in frustration slammed his hand on the table. 'None of us is going anywhere. This idea is madness!'

As soon as the words were out of his mouth he knew he had said the wrong thing. The expression on Zoe's and Kesiah's faces was identical. It was one of icy-cold determination.

'What I meant to say is that it's too dangerous.' He softened his voice and looked pleadingly at Kes and Zoe. 'What if you get caught, bio-assessment forgery… the Health Advisors won't turn a blind eye. You'd be in serious trouble.' He knew he had a valid point, but the continued ferocity of their glower was undermining any residual resistance.

'I have thought this through,' Zoe said, sounding like she was struggling to keep her temper under control. 'I *am* going back. I'm leaving Prima tonight, on the evening Subterranean.'

'But the curfew, and the contagion? This is serious. You can't just ignore the restrictions,' Silas objected, receiving another withering stare.

'Silas, I said I've thought this through!' Zoe repeated with far less patience this time. 'I didn't come to Prima to ask for your permission.'

'What time do you want me to be back here?' Kes asked excitedly, seemingly unaware of the tension between Silas and Zoe.

'Kesiah, I am not going to tell you what you can and can't do,' Zoe said, pursing her lips and looking pointedly at Silas. 'You are welcome to come with me. It won't be a comfortable journey, but if you are certain, then let's meet at the Subterranean station at five.'

Silas thought his head was going to explode with frustration. What was Zoe playing at? Why hadn't Soulsight shown him how much Zoe had changed? She was being utterly selfish! She was practically encouraging Kes go on this insane trip into the

Outerlands. Kesiah had no idea what she was letting herself in for. And he couldn't expect Zoe to look after her… she barely seemed capable of looking after herself. It was all made worse by no longer having Soulsight. Understanding Zoe was so much easier when he truly saw what was going on in her heart.

'Fine! You win! But this is a bad idea, Zoe.' He glowered at her, furious at having been forced into this position. She narrowed her lips and was about to fire back an angry retort when Kes let out an excited whoop.

'Yes! That means you're coming too, doesn't it?' Cheering with delight, she jumped up and threw her arms around Silas before dragging an unwilling Zoe into a group embrace.

'Here's what we'll do,' Kes said, releasing her hold on Zoe and Silas, oblivious to the undercurrent of hostility that ran between them. 'We'll leave a recording of both of our results on your Biocubicle and I'll tell my mum that I'm staying with you for a few days… to help you stay on level. I'm over at your place often enough so it won't raise any questions.'

'Fine,' Silas said grumpily looking at the floor. A small noise from Zoe caused him to glance up at her, and there it was again, that expression, like she was swallowing something incredibly bitter. What was wrong with her now? he thought, and at that moment he realised that he was not looking forward to spending any more time with her.

Chapter 7

How am I going to stop them from going? Silas thought, throwing his Vitality uniform into the laundry chute.

Dubiously he inspected the collection of winter clothes stacked in neat rows along one side of his closet.

Last time he had been to the Community it had been summer, and warm enough to wander around in the thin linen trousers that everyone wore. However, this time – he shuddered – this time, it was going to be miserable.

They would be cold, damp and exposed on the crater rim. What did Zoe think she was going to find there, anyway? It was only going to bring back bad memories, not help her to move on with her life.

This is all such a waste of time, he thought angrily as he pulled a burgundy smartfabric top from the shelf and slipped it over his head. Immediately the material made adjustments to begin insulating his skin from the cool air in the room. That would keep him warm even if the temperatures dropped below zero. Rummaging in the back of the closet he found a pair of green all-season running trousers. They were old and the smartfabric wasn't responsive, but they'd have to do.

As he lifted the clothes up, something fell out and landed with a dull thud on the floor. A battered sphere rolled a short way and came to rest by his toe.

It was Jono's sunstorer.

Silas picked it up.

It had always been his intention to give it to Zoe.

Unexpectedly, it all came flooding back, and the memories and emotions that he'd thought he had dealt with returned in full force. They were so raw and so painful that they took his breath away.

He closed his eyes and could vividly see the Community going up in flames. The sound and the smell of the fire, the sickening knowledge that Jono was lying dead at the base of the cliff, and through it all the sense of his failure and the fury that he, somehow, should have been able to prevent the brutal destruction.

Suddenly, Zoe's desire to go back made sense. Her grief was eating away at her and she could get no respite from it. Returning to the crater must be a last resort for her.

Poor Zoe. He sat heavily on the bed, his head in his hands. He was so stupid. She wasn't being selfish… he was! No wonder she had been giving him all those peculiar looks. She must think I am the most uncaring, self-centred…

'You have a visitor,' the house announced, cutting through his painful self-revelation.

'Who is it?' Silas asked, springing to his feet. He hoped it was Zoe. He had some apologising to do.

'Kesiah Lightman,' the house replied, and Silas flopped down on his bed again.

'Open the door for her,' he said, and moments later Kes burst into his room.

'Right, I've got a replay loop thingy with my details on it for your Biocubicle,' she announced, attaching a tiny gold square to the base of the unit, 'you just need to add yours.' She looked at Silas expectantly, waiting for him get into the Biocubicle. 'Oh, come on, everything is going to be fine,' she cajoled. 'What about your dad? Have you left a message for him?'

Silas shook his head, 'I've been busy packing.' He motioned to the feeble pile of belongings on his bed. 'Anyway, I don't want to lie… you know that.'

Kes rolled her eyes in frustration, 'I'll let him know you're with me. Just get in the cubicle,' she said as she stuck a separate gold square onto the control panel. Silas stepped in. The door slid shut and Silas heard Kes start her message.

'Hi, Anton. It's Kes. You probably already know, clinic is closed and so Silas is spending a few days with me…'

The Biocubicle kicked in, drowning out the rest of her message, and when he emerged she lined the two miniature recording devices up and tapped them once each. They responded with a tiny flicker of light.

'That's set. I've got to pack, too, so I'll see you at the Sub at five,' she said as Silas sank down on his bed.

'Don't be late,' Kesiah cautioned.

'I won't be,' Silas replied.

'I mean it.' Kes stood in the doorway, her hands on her hips, looking like a trainee Vitality Clinic coach. 'Zoe needs you. She may act like she doesn't, but she does.'

She turned to go, but Silas called after her.

'Wait, Kes. What do you mean by that? Did Zoe say something to you about me?' he asked hopefully.

'She didn't need to. I know what I saw. My Soulsight hadn't worn off.' Kesiah tapped her temple with her index finger. 'Zoe was terrified of going back. Why do you think I so enthusiastically volunteered? There is no way we could let her go on her own.'

'I didn't realise she was scared. Why didn't you say something?' Silas said with frustration.

'I can't get it right with you,' Kes sounded incredulous. '"Don't say everything you see" is what you told me. I don't know the rules of Soulsight.'

'There aren't any rules.'

'Don't blame me. I'm just getting used to it. Both of you became difficult to read. It all got a bit ugly. There was definitely anger, and a fair bit of jealousy.'

'Well at least you didn't mention that!' Silas said, cringing at the thought of his darker feelings being laid bare.

Kes rolled her eyes. 'What matters is that we are there for Zoe.'

'And that you get an adventure?' Silas added drily.

'That's a small bonus.' She grinned. 'So, hurry up.'

He was at the station at ten minutes to five. He wasn't going to risk being late. Not after what Kesiah had said.

He looked around impatiently. Where were they?

The concourse was busy with travellers and announcements echoed around the high vaulted ceiling.

'Curfew commences in one hour.'

'The next Subterranean departs in five minutes from Substation F.'

'Due to the current Health Alert, we recommend that you do not leave the Subterranean network after curfew. For your convenience, there are rest areas and Biocubicles located in all our stations.'

There was a sudden rush of people as another wave of passengers arrived at the station. Silas stood on tiptoe to try to see over the top of the crowds. How would he find Zoe and Kes in all this lot? Maybe he should go to the Substation; maybe they were meeting there?

'Hi, you're early.' A hand lightly touched his shoulder and he spun around.

'Zoe,' he said, relieved to see her. 'I was worried that I'd miss you in all the rush.'

'Move!' A passer-by barged into him, causing him to stumble forward and knock into her.

'Hey! Careful,' he called after the retreating figure who, after scowling over his shoulder, was soon lost in the mass of bodies.

'Sorry about that,' he said, 'and sorry for earlier,' he mumbled, trying to get all his apologies out of the way. 'I was angry. I didn't understand and…'

'It's OK,' she said, cutting through his explanation. 'I was tired and snappy. I don't have any right to… well… never mind.'

He looked puzzled, '"Right to" do what?'

'Nothing, it's fine. I'm fine.' Zoe frowned, looking far from fine.

He sighed, confused by Zoe's reticence, and they stood in uncomfortable silence, made more obvious by the noise and bustle that surrounded them.

If only I had an extra portion of Soulsight, Silas thought, wishing there was some way to fill the ever-expanding gulf between them. Where was Kes? She would inevitably create some kind of noise.

'I wonder when Kesiah will get here?' he eventually said out loud, unable to stand the silence any more. He craned his neck to look over the top of Zoe's head.

'I'm sure she won't be long,' Zoe said in a tight voice, turning away from Silas. 'She seems lovely, and... devoted...'

'Devoted?' Silas laughed, thinking about the term. Kes was wild and funny, contrary and unpredictable, but she had certainly stuck with him through all his ups and downs. 'Yes, I suppose she is,' he said in surprise.

'Hi!' A shout from across the busy concourse drew their attention. There she was at last. Dressed in pale pink leggings and a long-sleeved top, her blonde hair forming a dainty halo around her face, Kes was waving enthusiastically at them.

She looked every inch the Gold Standard. The harried crowds of impatient commuters were momentarily altered into a transfixed sea of admirers as they parted to make a way for her to walk through them. Indulgent smiles, envious glances and pure adoration flitted across the faces of those she passed, before they recalled the pressing nature of the looming curfew and continued on their journey.

'Wonderful,' she beamed at Zoe and Silas as she approached them.

'Wonderful,' Zoe echoed, sounding far from enthused as she turned away and shouldered her bag. 'Just wonderful.'

Chapter 8

'This'll do,' Zoe said, dropping her belongings onto the last cluster of four empty seats.

'These are great,' Silas said.

Zoe raised an eyebrow at his forced cheerfulness. 'They're empty because they are day-seats,' she explained. 'They don't recline.'

'I know that,' Silas said, growing irritated by her continual grumpiness. 'I mean, at least we can sit together. Why's it so busy, anyway? Is it because of the curfew?'

'It must be,' Kesiah said, settling into the chair opposite Zoe. 'Do you remember last time, Silas? When we first met, and the whole carriage was deserted? We played that game.'

Silas laughed. 'She got me climbing along the chair tops,' he explained to Zoe.

'Oh?' Zoe's interest was so obviously feigned that Silas immediately felt cross with her again. He swallowed down the bitter taste of anger and turned his back on her.

'I was exhausted but you just wouldn't let me sleep,' he smiled at Kesiah.

'Talking of sleep…' Zoe interrupted pointedly, before settling back onto her chair and closing her eyes.

Silas frowned and was about to say something – she was being so rude – but as he opened his mouth to speak, Kes put a restraining hand on his and shook her head.

'Leave her alone,' she mouthed at him, before adding aloud, 'It's a bit early for me but Zoe's right. Let's try to rest. It sounds like we will need to save our strength.'

Grumbling under his breath, Silas sat down next to Kesiah, deliberately leaving an empty chair beside Zoe. She deserved to sit on her own the way she was behaving, he thought irritably.

He hadn't felt tired, but as soon as the Sub started moving, the gentle hiss of the train rushing through the dark, endless tunnels combined with the steady rise and fall of muted conversations from the other passengers lulled him to sleep.

His dreams took him on a meandering journey from Zoe's front door to the tree house and, eventually, somehow he was at Vitality Clinic. Coach Hunter, his climbing instructor, was barking commands at him to climb faster and higher, faster, higher, and Silas was trying his hardest, but the coach was hanging on to his left arm, dragging him down.

Still he climbed upwards, with Coach still clinging on to his arm, putting unbearable strain on his shoulder joint. He would have to let go of the wall but, he remembered in his dream, he would be fine because his safety harness would catch him.

Then, with a sickening lurch he noticed that they weren't on the climbing wall in Vitality any more, they were dangling over the crater edge at the Community.

'Hold on!' he shouted to Coach Hunter, who, regardless of their predicament, was still instructing Silas to keep climbing.

Finally the pain in his shoulder was intense enough to push him out of his dream state, and he drowsily regained consciousness.

However, the ache in his arm didn't recede with the dream. It was as if a weight was crushing it.

Experimentally he lifted his other hand to his shoulder to see if he could relieve the burden, and felt under his fingers the soft, silky sensation of fine, long hair.

Kesiah. He ran his hand gently over her head. She had fallen asleep using him as her pillow.

He would have to move her; he was getting severe muscle cramps down his forearm. Slowly he opened his eyes, and blinked a couple of times to generate a few reluctant tears. As his vision came into focus the first thing he saw was Zoe. She was sitting bolt upright on her chair, wide awake, and silently watching him and Kes. Her expression was unreadable, an emotionless mask, but when she noticed that Silas was awake, she self-consciously looked away.

'You looked so peaceful together,' she said, with a catch in her voice, and a subtle rosy heat began to stain her brown cheeks.

Her embarrassment was peculiarly contagious, and Silas felt a blush spread over his own cheeks, as if he had been caught doing something wrong.

'I don't know about that,' Silas mumbled, attempting to cover his confusion. 'Her head weighs a ton.' He gently twisted his body away from under Kes and lowered her to lie across his chair. She barely stirred and Silas stood up and stretched his arm above his head, feeling the muscles relax and pull back into place again.

'May I?' He indicated to the seat next to Zoe.

'Of course.' She seemed pleased as she pulled her bag off of the seat to make room for him.

'How much further?' Silas asked, squinting at the display screen.

'Not too long now,' Zoe said.

Silas yawned and stretched again, and his gaze passed over his travel bag dumped under his chair.

'I nearly forgot. I've got something for you,' he said, remembering Jono's sunstorer.

'A gift?' Zoe said, sounding surprised and touched. 'For me?'

'Well, not a gift as such,' he said, rummaging in his bag until his searching fingers found the curved surface of the sunstorer.

'It was Jono's,' he explained, carefully placing the silver orb into her hand. 'I thought you should have it. I found it on the ground after… well, you know…'

Zoe was speechless as she gazed at the battered metal sphere. Silas held his breath. She was so unpredictable – what if she lost her temper and threw it back at him, or slapped him again? Surreptitiously, he covered his cheek with his hand.

'Thank you…' she whispered.

Relieved, Silas casually pretended to wipe something off his face before returning his hand to his knee.

She clicked the blockers open but there wasn't enough power left to produce even a flicker of light.

'I should have charged it,' Silas apologised.

'It's perfect,' Zoe smiled up at him and Silas was alarmed to see tears in her eyes.

'Don't cry! I didn't mean to make you cry!' he said in a panic.

The obvious horror in his voice and the stricken look on his face caused Zoe to give a half-laugh, a humourless spluttering noise in the back of her throat.

'I'm not crying, not really,' she said, swiftly blinking the tears away. 'It's just that it's difficult. Jono's gone, the Community's gone, you've…' She clasped the sunstorer in her lap.

'I haven't gone anywhere,' he said softly.

A sad smile played across her lips, but her gaze remained fixed on the grey sphere in her lap.

'I still don't fully understand why you are doing this,' Silas ventured, hoping he had interpreted her softened mood correctly. 'Are you sure you want to go back? It's not too late. We can get the next Sub home and we'll be back in Prima tomorrow. You can stay at my house until Nana comes home, if you like?'

Zoe didn't answer immediately; instead she turned the sunstorer over in her hands.

'It's not just about Jono, you know,' she said, eventually. 'He was my best friend, and for most of my life my only friend, and I miss him, but it's more than that. It's the whole Community, the people, the honesty and freedom, Soulsight, everything. I loved it there, and I loved them… I wanted to live there permanently.' She looked at Silas and registered his surprise. 'After I'd finished at clinic, I wanted to do what Bonnie did and just slip off the radar. I've never fitted in with Seen society. I mean, just look at me.'

Everything she shared struck a chord with Silas and he felt his heart respond to her pain. He didn't have the advantage of Soulsight, but at that moment he didn't need it.

'I am looking at you, and you look perfect to me,' he said with utter sincerity.

Zoe closed her eyes and Silas saw her shoulders begin to shake. It took a moment for him to realise that this time she wasn't sobbing, she was giggling.

'It wasn't a joke,' Silas said, trying not to feel offended.

'I know, I'm sorry.' Zoe tried to stop her laughing, but couldn't suppress it. She clamped a hand over her mouth to smother the noise, aware of the crowded carriage full of sleeping passengers around them. 'I look perfect!' she tried to say.

Suddenly he didn't care if she didn't believe him. He didn't care if she was laughing at him. All that mattered was that he had broken through the icy veneer she had constructed, and beneath was the warm, light-hearted Zoe that he knew and loved.

As her giggling fit subsided she relaxed back in her chair. 'Thank you,' she said eventually.

'For what?'

'For saying the right things, for coming with me even when you didn't want to, for being my friend.' She smiled, a full, warm smile that caused her eyes to sparkle. 'I'm glad you're here.'

The honesty of her words caused his heart to perform a stuttering flurry of beats, and he swallowed quickly.

His head filled with all the things he longed to say to her; that he would travel to the ends of the earth with her, that he would always be her friend, and more, if she would let him – and yet it all seemed too much. He couldn't risk pushing her away.

Instead, he held her gaze and simply said, 'Me too.'

Chapter 9

The Outerlands station was much as Silas remembered it. Remote and deserted.

They were the only passengers to disembark, and as the Sub accelerated away into the darkness of the tunnel, Silas experienced a rising sense of foreboding.

'There's the waiting area.' He pointed at a glass door, behind which was a series of wide benches, a nutrition dispenser and a Biocubicle. 'We will have to stay here until curfew is over. Where are you going?' Silas asked, nonplussed, as Zoe bypassed the waiting area and headed towards the exit.

'We have to travel tonight or we won't have enough time to get to the crater and back. It's OK. I've got it covered. Follow me,' Zoe insisted, marching up the ramp to the Overground platform.

'Zoe, wait, what are you doing?' Silas called. 'We won't be allowed to... the Unseen contagion and the curfew, remember?' But his cry fell on deaf ears as Zoe walked purposefully away.

Silas lingered on the platform, not knowing what to do. On the Sub, he had nearly told her that he would follow her wherever she went. However, his sweet and romantic notion had failed to take into account her unwavering single-mindedness.

Silas turned to Kesiah for help, but she just shrugged. 'She said she's got it covered. Let's go.'

They hurried up the exit ramp after Zoe, leaving the warmth of the sheltered Subterranean station behind them. A cold draught of air swept down the empty tunnel, and Silas' winter clothes began to adjust until only the exposed skin on his hands and face felt the chill.

They were nearly at the exit that led to the Overground station when Zoe stopped.

At the far end of the platform, two grey-cloaked Unseen were standing, patiently waiting for the next train.

'You see?' Silas said, hanging back from the tunnel mouth. 'The Overground is shared Seen–Unseen use. We can't risk it. We'll have to wait until morning.'

'We can't risk it as "Seen",' Zoe agreed, as she made a thorough inspection of the walls and ceiling of the exit tunnel.

'What do you mean?' Silas asked warily. He didn't like the surreptitious way she was now peering at the Overground platform. 'What are you looking for?'

She nodded towards the two distant figures. 'We can go wherever we like at night if we become like them. The tunnel seems to be a Safety Monitor blind spot. The authorities wouldn't expect Unseen to be coming from the Subterranean, so now's our chance.' She reached into her bag and pulled out lengths of grey fabric.

'What! You want us to wear those?' Silas stood in stunned disbelief. 'When you said you had it "covered", I didn't think you meant literally!' he hissed, watching, dumbfounded as Zoe separated the fabric into three Unseen cloaks.

'Kes, we don't have to do this!' Silas put a restraining hand on Kesiah's arm as she reached to take one from Zoe.

'I think it's a good idea,' Kes said blithely. 'It certainly beats being stuck in the waiting room. How boring would that be?' Her eyes sparkled with adventure as she slipped one of the robes over her head.

Silas watched, horrified, as Kesiah and then Zoe were transformed into nameless, shapeless Unseen.

'Hurry up,' said the shorter of the cloaked figures impatiently.

'I can't do this. I mean, is this even allowed?' he questioned, desperate to stall them. Putting on the Unseen clothing was the fulfilment of everything he most feared. All his striving at clinic and in the health suite, all the levels and targets he desperately fought to maintain were all focused on one thing and one thing only: staying Seen.

Zoe pushed her hood back. 'Silas, it's just dressing up. You are *not* becoming an Unseen.' She placed the last bundle of dull cloth in his hands, and he looked down at it without really seeing it. 'The only rules regarding the robes is that Unseen must not leave the house without wearing them. Seen can wear what they want,' she shrugged, 'and I want to wear this.'

'But it's still curfew, and whatever we are wearing we are still classified as Seen,' Silas insisted, struggling to grasp why Zoe and Kes seemed so relaxed about putting on the robes. Even the sensation of the fabric made his skin crawl.

'It's your choice. Come with us now, or go home,' Zoe said firmly. 'We haven't got long. Our connecting train will be here soon and I've asked Val to meet us on the platform. He'll be waiting.'

'Val's here?' Silas asked, the information breaking through the paralysing dilemma that Zoe's plan had caused.

'Who's Val?' Kes asked from under her grey shroud.

'He's a family friend,' Zoe said. 'An Unseen.'

'Val looked after us when the Community was destroyed,' Silas explained, looking past Zoe at the two Unseen waiting at the far end of the platform. Was one of them Val? It was impossible to tell. 'You should have seen him. I mean, with Soulsight. And Maxie, his wife... after all we'd gone through they simply accepted me. They made me feel safe.'

He stared at the grey cloak in his hands. What would Val think if he were to discover that I turned back because I was too afraid? he wondered.

'OK,' he said finally, shaking the garment loose. 'Just give me a moment.'

The visibility through the grey hood was far better than Silas expected. However, it still wasn't quite see-through enough to prevent him from treading on the back of Zoe's robe as they cautiously exited onto the Overground platform.

'Careful!' She adjusted her cloak. 'There's a monitor up there… don't look at it!' she whispered with greater urgency when Silas and Kesiah turned towards it. 'This way.'

They crossed the platform towards a large sign bearing the name 'Northwest 24'.

Underneath it, slumped in a heap of grey fabric, was an Unseen. As they approached, it gave a breathless greeting and started to stand. The movement seemed to trigger a coughing fit, and for a moment the figure was wracked by choking spasms.

'Hi, Val,' Silas said, hurrying to help his friend to his feet.

'Zoe, Silas, you made it.' Val said, eventually catching his breath. 'And you must be Kesiah. It's nice to meet you.'

'And you.' Kes' voice sounded surprisingly small as she timidly stepped forward.

At that moment the Overground train clattered into the station. It was an ancient vehicle, and the engine gave an agonising groan as it shuddered to a halt in front of them.

Silas headed for the Seen compartment in which he travelled last time, only to realise his mistake when the other three headed to the end carriage. Of course, they would have to travel in the Unseen part of the train.

The blacked-out windows looked forbidding, and, battling a building sense of claustrophobia, he followed Zoe through the narrow doorway. This was really happening. He had become an Unseen. He huddled behind the reassuring bulk of Val as he peered around the carriage with its many cloaked occupants. Then the doors slid shut, trapping them inside.

Sweat beaded across his forehead. He could feel it dribbling down the bridge of his nose. He was surrounded, hemmed in, the fabric hood was smothering him…

He stared around the packed carriage. He was supposed to be staying away from the Unseen. His dad would be furious. What if they were carrying the contagion? What if one of them had missed their Biocubicle scan, or the scan had malfunctioned? He had to get out!

'Calm down, Silas,' Zoe leaned back to whisper. 'I can hear your breathing. You are going to have a panic attack.'

'I can't do this; we shouldn't be here!' he whispered back.

'It's going to be OK,' she murmured. 'Close your eyes. Think about how it was at the Community. This is no different.'

He tried to do as she said, and thought about his initiation. Soulsight had let him see past the broken physical bodies of the Unseen who lived in the Community. It had been an incredible time, genuine, humbling…

The train swayed ponderously through the dark night. At each station some of the Unseen struggled off the carriage until only a few remained. Silas began to calm down. There were so many Unseen. An indistinguishable sea of grey shrouded figures, all unfit to be Seen.

'How are you doing?' Zoe asked softly.

'Better, thank you.' He leaned towards her. 'How many Unseen are there? Do you know?'

'I don't know an exact number,' she murmured back, 'I think it's about 30 per cent of the population.'

Silas mulled the information over. Nearly a third of the nation. At clinic he had been taught little about the Unseen, and his ignorance had only served to magnify his fear. In his mind they had become monsters. But his time in the Community had taught him that it wasn't the outside that made a monster; it was what lurked in the soul.

'Ours is the next stop,' Val said, his words deteriorating into a wheezing cough.

'Good.' Silas heard Kesiah mutter behind him.

She sounded so unlike her usual vociferous self. He glanced at her unremarkable grey-clad figure. No one would ever guess that under all that fabric was a clinic Gold Standard. She looked just like all the other Unseen. She must be finding this even more difficult than I am, he thought.

'Are you OK? We should have stayed in the waiting room,' he said quietly.

'I feel sad for them. Don't you?' she whispered back, her voice full of compassion rather than disgust.

'Er... yeah...' he said guiltily, trying to replace his aversion for the Unseen with a more virtuous emotion.

The train creaked to a stop.

Glad to be away from the confines of the Overground, Silas followed Val out of the station. It wasn't far to Val's house, and then he could remove the restrictive robes.

'Where are we going?' Silas asked suddenly, as he noticed they were heading away from the inhabited area.

'To... the... truck...' Val wheezed. 'Not far...' His condition had worsened since Silas had last seen him, and walking and talking was almost too much for him. He leaned on a crumbling wall.

'I want to reach the crater by dawn,' Zoe explained. 'We'll see Maxie when we get back.'

'I can't... go with... you... Biocubicle awaits...' Val said as they waited for him to recover, 'Take... the truck...' His breathing settled enough for him to walk a little further, then he pointed into a dark alleyway.

Squinting, Silas could just make out the outline of an open-sided shelter, under which nestled the bulky square front of Val's ancient and battered truck.

'No blindfold this time?' he asked half-jokingly, remembering his first terrifying journey to the Community, when the location was still a secret.

'No need,' Val said sadly. 'There's nothing... left to protect... just ashes... and ruins.' He handed a folded note to Zoe. 'Go straight on... for about... half an hour and then turn left... at the second crossroads. Then...' he pointed at the slip in her hands, '... follow these directions... You should be there by dawn.'

'Thanks so much for helping us,' Zoe said, as she opened the truck door. Kesiah and Silas slid across to the passenger side and Zoe climbed into the driver's seat.

'I hope... you find some kind of... reconciliation... with what happened... Remember to time... your return carefully. If needs be... use the Unseen robes... The curfew will be just as... rigidly enforced here,' he wheezed, then slammed the door shut for her. He turned to retrace his steps, and soon the night had swallowed his grey, shambling figure.

Chapter 10

Zoe fumbled with the dials in front of her.

'Do you need me to run and get Val, or do you know how to drive this?' Silas asked, after five minutes of them sitting in silence.

'Yes, sort of.' She made a tutting noise under her breath, and roughly pulled the hood away from her face. In the blanketing darkness, all Silas could make out were black pits where her eyes should be. 'I've steered a motorboat. It's the same kind of thing. I'm just finding the... aha!'

There was a click and a hum before the truck obligingly sprung to life. Lights flickered across the dashboard, casting an eerie green glow over Zoe's face. It was meaningless to Silas. He wouldn't know where to start.

'It's fully charged, just like Val promised,' Zoe said, and placed her hand on the steering panel. Gently she angled the panel forward and the truck rolled out of the alleyway and onto the road. She tilted it further and it began to pick up speed.

The quality of the road began to deteriorate as soon as they left the outskirts of the town, and the old truck seemed to hit every rut and pothole.

'Mind out!' Silas shouted as Zoe swerved to avoid a large crater in the road that would have tipped the truck over.

'I saw it!' she barked, and Silas wasn't sure if she was angry with him or the road, but she slowed down and squinted through the windscreen.

'This is too difficult,' Silas said, bumping into Kes as the truck hit another hole. 'Maybe we should wait for daylight. At least we can avoid the worst bits.'

'I want to be as far away from town as I can be before sun-up. I'll just take it slow,' Zoe insisted, as she dropped the speed again. 'Let's push on.'

The truck crawled along as Zoe carefully picked the best route.

Kes and Silas tried to help by calling out the more severe damage as they came up to it, but in the end it took them over an hour to reach the second crossroads. They approached the intersection and the truck headlights lit the derelict buildings that littered the sides of the road.

Zoe angled the driving panel to the left, and as they turned the corner the light skimmed over damaged house fronts and empty windows.

A shudder rippled down Silas' spine. It was even bleaker than the Uninhabited areas back home. A genuine ghost town, neglected and forgotten as the population contracted, and the roads became less frequented and eventually completely abandoned.

All three of them were focusing intently on the route ahead as it petered out to little more than a faint muddy track across the ground.

'Are we still going in the right direction?' Kesiah asked. 'Where are the instructions your friend gave you?'

Zoe fumbled in her lap and passed the crumpled sheet to Silas.

'Do we have a light?' he asked..

'Here.' Zoe flicked open a compartment by the steering panel to reveal a row of sunstorers, all connected to the truck's solar charger. He took one and opened the blockers so that a thin ray of bright light spilled across his lap.

'"Twenty-five kilometres north",' Silas read out. 'How do we know when we've done twenty-five kilometres?'

Zoe pointed to one of the faintly glowing numbers on the driving panel. 'This one,' she said and double-tapped it to return it to zero. Five minutes later the number read '1'.

Silas looked at the list of directions. It's going to be a long journey, he thought grimly.

A couple of hours later the pitch-black of night was fading to grey, and Silas was able to get a better look at the terrain.

He had imagined there would be life – trees, grass, something – but there was nothing but bare, rock-strewn earth stretching far into the distance.

'Are you sure we are going the right way?' he asked, remembering how plant and animal life had thrived in the crater.

'I'm sure,' Zoe answered, keeping her eyes fixed on the almost non-existent track.

'We've reached twenty-five,' Kesiah said, pointing at the dial. 'What next?'

'Bear north-east until the riverbed,' Silas read, 'then head west.'

Head west at the riverbed, he repeated over and over in his head, until the monotony of the landscape and the dull hum of the engine numbed his thoughts and his eyelids began to droop.

He jerked awake as the truck hit a rut.

West at the riverbed…

He came to with a guilty start. The truck was at a standstill and he was sitting alone on the front seat.

How long had he slept?

Daylight filtered through the dusty windscreen and he could make out Kesiah and Zoe, still wrapped in their Unseen cloaks, grey cloth flapping wildly around their ankles. Kes had her arm resting around Zoe's shoulders as they stared into the distance.

The biting wind was cold enough to penetrate through his winter clothing as he stiffly climbed out of the truck. Shivering, he held his own cloak closer to him.

'Hi,' he said as he approached, but the greeting died on his lips.

Heedless now of the bitter cold and the fierce wind, all his senses were consumed with the vision at his feet. They were standing at the crater edge.

No birds swooped over any distant woodland canopy; no deer grazed the lush pasture. Gone was the thick forest and the verdant grassy plains, replaced by blackened earth and scorched stumps.

The lake remained, but its once blue waters were dark and oily. The destruction was complete. What had been a haven of life was now little more than a scarred and ruined wasteland.

It should not have been like this, Silas thought, as the agonising clench of impotent rage gripped him. The Community had never been a threat. They'd had something special. A perfect place where what was valued was the beauty of the heart. Seen and Unseen had been obsolete titles. A soul that was strong in love and self-sacrifice, generosity, trust… that was what had mattered.

Yet with one order, Helen Steele's Health Advisors had obliterated a home and a hope. Silas had stopped trusting Viva and Helen Steele when he had witnessed the full extent of her fear and hate. But being confronted with the devastation that she had ordered was a stark reminder of her intent to destroy anything different from her own idea of what was perfect.

And this was Jono's tomb. His final resting place. It felt oddly appropriate. Jono had lived free and had died free. He wouldn't have coped as an Unseen. Monitored, regulated and controlled. That wouldn't have been enough of a life for him.

Silas took a deep breath and gazed at the vast, ruined crater. The painfully tight knot of anger had already dulled. All he had now was a weight, a heavy, leaden ache in his throat.

'Do you want to go to the crater base?' he asked Zoe, moving to stand beside her so she could hear him above the wind. She remained resolutely staring over the edge.

She had been crying. Her eyes were red and there were faint, wind-dried, white salt tracks that stopped halfway down her cheeks.

'No.' Shaking her head, Zoe stepped free from Kesiah's supporting embrace and fiercely rubbed her face with her hands.

'I've seen all I want to.' She sighed unsteadily and dragged her eyes from the crater to look at Silas.

Although she was now facing him, her gaze was strangely unfocused. He wanted to offer some words of comfort, but she seemed so unreachable in her grief and pain... distant... broken.

Abruptly she turned her back on the crater and walked towards the truck, her grey cloak billowing around her like an extension of her sorrow.

Wordlessly, Silas and Kes followed her. She opened the rear door of the truck and the three of them climbed in.

Sealed inside, away from the howling wind, the silence was deafening. Zoe sat on one of the benches, leaned her head back against the window and closed her eyes.

'I can never go back,' she said, quietly.

Chapter 11

Silas stared at her with a mixture of pity and frustration. *I tried to explain that we couldn't recapture the past when we were still in Prima,* he thought unkindly. *You didn't need to drag us all the way out here to prove it!*

'I needed to put this to rest.' She opened her eyes, but kept her gaze fixed on the metal roof of the truck. 'I've been living, eating and breathing thoughts of the Community for the last six months. I've gone through all of the "ifs" and "onlys", and there is nothing I could have done. I see that now.' Zoe's voice should have been bitter, but instead it was full of a deep sadness. 'Helen Steele was determined to destroy everything so utterly. It wasn't just the people she took. Nothing and no one can live here ever again. Our Flawless Leader has made sure of that.' Finally she looked at Silas and Kesiah. 'Thanks for coming with me. It would have been too much to do this on my own.'

Silas couldn't hold her gaze, ashamed of his mean-spirited thoughts, but Kesiah smiled. 'That's what friends are for,' she said gently.

'What do you want to do, Zoe? Are you ready to head back to Maxie and Val's?' Silas asked eventually.

'Not quite yet,' she answered, beginning to sound less fragile. 'There is another thing I want to try, now that it's daylight, but first we should have something to eat.'

Neatly packaged under the benches were labelled boxes of provisions.

'Nutrition,' Kesiah said pulling one of the boxes free and lifting the lid. Inside were multiple silvery packages.

'Protein portion,' she read before tearing one open. A pale brown paste oozed from the packet.

'I wish you could have tried some of the food they used to make here, Kes,' Silas said, helping himself to a packet of nutrition. 'It was delicious. Stew... bread... waterberries!'

'Deer meat? I remember you didn't like that so much!' Zoe interjected, a half smile playing across her lips. 'Oh, yes, and the crayfish... and the eels...' she continued mischievously.

Surprised by her teasing, he caught her eye and grinning, raised his hands in surrender. 'All right! I'll admit, some of the food was completely disgusting,' he laughed. 'Now pass me another nutrition pack.'

They had eaten enough to constitute a balanced breakfast, and Silas peered out of the window at the inhospitable terrain. 'So what else did you want to do here, Zoe?' he asked, hoping it would be something quick so they could reach Maxie and Val's before sunset.

'I want to find the Soulsight cavern,' Zoe said.

Initially, Silas thought she was joking, but his smile faded as he caught her serious expression.

'Wha...? Zoe, no...' he exclaimed. 'We are not climbing that waterfall again. That's suicide!'

Zoe held her hands up, placatingly, but Silas was too shocked to let her speak. 'We barely made it out with our lives last time, and that was with Jono helping us. I'm not letting you back out there if that's what you are going to attempt.' He moved to block the truck's rear door and crouched down with his arms folded.

'Come and sit down,' Zoe said, tempering her exasperation with a smile. 'I'm not completely stupid. Do you think I'd do that horrific climb again?'

'I don't honestly know what you'd try to do,' he muttered, reluctantly returning to his seat.

'My main reason for coming here was to say goodbye... to let go of the past. I feel able to do that now, to move on. However, there is something else here that I want.'

'Soulsight,' Silas said quietly.

'Yes,' Zoe agreed. 'Not only do I want to see with it again, but also I want to take some back with me.' She looked imploringly at Silas. 'I've been thinking about how perfect the Community was, how free we were, how secure. You remember, Silas? What if we had something like that in Prima? Where the Seen–Unseen barriers were broken down...'

He shook his head at the impossibility of the existence of such a place. 'Zoe,' he said gently, 'you have to be practical. Without going through the waterfall, how are you going to get to the cavern?'

'Through the other entrance,' she said, sounding surprised that Silas had needed to ask.

Silas frowned. 'You can't mean that tiny space we squeezed out of last time? You will never find that! Look out of the window. There are no landmarks or handy signposts. It's just flat nothingness.'

'I know.' She seemed undeterred. 'I have a plan.'

Her plan was simple, but to Silas' mind, hopeless.

They had driven to the edge of the crater that was directly above the waterfall. It spewed from a mouth halfway down the cliff face, but even through the closed door of the truck Silas could hear its roar. He had no desire to look over the edge.

'I've worked out a rough distance. Seven to eight kilometres that way,' she said, pointing at the barren horizon.

Her calculations were based solely on her memory of the desperate journey they had taken in their attempt to rescue Jono from the Health Advisors. Silas remembered parts of that night vividly – the huge scanning craft settled on the edge of the precipice and the sound of the sedating gas that was pumped into the crates containing their friends. He recalled the moment that the Chief Advisor cheered as Taylor leaned over the crater edge and fired the lethal disruptor that killed Jono – all these memories readily bubbled to the surface of Silas' mind. But as to the distance they had covered or the speed with which they'd moved, he could not have ventured a guess. Zoe, on the other hand, seemed completely confident.

'Let's see if we can find it, then,' Kesiah said, wriggling enthusiastically in her seat.

Silas glowered at her. She was enjoying this too much.

If Silas had thought that the track to get them to the crater was bad, he realised that true off-roading was appalling and, after banging his head for the hundredth time, he made Zoe stop and he got out and walked.

'Of all the lame ideas! This is such a pointless waste of time,' he grumbled to himself as he marched alongside the slow-moving truck. 'Pointless!'

'You say something?' Zoe shouted over the high-pitched whine of the truck's labouring engine. Her eyes were alight with purpose and hope and, remembering again how much she had lost, Silas didn't have the heart to complain.

At least I feel warmer now, he thought, piling his Unseen cloak into the back of the parked truck. Dust from his trek had coated his sneakers and he idly kicked his feet against the tyre as he listened to Zoe's futile instructions.

'Kesiah, you head west,' she said pointing directly ahead, then handing Kes a canister of marker paint. 'Take the red one. If you walk for twenty minutes, leaving a mark every minute or so, then come back to the truck and head out at a different angle. That way we know exactly what ground we have covered. It shouldn't take long to find, not with all three of us searching.'

Kes shook her paint can and nodded.

'Do you remember what you are looking for?' Zoe asked.

'Yep,' Kesiah held her hands out at a distance only slightly wider than her shoulders. 'A hole in the ground. Not much bigger than this. Grass around the edge and it's in a dip... a gully.'

'Great,' Zoe said, 'if you find it, then come back here and wait for us. There are plenty of sunstorers in the truck. We can explore it together.'

Fanning out from the parked truck, they turned their backs on each other. Kes continued west, Zoe faced north and Silas started walking south, up gradual hills and down shallow gullies, the fierce wind numbing all exposed skin and any sensible thought.

Every few paces Silas stooped and coloured another patch of earth in vivid blue. But there was no sign of the hidden cave entrance; nothing except rock, wind stunted shrubs, sickly grass... and dust.

After twenty minutes of walking he retraced his steps, then took a slightly different path from the truck into the barren wasteland. He wondered how long it would take until Zoe recognised the hopelessness of the task.

As the day went on, the wind began to get stronger, and clouds of dirt started to billow up from the ground. Silas shielded his eyes from the dust storm. Clambering up a slight rise in the undulating plain, he looked around for Zoe and Kesiah. He couldn't see them anywhere.

'Kes? Zoe?' he called, suddenly feeling alone and vulnerable. He spun around, 360 degrees. The quality of the light changed again, darkening into a brown murk, further reducing the visibility.

Crouching down, he looked for the patches of blue paint that would lead him back to the safety of the truck; however, the top layer of dust began to lift and twist in fiendish swirling spirals, taking his carefully applied blue paint with it. Soon he was swallowed by a vortex of stinging grit and sand.

'Kes?' he called again.

With his eyes almost completely closed against the damaging dust storm, he twisted around again, looking for any signs of the way back. At last he saw a faint glow of light. Zoe and Kes must have reached the truck and were using it as a beacon, he thought. Then over the howl of the wind he heard a shrill blast of noise.

With one hand up to cover his eyes and another across his mouth, he battled blindly across the savage terrain and found the truck parked in a shallow dip where they had left it, lights blazing and horn blaring.

He opened the door and half-climbed, half-fell into the back of the truck. His eyes were streaming with tears and he blinked to try to clear them. His face and hands felt sore, as if they had been aggressively scoured, and in places there was clear fluid leaking through his damaged skin.

'We need to get out of here, Zoe. We can't stay; we'll be blown away! Can you get us back to town?'

It was only when Zoe failed to answer that he noticed...

'Where's Kes?'

Chapter 12

They kept the engine running and the lights blazing until the truck eventually lost charge. Then Zoe took all the sunstorers and placed one in each window.

The remnants of murky brown daylight were swallowed by the terrifying black of night as the wind continued to rage and howl around them. The power of the storm was frightening in its ferocity, rocking the truck from side to side as if to try to turn it over, while claws of dust and stones savagely scraped over the doors and roof.

'She must have found somewhere to hide... some kind of shelter,' Silas shouted over the noise. 'She has to be all right.'

'Maybe...' Zoe said, her expression bleak as by the feeble light of the sunstorer she watched the maelstrom of dust and grit whip past the window.

For the most part, Zoe and Silas sat in anxious silence. Neither of them could sleep, but just as dawn was beginning to break, Zoe sat up a little straighter. 'The wind's dying down and it's getting lighter,' she said.

'At last!' Silas was instantly alert and pushed the door of the truck open. It was stiff, as if it had aged and rusted overnight, and it creaked alarmingly as he forced it to move. The wind was still strong enough to snatch the breath from his mouth, but it was no longer armed with the million particles that had given it teeth.

As he held on to the truck to orientate himself, he became aware of the fine scratches covering the painted metal surface. His stomach clenched as he thought of Kes' exposed face and hands.

'Kesiah!' he called, but his cry was immediately dispersed by the buffeting gusts.

'She was heading west, let's follow what's left of her trail,' Zoe said, grabbing an emergency aid kit from the back of the truck. 'Silas, I am so sorry...'

'Stop it.' His fear turned to anger and he rounded on her. 'What good are your apologies? None of us should have even been here. Why did you have to come? What was the point? Just to relive some shattered fantasy? Well, wake up. It's all gone, it's all lost, and now Kes is lost too!'

'I know,' she mouthed, tears collecting in her lashes.

'Don't...' He grimaced with frustration. 'Look, this isn't helping Kes. Let's find her first. Save "sorry" for later, OK?'

He walked away. There wasn't time to worry about Zoe's feelings. Kesiah was still out there somewhere, and she needed them.

The storm had obliterated most of Kes' trail of paint, but occasionally they would find a boulder or tree stump liberally sprayed red to show them they were still on the right path.

Over and over they called her name, until their throats were hoarse, but there was no answering cry.

'It's no use!' Silas clambered onto a small rocky outcrop, just a few feet off the ground, and gazed around him. The early morning sun was behind them and cast their long shadows across the empty ground.

Even from his elevated vantage point, he could see no trace of Kes. But that meant little. The barren landscape wasn't completely flat. Even the truck was hidden from sight in a shallow dip. Kes could be lying injured in any one of the surrounding hollows.

'Maybe she's made it back, now the wind's died down... shall we go and check?' Zoe sounded exhausted, having missed another night's sleep. He briefly glanced at her as she wearily turned and began retracing their steps alone.

A sharp prick of guilt needled his conscience. It had been Kesiah herself who had insisted on coming to the Outerlands with Zoe. And none of them could have predicted this.

'Zoe, wait.' He jumped down from the viewpoint, and was about to follow her when he heard a faint sound.

He froze, poised and alert, trying to work out exactly what he had heard.

It had been barely discernible. A high-pitched cry, like a birdcall, but it hadn't come from the sky; it had come from ground level.

Crouching low, Silas listened. There it was again! But it wasn't like any bird sound he had ever heard. It was more catlike, he decided.

Slowly moving his head from side to side, he tried to locate the precise source of the sound.

Zoe's crunching footsteps drowned out the next cry, and he held his hand up to stop her moving.

'Shh... I heard something.'

'Kes?' Zoe asked hopefully.

'I don't know. I don't think so. It doesn't sound like any noise a human would make, not unless...' He clenched his jaw tight, trying to stop himself from voicing the awful conclusion that his mind had already reached. Not unless she was in terrible pain.

'There!' he said, hearing it again.

'I heard it too.' Zoe circled around the rocks that Silas had used as a viewpoint. 'It came from down here.' She dropped to her knees as the faint, eerie call sounded again.

'Look!' Zoe crouched lower, peering under the rocks. 'There's an opening.'

Crouching beside her, Silas could see the gap which had been partially concealed by a jutting lip of stone.

Experimentally, he pushed his arm into the space. 'Have you got a light?' he asked, manoeuvring on to his belly, and ignoring the sharp gravel digging through his clothing.

'Here,' Zoe handed him a sunstorer, but there was little charge left in it and it flickered dimly.

The noise came again. This time it was more drawn out and pained.

'What is making that sound?' Silas said, wriggling forward, until his head and shoulders were through the opening's narrow mouth. He held the sunstorer higher, and in the wavering light saw the start of a sloped tunnel, which seemed to widen as it descended into the darkness.

'It goes down a long way, and it opens up into some kind of passageway,' he said, shuffling back out from under the rocks. 'The noise is definitely coming from down there, but I can't see anything. Can we get more light?'

Zoe jumped up. 'I'll see what I can get from the truck,' she said. 'I won't be long. Stay there.'

Dropping the emergency kit, she set off with renewed energy, running in the direction from which they had come.

Silas lay down again on the stony ground and peered into the tunnel, straining to catch the faintest sound.

Carefully he wriggled further into the opening, using his elbows to propel himself forward until only his feet were protruding above ground. He opened the sunstorer fully and held the feeble light as far forward as possible.

A glint of colour caught his eye. Further down the slope something shiny and red reflected back at him. His heart performed a swift double tap of extra beats as he recognised the canister of red paint.

Kes had been this way! She must be down there somewhere.

At that moment the sound of another faint but spine-chilling cry filled the tunnel. It made the hairs on Silas' head stand on end because he immediately knew that the noise was not an animal howl; this was the scream of someone in absolute agony.

'Kes!' Silas shouted into the darkness. 'Hold on. I'm coming to help!'

Pushing rapidly backwards out of the tunnel, Silas jumped on top of the outcrop looking for Zoe. Where was she?

His gaze fell on the emergency aid box lying on the ground where Zoe had dropped it. Silas wrenched it open and grabbed handfuls of bandages, then he saw a pack of single-use light sticks.

In a split second he had made his decision. He could no longer wait for Zoe to return. Pulling the blue paint spray from his pocket, he hurriedly wrote 'KES' next to a downward-pointing arrow on the rocks and, stretching out fully on his stomach, he wriggled forward through the opening.

The tunnel soon grew wide enough for Silas to stand. The walls shone deathly white in the glow of the light stick, and he carefully clambered across the uneven floor. He picked up the red canister as he passed and stood it upright on a large rock, adding another blue arrow. Zoe would need a trail to follow when she returned.

Again, a pained cry echoed up the tunnel, and Silas hurriedly pocketed his paint can and carried on.

The tunnel began to narrow and soon Silas found himself trying to squeeze through a gap that was now barely a hand's-breadth wide. Frustrated, he pulled back. There must be a way through, he thought, pushing with all his might against the rock wall as if his desperation alone would be enough to widen it.

He cupped his hands around his mouth. 'Kesiah?' he called through the narrow gap.

Another wordless cry echoed through the tunnels, and Silas pressed his ear to the crack in the wall, only to discover that the sound wasn't coming from there at all.

How was that possible? he thought. I haven't missed a turning. Kes came this way. She's down here somewhere.

Frowning, he triggered a second light stick, and with the extra illumination he slowly retraced his steps.

The cries seemed increasingly pitiful, and Silas could hear exhaustion creeping into them. In his head he could clearly picture her lying, hurting, deep in the tunnel. Maybe she had fallen and broken a bone, maybe the dust storm had torn at her face and hands before she had found shelter...

'I'll find you!' he shouted, searching every corner of the walls and ceiling of the rough-edged tunnel.

Suddenly he spotted it. A vertical slit in the wall, hidden by an outcrop as he had descended the tunnel, and only obvious as he returned upwards. That was where the sound must have come from. Leaving another blue mark for Zoe, and holding the light in front of him, he squeezed through.

His foot touched the edge of something soft, and Silas looked down at a thick dark carpet of vegetation. The plant layer seemed to shiver as it reflected the light sticks gripped in his hands. Then, as if it were being awoken from sleep, the floor, walls and ceiling of the new tunnel began to glow and shimmer, becoming brighter and more beautiful by the second.

'Soulsight,' Silas whispered. 'I've found the Soulsight caverns.'

Chapter 13

He took a tentative step forward, marvelling at the colours and patterns radiating over the cavern walls. Wave after wave of swirling whorls and spirals flowed around him.

Lost in wonder, he ran his hands gently across the slick surface, creating a riot of dancing colour. The luminescence began to spread, drawing him deeper into the cave system. It was tempting to let the light slowly lead him forward, but then he remembered Kesiah. Finding her was his priority.

Closing his eyes to the distracting light show, he listened.

Moisture dripped and popped through the layers of wet plant, and from somewhere up ahead there came the faint sound of trickling water, but the cries seemed to have stopped.

Alarmed, he snapped his eyes open and hurried forward, oblivious to the spectacle surrounding him, and only conscious of the sickening feeling that he was too late to help Kes.

Moving faster now than the steady progression of the Soulsight chain reaction, he once more held his light sticks aloft. The tunnel began to widen until Silas could no longer touch the sides. He paused to allow the plant layer around him to respond and spread, and saw that the narrow tunnel had opened up into a beautiful cave.

Ancient pillars of coated rock glimmered in reds and greens. As he brushed past the shining surface, tremors shimmered across the huge shapes as if giant creatures were stirring in their sleep.

He rounded a pillar and opened his mouth, about to call out for Kes again, when the most unusual sight confronted him.

There, in the middle of the cave, was a large wooden box.

Silas stared at it. It was so unexpected and out of place, such an ordinary item set in the midst of the most extraordinary phenomena.

How had it got there? Had it been carried there by some of the Community workers, or had the Health Advisors left something behind?

Silas took a step closer. The box was large, nearly waist-height, and was made of smooth wooden planks, neatly joined to form a seamless exterior. A partial word was printed across the bottom left hand corner... *utrifa*... There was no lid, and Silas edged forward, unaccountably afraid of what he might see in there.

He looked and blinked rapidly. He could hardly believe his eyes.

I can see... a child! he thought with amazement.

Curled up in a bundle of blankets was a sleeping baby. Its head was covered with downy curls, and its long eyelashes fanned down on to chubby cheeks.

I must be hallucinating, Silas thought, rubbing his eyes and trying to clear the fog of fatigue that was creeping up on him... or am I dreaming?

He held the light sticks up a bit to get a better look and maybe dispel the strange vision, but the change in the light quality caused the child to wriggle and screw up its eyes.

'Don't wake him!' came an urgent whisper from across the cave.

Startled, Silas looked up. 'Kes?' he exclaimed, briefly considering that she may be part of the same hallucination.

She hurried towards him, and he reached out a hand to touch her.

'I found you... You're not hurt!'

The colourful Soulsight lights played across her features, staining them red and blue, but as far as Silas could tell, she didn't appear to have so much as a scratch on her face or hands.

'I thought you were injured, trapped...'

The child whimpered.

'Shh!' Kes, warned, and grabbed his outstretched arm to pull him away from the sleeping baby. 'He's only just gone to sleep! He's been screaming for ages. It sounded like a dying cat. But you are not going to believe who else is here.' She opened her eyes wide with excitement.

'What do you mean? Who's here? Are there Health Advisors? Did they follow us?'

Panic made his voice loud and Kesiah shushed him again as she manoeuvred him even further away from the wooden box-crib. 'Not Advisors,' she whispered. 'Jono is here! I got lost in the storm and was sheltering by some rocks, shouting for help. He had just been collecting his sunstorers and heard me calling out, and brought me here to shelter.'

The swirling Soulsight patterns didn't help Silas' spinning head as he tried to make sense of Kesiah's words. 'What did you say?' he cried, forgetting to be quiet. 'You said Jono…?'

A thin wail echoed around the cave, rapidly strengthening into an ear-splitting scream.

'Silas! You woke him up!' Kes rolled her eyes in exasperation and hurried over to the box.

'Kes!' Silas whispered, chasing after her. 'What do you mean?'

'There's no point trying to be quiet now,' Kes scooped up the scrunched-faced, crying infant and scowled at Silas. 'Don't worry, little one, I'm here.'

'Kes, please. You said Jono, didn't you? Why would you say that?'

'Because a man who introduced himself as Jono heard me shouting for help and invited me to shelter from the storm,' explained Kes, with exaggerated slowness.

Silas shook his head, unable to comprehend what she was telling him.

'It must be someone else,' he rationalised. 'Are you certain you heard his name correctly, Kes? I saw my friend Jono killed here six months ago – he was shot with a disruptor. Remember, I told you about him. This cannot be the same man.'

Kesiah smiled. 'He's much nicer looking than you described him.'

Silas' frown deepened. That report didn't fit Jono at all. 'You thought he was nice looking?' he queried.

'Yes, perhaps not initially, but...' Kes was momentarily discomfited, and Silas was sure she was blushing, but it was hard to tell under the continually shifting colour spectrum. '...anyway, as soon as I mentioned you and Zoe, he has been desperate for the storm to stop so he could find you.'

Silas shook his head. 'Jono is dead,' he said, sadly. 'I don't know who you met, but it was not my friend.'

Kes sighed. 'Tall, long legs, one short arm...' she said brusquely, then her voice softened. 'Also kind, generous, charming, attractive...'

Perplexed, Silas stared at her. 'The first bit sounds like him, but how can he be alive? I don't understand.'

'Now, why doesn't your lack of comprehension surprise me?' laughed a deep, booming voice.

Silas spun around, his jaw hanging slack in amazement as an incredibly familiar figure strode across the glistening carpet of Soulsight.

'Jono!' Silas cried in disbelief. 'How...? It *is* you!'

Jono's peculiarly elongated legs carried him rapidly towards Silas. His good arm was held outstretched, while the other, a short withered stump, swung uselessly at his side.

Tentatively, Silas reached out to touch him, afraid that he would be insubstantial – merely some type of clever projection – and that his hand would pass right through.

'But how? They shot you with a disruptor... you fell off the crater wall! Are you truly alive or is the Soulsight playing with my head and making me see what I want to see?'

Jono laughed and flung the real and considerable weight of his good arm over Silas' shoulders.

'"A spirit I am indeed; But am in that dimension grossly clad Which from the womb I did participate",' he responded with a shout of laughter, his huge plain face crinkling into a smile of utter pleasure.

Silas grinned along with him, slapping him hard on the back. 'Oh, it is you, all right! No hallucination of mine could quote nonsense Shakespeare as fluently as that. But what... I mean... how? Jono, I don't understand. You fell...'

'I did,' he confirmed with another laugh. '"O time, thou must untangle this, not I. It is too hard a knot for me t'untie."'

'You're not dead.' Silas slowly enunciated each word as if giving them time to sink in, and then gave a joy-filled shout of incredulity. 'You're not dead!'

It was then that Silas noticed Zoe standing a bit further back from Jono. Her face was lit with a beatific smile, and the wonder in her expression gave her an other-worldly radiance.

'Jono's alive!' she cried, ecstatically.

Perhaps Silas had begun to absorb some vaporised Soulsight from the damp cave atmosphere and his vision was already altered, but he had never seen Zoe look more perfect, as if the one piece of her life that was missing had been restored, and she was once more made whole.

At that moment he felt a small part of his own heart splinter away. Zoe's smiles, her overwhelming happiness, her joy... it was all for Jono.

Immediately the old feelings of jealousy bubbled up.

'Jono's alive,' he echoed, trying to recover his initial enthusiasm, and hoping his smile didn't seem forced as he attempted to disguise the unpleasant resurgence of bitter envy.

'I think your baby wants you,' Kes said, interrupting their reunion. The child was straining and complaining in Kesiah's arms, eager to reach Jono, the only person it recognised.

Silas was grateful for the distraction. Soulsight exposure would mean that soon Zoe would be able to see his internal conflict. He just needed a moment to compose himself.

He focused on the advice that Bonnie had once given him. All he had to do was embrace the things that made Zoe happy.

And Jono was the one person who seemed to be able to do just that.

He glanced again at her and caught the full power of her glowing smile as she watched Jono take the child from Kes. I can do this, he thought. I can be happy for her.

'I expect you are hungry,' Jono laughed as he cradled the infant in his one good arm. He smiled at the baby, who returned the expression with an open-mouthed grin of his own. 'How can I resist you,' Jono cooed, 'even though "He hath eaten me out of house and home, he hath put all my substance into that fat belly of his".'

The baby's grin grew wider and Silas groaned, 'You've taught the baby to like Shakespeare, haven't you!'

Chapter 14

With Jono's help, the child had messily consumed two packets of nutrition and was now contentedly playing with the empty silver containers.

Clasping his own nutrition pack in one hand, Silas sat on a spongy, vegetation-covered rock and watched.

As the Soulsight enriched atmosphere steadily took effect, Silas could do little else but admire the change in Jono. No wonder Kes had been so enthusiastic when she had described him. The words she had used hadn't done him justice, though. 'Charming' and 'attractive' sounded trite and hollow compared to the richness of Jono's soul.

The person he had known six months earlier had been a complicated mixture of conflicting traits... incredibly loyal, yet also angry and suspicious. However, now there was no warring emotion to mar or scar, just a golden brilliance that shone through his broken, misshapen body and transformed him.

Silas recognised the appearance of this trait immediately. Bonnie had looked similar with Soulsight, and he had been told it had also been the distinguishing feature of his own mother's soul.

This was what self-sacrificial love looked like.

Yet, despite Jono's impressive appearance and Kesiah's simple pure beauty, Silas was continually drawn back to Zoe. She was so incredible, so perfect... so complete.

He couldn't tear his eyes away. Even when she caught him staring he didn't look away, and was surprised to notice that she seemed as riveted by him.

The intensity of the moment was finally broken by Jono who, with a voice thick with emotion, gruffly said, 'I see you Zoe, Kesiah and Silas.' He lifted his hand to his eyes and pointed at each of them in turn.

'I see you, Jono,' Kesiah and Zoe replied.

Reluctantly Silas turned his attention from Zoe. 'I see you, Jono,' he said, brushing his fingertips across his eyes and reaching towards Jono. 'Although, I still don't understand *how* I am seeing you. You are here, but you were shot... by a disruptor.'

'We saw Taylor acquire your brainstem signal and press the disrupt button,' Zoe agreed, in a small, hollow voice as she recalled the terrible moment.

Jono nodded seriously. 'Her hate for me, for what I am, was terrifying. She wanted me dead. I had to get out of range of the disruptor, and as I couldn't climb down the cliff fast enough, I had to jump.'

'The Chief Advisor said you'd fallen.' Zoe interrupted. 'And we saw Taylor with Soulsight. She twisted up on herself and we knew that she had killed you.'

Jono shrugged. 'Perhaps her appearance altered because her intention had been to kill; she had committed murder in her heart. All I knew was that my only hope was the waterfall. I could hear it, but the crater wall was too dark and I couldn't see it. I knew that if I could get above the point of its outflow I would have a chance. So I climbed down as fast as I could and let go. I don't even remember hitting the water; I think I may have blacked out for a few seconds.'

'You deliberately jumped to put distance between you and Taylor? You jumped... into the plunge pool...?' Silas said with a slow realisation as his mind struggled to cope with the facts. All the nightmares he'd had of Jono's corpse falling from the crater and being smashed to pieces on the rocks below had been so vivid, so real.

'I thought I was going to drown,' Jono admitted. 'The falls kept pulling me back under. I had to fight with every ounce of strength to escape. Eventually I got clear and let the river carry me downstream, thinking that it might be best to stay looking dead, in case the Advisors sent out a search party. When the forest went up in flames I saw the boat, just floating in the middle of the lake, and in it was this little one.'

Jono bent down and scooped the child up to sit on his knee. The baby giggled and tried to push his fingers into Jono's mouth.

As he looked at the infant, Silas felt a sudden need to protect him, to love and nurture him, and with that came recognition. He knew who this child was.

'It's Bonnie's son!' he gasped. 'Zoe, you said he was lost, but he's been here all along.'

Zoe had obviously reached the same conclusion, and joy spilled from her, making Silas feel giddy with shared delight. 'Bonnie will be so happy,' she said.

'What was he doing in the boat?' asked Silas, once more finding it difficult to look away from Zoe.

'I don't know,' Jono admitted, 'but he was tucked right under the seat, covered by the crayfish net, and there was some other stuff there too... a bag, some clothes and food. I think Bonnie may have been trying to escape with the twins and hid him when she was taken.'

'But how have you survived this long?' Silas asked. 'We saw the crater. It's a charred mess, nowhere to live, no food, nothing to hunt.'

'It was tough to start with,' Jono agreed. 'I didn't think the baby would make it. There were a few supplies in the bag, but when they were gone he became weaker and weaker. Then I found a patch of waterberries that had escaped the fire, and eventually the forest cooled enough for me to get to the supply caves. The food stores and medical kit were still there, hidden in the back caves, and we've survived off of those. We're running low now, though. Another couple of months and we'll have to head out and try to find the town.'

Jono shuddered at the idea, and a tiny shadow of fear ruffled his otherwise perfect countenance. For Jono, the town would mean classification, and life as an Unseen. And the same would be true for Bonnie's baby. Destined to grow up shrouded and hidden because of one small growth on his back. Silas looked at the infant again and felt a fierce love for him. He would never allow that to happen.

'Did you give him a name?' Zoe asked, moving closer to Jono and smiling at the child.

'It wasn't really my place because he's not really mine and, after all, "What's in a name?" Jono looked down at the baby boy with adoration. 'But yes, I named him. I couldn't call him "baby" all his life so I named him William. After…'

'After William Shakespeare, we get it.' Silas finished for him, laughing at the choice. 'I hope Bonnie likes it!'

'She'll be so glad to see him again, I don't think she'll mind what you've called him,' Zoe said, 'and I can't wait till Bonnie and Nana find out that you are alive and well!'

'I'd like to see them too,' he said thoughtfully, smiling at the child, then glancing at Zoe. 'It does seem incredible that you are even here.'

'I can't explain it, but I had to come,' Zoe said. 'I didn't expect you… and this… but maybe, somehow, deep down I knew.' She laughed with pleasure, letting her eyes wander over the sparkling cavern.

Jono grinned. 'Well, you have found me and the caves, and perhaps, now you are here, you would like to view the true wonders of the Soulsight caverns? You wouldn't believe some of the places I've found.'

'I would love that,' Zoe immediately responded, as if exploring with Jono was the most exciting opportunity she had ever been offered.

I'm not going to be jealous, Silas told himself firmly. If Zoe is happy, then I am happy. She and Jono were always meant to be. I am her friend, just her friend.

He watched her help to arrange the baby in a sling of fabric, securing him to Jono's chest. The child objected at first, but settled as soon as Jono and Zoe began to walk away.

'Come on, Silas.' Kes prodded him with her foot. 'We're not travelling all this way to miss out on seeing the caverns.'

Zoe slipped her arm through Jono's as they crossed the cave and reached one of the many tunnel openings branching off of it.

'Stop sulking,' Kesiah said, stretching out her hand.

'I'm not!' Silas retorted grumpily, annoyed that Soulsight laid all his emotions bare. 'I'm just tired. I spent most of the night keeping a lookout for you, remember.'

He grabbed her proffered hand and she pulled him to stand.

'Right. Just tired,' she teased. 'Let's catch up with Jono. He's incredible, isn't he?' Her appearance suddenly intensified, as if she had been lit up from the inside.

'Hmm,' Silas grumbled as Kes hurried after Jono and Zoe. 'He certainly seems irresistible to you and Zoe.'

Chapter 15

Silas' gloomy mood lifted as Jono led them through the extensive network of caves. They were far larger and grander than any they had seen on their last desperate escape through the tunnels, and this time they could pause to enjoy them.

As they entered each new cavern, Jono would allow a brief flash of light to fall on the closest section of Soulsight. Waves of colour would roll and billow over the floor to spread up the walls and coalesce on the ceiling.

Thick strands of Soulsight fell in tangled cascades, and as they brushed past, new colours and patterns danced around them.

Kesiah stood next to Silas. She seemed subdued, as if the caves were too much for her. Giving her a sideways glance, he noticed that she was hardly sparing a moment of her attention on the light-show before her. She was completely focused on Jono.

He felt a pang of sympathy for her. He knew what it was to lose your heart to someone who didn't feel the same way back.

'Hey, Kes,' he said, trying to distract her, 'watch this!'

He bounded in giant leaps across the cushioned layers of Soulsight on the cave floor. Where his foot stepped, the Soulsight glowed deep purple, surrounded by a ring of blue, then green, yellow and red, until there were circular rainbows of colour filling the whole floor.

With a delighted giggle, Kes broke free from her silent adoration of Jono and sprang across the floor, performing a series of high somersaults in mid-air to land perfectly in a blaze of golden light that rippled from her feet.

'Very nice!' Jono called across to them. 'But if you like this cave, you are going to love what is around the corner!'

Eagerly they followed Jono as he opened the sunstorer to its full capacity and sent out a longer burst of light.

Jono halted. One by one, they came to stand next to him.

Silas gasped in astonishment as he saw that they were standing on a sheer edge. Below, above and to the sides, the light wave flowed across the Soulsight, gradually illuminating an immense cavern. The roof was easily as high as the Vitality Clinic main building, and the floor dropped vertically for a similar distance below them.

'Whoa!' Zoe exclaimed, stepping hastily back from the edge. 'That's as far as I go!'

'Wait, Zoe,' Jono said, sitting down and dangling his long legs over the sheer drop. 'Watch this!'

'Jono!' Zoe had retreated to the safety of the tunnel, but the fear was clear across her face and in her voice. 'What are you doing? You're still carrying William!'

'It's fine,' he assured her. Then, to Silas' horror, he wriggled to the edge of the precipice and dropped over.

'What? Jono!' he cried, leaning over the edge and shielding his eyes from the blinding glare of light as Jono's falling body stirred up the Soulsight on the steep cavern wall.

The agitated plant layer began to dim, and Silas could just make out his friend, still seated, as he reached the floor of the cave and slid away from the wall before coming to a gentle halt.

'Come on! Have a go,' he called, laughing and staring up at them. 'The Soulsight makes it into a slide. It's not that steep once you are on it.'

Kesiah didn't need a second invitation and immediately sat on the edge where Jono had been seconds before.

'Kes!' But before Silas could warn her of Jono's reckless behaviour and how he had no concept of safety, she pushed herself neatly over the edge, and her squeals of terror and excitement echoed around the vast cavern.

Silas gingerly peered over the edge to see Kes arrive at the bottom of the cave with a bright trail of light, like a comet's tail, behind her.

Jono helped her to stand, and she looked up into his eyes with open adoration. Silas was about to shout down, but the words froze on his lips when he saw the way that Jono continued to support Kes even though she was already on her feet. Maybe it was the residual glow from the disturbed Soulsight, but he was certain that Jono was looking at Kes with the same measure of intensity.

What's Jono doing? thought Silas angrily. One minute walking arm in arm with Zoe, and the next gazing into Kesiah's eyes.

'Are they OK?' Zoe asked from behind him, stepping gingerly towards the edge and trying to peer over.

'Oh, they look fine to me. It's just a big slide. Trust Jono to jump off something!' Silas answered with a light-hearted laugh, stepping in front of her to block her view. Something was going on between Jono and Kesiah, and he wasn't going to let Zoe get hurt by him... not when she had just found a measure of happiness once more.

Concern clouded Zoe's expression. 'What's the matter? What are you not showing me?' she demanded, trying to push past him.

'Nothing,' he said, trying to sound innocent, but glancing down at Kes and Jono served to confirm his suspicions. They seemed transfixed by one another, oblivious to their surroundings.

I've got to do something before Zoe sees them, was Silas' only clear thought as he abruptly sat down and levered himself over the edge.

The initial lurch left his stomach high in the air as his body dropped in freefall. Then his backside connected with the slippery cushion of Soulsight, and he let out an undignified squeal of horror that turned into a whoop of exhilaration as he rushed downwards.

'That was insane!' he shouted, slowing to a halt near his friends' feet. He started to laugh as the buzz of adrenaline receded.

Jono moved to help Silas to stand up. 'So you liked it, then? Do you want another go?' Jono said, grinning from ear to ear.

'Absolutely not!' Silas said, recovering from the shock of his own boldness and looking long and hard at his friends. Jono seemed unchanged; no hint of duplicity warped his appearance. Maybe I misinterpreted the look between them. If Jono was playing with Zoe's feelings then surely Soulsight would show some twist or distortion. Instead, the opposite was happening, Jono was becoming increasingly radiant, almost too perfect, and Silas felt the need to avert his gaze. It took him a moment to realise what was going on.

'I'm overdosing,' he groaned, blinking his eyes tightly shut, then glancing at Jono again. Now his friend's face was consumed with the fury and bitterness of his past. The fear he had known as a lost and abandoned child choked his eyes with thick shadows.

'Ugh!' Silas blinked again, shaking his head to try to alleviate the effects of the Soulsight overload.

'It'll even out,' Jono said, laughing at Silas' struggle. 'Kes doesn't seem to have a problem.'

Silas risked looking at Kesiah, and was relieved to see his view of her remained steady. Then in an accelerated display, her appearance abruptly shifted.

Kes' soul had always reminded Silas of a pool of clear water, but now it was if he were looking into a vast, pure sea. He could see the far reaches of her heart. His head began to spin as if he were standing once more on the cliff edge, and he had to look away from her as well.

'How come you don't have a dark and bitter past like everyone else, Kes?' Silas asked, keeping his eyes fixed firmly on the thick, flickering Soulsight carpet under his feet.

'I don't know... just lucky? Maybe I've got a dark and bitter future lined up!' She said it as a joke but, out of the corner of his eye, Silas saw Jono flinch and step closer to Kes, as if shielding her.

'Hey!' Zoe shouted from high above their heads. 'Are you coming back up here?'

'"She speaks! O, speak again, bright angel",' Jono immediately called back, and Zoe's distant laugh echoed around the cavern's vaulted ceiling.

Silas rolled his eyes. Zoe always laughed at Jono's lame Shakespeare quotes. '"You are as glorious as an angel tonight,"' Jono continued. '"You shine above me, like a winged messenger from heaven who makes mortal men fall on their backs to look up at the sky."'

It took Silas a moment to realise that Jono's words were no longer loud enough to reach Zoe, who was still cautiously peering over the high edge.

Jono was talking to Kesiah.

'So how do we get back up… to *Zoe*?' Silas asked crossly. He wanted to shake Jono. Why was he acting like this?

'What?' Jono said, struggling to tear his eyes away from Kesiah.

'The way to the top…' Silas spelt it out for him by adding stepping motions with his hands.

'Follow me,' Jono grinned, and bounded to the edge of the steep slide.

Chapter 16

Where the face of the rock-wall slide was completely smooth, the sides consisted of a haphazard pile of rocks and boulders. The Soulsight layer still made it slippery, but it was simple enough for Silas to push his hands and feet under the thick green strands and find secure footholds.

Soon they were back on the ledge, where Zoe, sitting a safe distance from the edge, was waiting for them.

Silas felt his chest painfully constrict. With Soulsight still overloading his system, she appeared so wonderful that he could feel the pinprick of tears forming at the corners of his eyes.

He swallowed the lump in his throat and forced himself to look over to where Jono was gallantly helping Kesiah up the last few steps. To Silas' surprise, Kes was allowing him, even though she could have walked up the steep incline on her hands had she wanted to.

He could understand Kesiah's infatuation with Jono, but what he was struggling to make sense of was why Jono was giving her so much attention in return. Soon Zoe would notice, and her wholeness that had only just been restored would be shattered.

I'll have to tell her, Silas decided. It was what a friend would do. She may not want to hear it, but far better that I warn her gently now than have Jono hurt her. All I need is a moment to speak with her alone.

The opportunity presented itself almost immediately.

On reaching the top of the rocky ladder, Kesiah peered over the edge. 'I am going down again,' she announced with a grin, and promptly sat on the edge of the vertical drop and disappeared out of sight. Once more her squeals of excitement filled the cavern.

'Please don't, Jono!' Zoe called, as he sat on the edge, ready to follow Kes down the slide again.

'Why not?' Jono asked, sounding innocent enough as his exposed soul wildly fluctuated between bitterness and love.

Silas almost shouted at him, to tell him not to be so callous; however, Zoe simply said, 'Not while you are carrying baby William.' She stretched out her arms. 'You can throw yourself off as many cliffs as you like, but give the baby to me while you do it!'

Laughing at her concern, Jono retreated from the precipitous edge and swiftly untied the swathe of fabric that kept Bonnie's baby secure. Remarkably, the child was fast asleep.

'Takes after his Uncle Jono,' he said, and gently passed him to Zoe before eagerly following Kes down the steep drop.

'Aren't you having another go?' Zoe asked Silas, inclining her head towards the glowing edge.

'No way!' Silas shuddered. 'I don't know what I was thinking the first time. You had the right idea.' He smiled, but couldn't trust himself to even glance in her direction. The overdose was still far too powerful. To keep a clear head, he would have to avoid looking directly at her while they talked.

'Can I join you?' he asked, indicating a patch of damp spongy floor next to her.

'Of course,' she said, but her gaze was fixed on the bundle in her arms. 'Isn't he beautiful?' she sighed.

'Let me have another look,' Silas said softly, moving closer to peer over her shoulder. Once more, he felt the incredibly strong instinct to protect the child. Unfortunately it was accompanied by the irresistible desire to weep. Trying to suppress it, he decided that his safest course of action was to avoid looking at anyone for another couple of hours. Perhaps he should just keep his eyes closed…

Leaning back against the wall, Silas heard squeals of laughter coming from the base of the cavern and he knew this was his chance.

'Kes and Jono seem to be getting on well,' he said, as nonchalantly as he could.

'Yes. Kesiah is quite... um... unique, isn't she?' She seemed to be choosing her words with particular care. 'Very friendly... How did you get together?' Zoe asked, keeping her gaze fixed on the sleeping infant in her arms.

Silas' heart sank. She's noticed, he thought, and she thinks it's all Kes' fault.

'We met after last season-break. I told you about it on the train, remember? She kind of... I don't know... looked after me, I suppose.'

He didn't want Zoe getting the wrong impression. Kesiah may be acting completely love-struck, but then Jono *had* rescued her from the dust storm. 'Kesiah's really kind, and has become almost like a member of the family,' he added enthusiastically.

Almost imperceptibly, Silas felt Zoe's body tense, as if she were bracing herself against an impact, and when she spoke, her words sounded brittle.

'She certainly is charming,' she admitted, sounding far from enthused. 'I have been wondering about her, though.'

'What's that?' he asked, trying to keep his voice light, although his hands twisted anxiously in his lap.

'Do you think she has some measure of natural Soulsight abilities? There is a lot of good in you. The time with the Community, and the things we went through have made you... wonderful...' Zoe stumbled over the word, as if embarrassed by her admission, but it wasn't lost on Silas, who felt a pulse of adrenaline tingle down the length of his spine.

'And besides,' Zoe rushed on, 'she seemed particularly accepting of me. When she first met me she described me as lovely.' Zoe gave a short laugh. 'I thought she was being sarcastic, but it was only later that I realised she meant it. It's no wonder that you like her so much.'

'Yeah,' Silas agreed. 'She's great. Everyone loves Kes. Even Manager Gilroy seems to have warmed to her, and that man doesn't like any Vitality students. Maybe she *has* got something special, some kind of inbuilt Soulsight going on. She doesn't seem impressed by "levels". I've lost count of the amount of times the other Gold Standard has asked her out. You'd think he'd get the hint.' Silas chuckled, remembering the bemused expression on Tony Watts' face the last time Kes had turned him down.

'Really?' Zoe sounded surprised.

'Of course,' Silas laughed. 'She's the Female Gold Standard and he thinks it's expected of him, or something. Kes is always polite to him, though. I think that confuses him even more.'

'I mean, he asks her out even though she's already your girlfriend?' Zoe was studiously avoiding looking up. 'I know it's none of my business…'

'Girlfriend?' Silas laughed with surprise. 'Kesiah isn't my girlfriend.'

'She isn't?' Zoe sounded puzzled.

'No,' he exclaimed. 'What on earth gave you that idea?'

'Are you kidding me?' Zoe said, sounding heated but still averting her gaze. 'I can't even look at you to check until the Soulsight settles. You are telling me that you and Kes aren't… you know… together?'

'Not like that,' Silas was staring at Zoe's profile now, confused by the way the conversation was going.

'But… but…' Zoe was floundering now. The baby in her arms must have felt her distress as it began to twitch and move in its sleep. 'But she stays at your place. She keeps her clothes in your closet…' Zoe said weakly.

Silas nodded slowly. 'Sure, she sleeps over sometimes. Mainly so she could help me stay on level. She's a brilliant friend, completely rock solid, and I don't know where I'd be without her… but she is *just* my friend.' Another thought popped unbidden into Silas' mind and he couldn't resist testing it out. 'Zoe, did you think… I mean, have you been jealous?'

'I don't know what you mean!' she said huffily, wrapping baby William up in his cloth blanket, as if she were getting ready to go.

With a sudden clarity of insight, everything made sense. The reason Zoe had been so difficult, so prickly and awkward, was because, all this time, she thought he and Kes were together.

'Zoe, wait, stay here.' Silas rested his hand gently on her arm.

Reluctantly, Zoe stopped trying to leave and turned her face towards him.

Immediately, he was lost in her, overwhelmed by her. Explanations, words, even thought, seemed to wither in his mind.

He gulped and tried to form a coherent sentence. 'Kesiah is… but, surely you know, you realise… my heart… it's…'

She lifted her eyes to meet his and, reflected in her gaze, was an openness and a vulnerability that he had never seen before. Instantly some deep part of his heart seemed to connect, to link, with hers. He stopped struggling to rediscover the words that he wanted to say, because he knew they were no longer necessary. She was experiencing the same indescribably profound bond with him.

Chapter 17

Gradually the intensity of the shared moment began to fade. Silas didn't know whether to feel saddened or relieved. He knew he couldn't sustain the powerful level of emotion that the Soulsight had produced in him, but at the same time he guessed it had been a one-off. A perfect and beautiful coincidence, the peak of the overdose fluctuation combined with complete unrestricted honesty.

What remained was a new level of understanding between them, a mutual trust and security where he could be completely free and unembarrassed.

'So, when did you start to like me?' he asked, curiously.

'From that first day, back in Vitality Clinic, when you helped me,' she answered with the same unaffected candidness. 'Do you remember it?'

'Even back then?' Silas was surprised. 'I was such an idiot then. I treated you so badly.'

'No, you didn't,' Zoe demurred.

'But why didn't you say anything?' Silas asked. 'You must have noticed how I started to feel about you.'

'I was worried that you liked me under false pretences. I was the first person you ever saw with Soulsight. I couldn't be sure that what you were feeling wasn't a temporary infatuation.'

Silas remembered that first time he had truly seen her. She had transformed before his eyes. 'There has been nothing temporary about my infatuation with you, Zoe Veron,' he murmured, moving closer to her so their shoulders touched.

Zoe leaned into him. 'Also, I knew that after I'd done my final year at clinic I wanted to make the Community my home for good. It wouldn't have been fair of me to tell you how I felt, then expect us to live so far apart.'

'We would have worked something out…' Silas protested gently.

'Then you started treating me like a friend only,' Zoe continued, 'and I thought you'd got over me, so I reconciled myself to that.'

Silas shook his head in amazement. All his hopes, his longings… and all this time she had felt the same way about him.

Zoe rested her head on his shoulder and he rubbed his cheek on her thick hair, delighting in the sensation.

'I thought I was doing the noble thing… you know, making space for you and Jono. You seemed perfect together,' he said quietly.

Zoe laughed. 'Jono is the big brother I never had. He sees it as his job to protect me. He'd do anything for me, but I have never felt… well… like *this* about him, or anyone else, except you.'

With that final confession, Zoe angled her face to look up at Silas, and it was the most natural thing in the world for him to tilt his head towards her.

'Waaahhh!' The scream rent the air, and Silas lurched backwards.

On waking from his nap and recognising neither of his carers, William chose that moment to show his disapproval in the loudest possible terms.

'Great timing!' Silas said, rolling his eyes. 'Whose side are you on, buddy?'

Zoe giggled, and swiftly kissed Silas on the cheek before turning her attention back to William. 'I don't think he'll be happy until he sees Jono,' she said, levering herself upright.

'Stay there, I'll get him,' Silas said with feigned irritation. He was actually ecstatically happy. At long last they had shared their hearts. It was all too good to be true.

His feet seemed to barely touch the floor as he drifted to the ledge at the top of the Soulsight slide.

'Jon...' he began to shout, but, looking down into the crater, he could see Jono was busy.

'How come he gets to the kissing part?' Silas grumbled.

'Oi! *Uncle* Jono! You've got responsibilities up here. Your baby is crying!'

They didn't rush to separate, and seemed totally unconcerned when they did.

'Jono and Kesiah, that's what I wanted to talk to you about,' Silas turned back to Zoe, as Kes and Jono meandered, hand in hand, towards the rocky steps.

'What about them?' Zoe asked over the furious cries of the baby.

'They're... um... together.'

Suddenly the whole situation seemed comical, and Silas began to laugh. He walked towards a surprised Zoe and wrapped his arm around both her and the howling baby and finally kissed her.

'About time!' Jono crowed, as he and Kesiah eventually joined them on the ledge. 'The tension between you two has been that thick, I could have cut it with a knife!'

Silas laughed, but felt no embarrassment. There was nothing to feel self-conscious about. Everything was perfect.

Jono's appearance had almost settled now, but the golden aura that surrounded him made him look unreal, as if he himself were a source of light.

'I thought you said William was upset?' he asked, letting go of Kesiah's hand to take the child from Zoe.

'He was. He seems to have calmed down,' Silas said.

Far from screaming, William was now babbling happily as he held on to Jono's ragged jumper with his tiny fists.

'I completely agree,' Jono responded, nodding seriously at the infant. '"The sight of lovers feedeth those in love."'

Kesiah smiled and wound her arm around Jono's waist, gazing up at him. Their souls seemed to merge at the edges, and

Silas wondered if he and Zoe were beginning to show the same phenomenon, or whether it was just a final effect of the Soulsight overdose.

Zoe must have thought the same thing as she slipped her hand into Silas'. 'It seems amazing that you two have only just met,' she said. 'You seem made for each other.'

'Ah…' Jono sighed, looking at Kes again. '"Hear my soul speak. The very instant that I saw you did my heart fly to your service."'

Silas smiled at Zoe. She had liked him from the first moment she'd seen him. His heart was so full. He had never known such complete happiness.

'I love you, Zoe,' he said, not caring that Jono and Kes could hear, not caring about anything else except the clear response, initially written across her face and then reinforced by her words.

'I love you too.'

Silas barely noticed walking back through the caverns. The wonder of the lights and patterns of the Soulsight plant became a glittering blur as he only had eyes for Zoe and, more by luck than judgement, they managed to follow Jono to the corner of the caverns that he had made into his camp.

Jono lit a fire and the tendrils of smoke curled and writhed across the ceiling before being absorbed by the perpetually dripping, plant-coated walls.

Silas sat down and tried to suppress a yawn, but another quickly followed, and soon he couldn't stop yawning.

'I'm so tired!' he reluctantly admitted.

'Here,' Jono said, handing out some large silvery blankets. 'The Soulsight makes for a pretty good mattress, but it's damp. We can spread these out close to the fire and sleep here tonight.'

Silas unfolded the fabric. It crinkled as he tried to smooth it flat, but it was large enough to lie on, and gratefully Silas stretched out.

'There's room here for you,' he called to Zoe, patting the space beside him. 'You can put your blanket next to mine.'

'You get some rest,' she said gently. 'I just need to talk to Jono.'

'OK,' Silas smiled at her through fast-closing lids.

'What's up, Zoe?' Jono asked.

'What are you going to do next? We have to leave tomorrow. Maxie and Val will be worried. But are you staying here?'

Silas tried to stay awake and listen to the answer, but he was just too tired, and the words merged into dreamscape as he fell asleep.

Warm air was moving across his face in little gusts.

Silas slowly awoke and frowned. What was causing that? Was the heating in the house faulty? He began to process his memories. Oh yes! He was in the Soulsight caverns and they had found Jono. That was fantastic, but it didn't quite explain the reason why he felt so happy. Then one thought crystallised.

Zoe!

She's lying next to me! Silas realised with wonder; that's her breath I can feel on my cheeks. Thrilled, he opened his eyes, only to screw them closed tight again.

Jono! Not the face he wanted to see when he first woke up in the morning, and certainly not in such close proximity! Where was Zoe, though? He rolled over, escaping the unappealing sensation of Jono's breath in his face, and felt damp Soulsight under the palm of his hand.

'Hey, sleepyhead,' Zoe gently called from the other side of the fire.

Levering himself up on to one elbow, he looked around. 'What's the time?'

'It's time to get up,' she smiled, completely perfect in the half-light from the dim sunstorers.

'Have you slept?' he asked her groggily. 'Is it day or night still?'

'It's morning, I think...' she said, dragging her silver blanket over to sit next to him.

'What's the plan for today?' Silas asked, reaching out to cover her hand with his. Her skin felt so soft, so warm. He could still hardly believe that yesterday had happened... she *loved* him! He didn't want to move from this place, this moment, in case something broke the spell and they had to return to the uncertainty and insecurity of the past.

'Good morning,' the deep grumble of Jono's voice effectively shattered the bubble that he had been trying to create around himself and Zoe.

'Morning, Jono,' Zoe replied brightly.

'Where's William?' he asked.

'Kes has him,' she reassured.

Jono grunted his approval and then stretched out fully. 'If she needs me, I'll just be getting cleaned up.'

Silas thought nothing would prize him from Zoe's side, but he suddenly became aware of his own overwhelming stench. The need to feel clean and smell a little more human caused him to let go of Zoe's hand.

'Where do we wash?' he asked.

'Follow me,' Jono said, springing to his feet. 'But I warn you now, the water is always cold.'

Cold was an understatement. Stripped to the waste, Silas splashed icy water over his chest and held his head under the miniature waterfall that was spewing down the green-coated wall for as long as he could tolerate.

Jono passed him a bottle of cleanser.

'Thanks,' Silas said, rubbing it into his hair and skin before braving the frigid water once more.

'That's better!' he said through chattering teeth, as he pulled his top over his head. The fabric immediately absorbed the excess moisture from his skin and deposited it as droplets on the outer layer of his jumper, which he brushed off with one flick of his hand. Within seconds his body was warm and he had stopped shivering.

'What did you decide on last night?' he asked, as Jono vigorously towelled himself dry and started redressing himself in layer after layer of thin cotton clothes, some little more than rags. 'Are you staying in the crater?'

Jono shrugged as he pulled on the last thicker, woollen layer. 'I don't know if "decide" is the right word,' he chuckled. '"From women's eyes this doctrine I derive", or, to put it another way, Zoe told me what she thinks should happen, and let's just say, she's probably right.'

Silas laughed as well. 'That sounds like Zoe. If it wasn't for her telling *us* what to do, we would never have come back to the crater and found you.'

'Very true,' Jono nodded.

'So… what are you going to do?'

'One option is to stay here. Zoe would ask Maxie and Val to send regular supplies to me.' The lack of conviction in his voice was reinforced by visible doubt and accompanied by a tiny grey shadow of fear.

'And you don't want to do that,' Silas surmised.

Jono shook his head. 'No. I've been alone for long enough. The Community was my family and I miss them. Caring for William has been the only thing that has kept me going, but he needs to be with Bonnie. He will return with you and so, I think, shall I.'

'The only way to survive will be to register for classification. When that happens you will have to become an Unseen. No more daylight,' Silas warned.

Jono nodded. 'I know, but why would I stay here when the people I love are out there? William, Zoe, Nana…'

'And Kesiah,' Silas finished the list for him, and at the sound of her name, the tendrils of fear that had been lurking in the corners of Jono's eyes receded.

'I will go where she goes,' Jono said, resolutely.

'I know that feeling,' Silas said, thinking of Zoe.

Chapter 18

It had taken most of the morning for Jono to sort through the assortment of belongings he had accumulated in the cave. Metal cooking pots, tools, items of clothing... anything that had escaped the destructive fire in the crater he treated like priceless treasure.

Silas understood why. This was the last link to Jono's childhood home, the final physical pieces that ever proved the existence of the Community. He packed a few boxes with his most precious possessions, and they persuaded him to store the rest in William's wooden crib.

While Kes helped Jono, Zoe and Silas took the opportunity to gather armfuls of Soulsight. Finding several empty Nutrifarm boxes, they filled one for each of them and stacked them next to Jono's few belongings.

'We'll com-link Nana as soon as we get to Val's house. She'll know what we should do for the best. If we can get Jono and William to Prima somehow, before...' Zoe couldn't finish her sentence. None of them wanted to think of Jono, shrouded in grey, feared by the Seen, an outcast, confined to the night and never seeing the sun again.

'Are you sure about this?' Kesiah sounded worried, but Jono was quick to reassure her.

'Yes, Kes, I am sure. I don't want to stay here on my own. If I try to get classified in Prima then at least I can be near you. I've got all I need. William has been fed. Let's go now. "There is a tide",' he began, deliberately adding volume and depth to his voice, and the rich, resonant cadences sent a shiver of light across the Soulsight layer, '"which, taken at the flood, leads on to fortune; Omitted, all the voyage of their life is bound in shallows and in miseries. On such a full sea are we now afloat. And we must take the current when it serves, or lose our ventures."'

Silas nodded. He understood – maybe not the words, but the gravity with which they were spoken and the pure and genuine courage that emanated from Jono.

They followed Jono through twisting tunnels and vast caverns, each carrying a box of Jono's belongings and a box of Soulsight.

'All the passages interconnect,' Jono called over his shoulder. He had William strapped to his chest and a large carton hooked under his arm. 'But we'll have to go the long way round to avoid any clambering.'

'That's good,' Silas said, resting his chin on the lid. 'The flatter the better. I can't see where I'm putting my feet.'

The Soulsight coating on the walls began to thin the further they travelled from the central caves, and before long the only light came from their sunstorers. The route suddenly narrowed, and through a thin opening above their heads came a draught of fresh, cold air.

'Is this the way out?' Silas asked. 'It looks different. Even smaller than I remember. No wonder we couldn't find it.'

Pushing his boxes ahead of him, he clambered out of the narrow confines of the underground caves.

A cloudless black sky stretched above them, and countless stars sparkled brilliantly in the frosty night air. A full moon hung low on the horizon, casting pale light across the barren land.

'I've lost track of time. How long were we in the caverns?' Silas asked.

'This is our third night here... I think...' Zoe said, also looking confused. 'Come on,' she said, 'the truck should be over here.'

They found it easily enough. It looked like an abandoned wreck. Silas ran his hands over the bonnet, feeling the coarsely scratched bodywork. 'We ran the power dry through the dust storm, so will it start?' he asked anxiously.

'I hope so,' Zoe muttered. 'It's old, but as long as the recharge panels had enough sun yesterday it should be OK. Otherwise we've got a long walk.' She opened the front door and powered the ignition. With a complaining whine, the vehicle reluctantly spluttered to life.

After helping Jono and Kes load up the back of the truck, Silas clambered in next to Zoe, carefully resting his bag and box of Soulsight on his knee.

'Are you all right?' he asked Jono, who had chosen to sit on the metal floor instead of the benches.

'Too tall,' Jono explained, and lay the baby on his outstretched legs.

'I'll drive as carefully as I can,' Zoe said, 'but the track is awful. I hope William will be OK.'

'He'll be fine. Let's go,' Jono said.

Silas helped Zoe as best as he could, trying to use Val's handwritten instructions in reverse. They had to stop a couple of times to get their bearings until they reached the start of the firmer road, and the journey immediately became far more comfortable. That comfort, however, was only physical, for they were all preoccupied with the painful reality that the closer they got to the town, the sooner Jono would become an Unseen.

They arrived at the outskirts of the Uninhabited area just as the concealing black of night began to fade to a pre-dawn grey.

'We need to get you to Val and Maxie's house fast, before the sun comes up,' Zoe said, passing one of the Unseen robes to Jono. 'We only have three coverings, so Kes, will you stay in the truck with William? It will be far easier to carry him during Seen hours than to try and smuggle him through town now. We need to move quickly and stay quiet. If William starts crying, he'll draw too much attention.'

'Of course I'll stay,' Kesiah responded. 'He knows me better now. I'll look after him.' Gently she lifted the sleeping child into her arms.

They could clearly see the internal battle Jono was experiencing. Relinquishing William was the first difficult step in an exceptionally hard journey.

'Are you ready?' Silas asked, looking Jono full in the face.

'No.' Jono replied, but pulled the long grey cloak over his head anyway, hiding his fear under the shroud. Silas quickly covered himself and climbed out of the truck.

'I'll come back for you after sunrise,' he said to Kes, who took Jono's place on the floor, trying to stay out of sight.

The robe stopped at Jono's knees. It looked ridiculous and glaringly obvious that it wasn't his.

'We'll have to stay close to him so no one sees his legs,' Zoe whispered to Silas. Flanking Jono, they tried to move quickly and silently through the shadowy alleyways.

It wasn't dark enough. Dawn was starting to break, and Silas tried to hasten Jono and Zoe along as they joined a deserted main street. The lack of any other movement made Silas feel more exposed, and he was acutely aware of the sound of their hurried footsteps echoing off the buildings around them. This was the interlude between the start of the Unseen curfew and the end of the Seen one, and any moment he expected to hear a shout from a patrolling Health Official.

'This one,' Zoe said breathlessly, as they crowded around Maxie and Val's front door, knocking urgently, just as the sun began to rise.

The door opened and they barged inside. Maxie sidestepped out of the way and Silas pushed the door shut behind him.

'Thank goodness you're safe. Val and I expected you back yesterday!' she cried as she helped them remove their outer robes. Then, reaching Jono, she stepped back in shock. 'Who? How can this be possible? It can't be… Jono?'

'I see you, Maxie,' he said in his deep, resonant voice.

The excitement was almost too much for Maxie. 'Val,' she shouted. 'Come and see… Jono's here!'

The 'I see you' greetings, hugs and half-explanations all took place in the narrow hallway, until Maxie eventually steered them into the larger room at the front of her house. It was the same as Silas remembered from his last visit, except for the addition of a Biocubicle. Shiny, smooth and strangely ominous, it was identical to the model that he had seen in the Unseen house back in Prima.

Finding one here, in Maxie and Val's house, seemed like an invasion. As if the cubicle were waiting to ensnare and devour rather than merely assess and advise.

The stark reminder of the world he was introducing Jono into was unsettling. Maybe he should encourage his friend to head back to the crater while he had the chance. His concerns, however, were forgotten as Val swept him into one of his strong bear hugs.

Val's approval and affection seemed limitless as he continued to hug each of them in turn until he became too short of breath and had to sit down.

'I can't believe it... You're alive!' he wheezed, gazing in wonder at Jono once again. 'Don't tell me... the crater is green once again, and Bubba Gee... is making more waterberry rum!'

'Sadly not,' Jono smiled wryly.

'There is other good news, though,' Zoe interrupted. 'Isn't there, Jono?' Then, without giving him a chance to answer, she carried on talking excitedly. 'Bonnie's son, the twin that was lost. He's been in the crater all this time! Jono found him and has been looking after him.'

This news was too much for Maxie, and she suddenly had to sit down beside Val. Her heart looked fit to burst as a palpable wave of joy emanated from her, lighting up the room with happiness. It was contagious, and Silas found his own spirits begin to rise until he wasn't sure he could contain his delight.

'You must com-link Nana immediately and tell her!' Maxie said, looking from Zoe to Jono and back again, adding in a more confused tone, 'But where is the child?'

'Kesiah has him in the truck. We didn't have enough robes for all of us to get through the curfew, so we were going to bring her and the baby after sunrise,' Silas explained.

'It will probably be safe to go now,' Zoe said trying to peer through Maxie's darkened front window. 'I'll come with you, Silas. There's quite a lot to carry. We'll com-link Nana when we get back. Then she can see the baby with her own eyes.'

It was a relief to be moving freely in the daytime without the hindrance of the Unseen robes tangling around his ankles, yet Silas was reluctant to rush.

This was the first moment that they'd had to themselves since their kiss. He glanced at Zoe, and then found he was unable to look away.

'Zoe Veron, you take my breath away!' he said, reaching to grab her hand and pulling her towards him. He wanted to imprint this moment on his memory, so even when his Soulsight faded he wouldn't forget that *this* was who she was. This perfect vision was the real Zoe.

As they embraced, she stroked his cheek. 'I've never seen you so happy,' she said, gazing up at him.

'There's a lot to be happy about.' He smiled and brushed his lips against her forehead. 'Just think… Jono's alive, we have found Bonnie's lost child, and…' he paused, still overwhelmed by the richness and depth of his feelings for her, '… we have each other.'

Silas held her gaze, seeing her love for him as clearly as if she had once again spoken the words out loud. He could have stood there for hours.

'We're supposed to be getting Kes,' Zoe said, when Silas didn't show any sign of letting go. 'She'll be worried about Jono,' Zoe prompted again.

'You're right,' he said, reluctantly releasing her from his embrace. 'Let's go.'

Chapter 19

Curfew had ended, and the Seen citizens of the town were beginning to stir.

Seeing them with Soulsight was a curious experience. Normally the streets would be full of a uniform perfection, with every Seen citizen dressed impeccably in the latest, tailored, physique-enhancing outfit, flaunting their outstanding health.

Now, however, Silas could all too clearly see the mixture of insecurities, fears and jealousies that seemed to characterise so many of the Seen. He tried not to stare, but it was a fascinating mismatch. The confidence with which these ugly and distorted people strutted along the street was astounding.

'If only they could see themselves,' he whispered to Zoe, 'what they truly look like.'

'Shh,' she hushed him. 'Were we so different before Soulsight?'

'I guess not,' he admitted, remembering the first time he'd seen the twisting shadowy fears that deformed his own true reflection.

None of the Seen, however, gave Silas and Zoe a second glance as, hands interlocked, they retraced their steps up the hill to the alleyway where Val's truck was parked.

Kesiah was pacing impatiently outside the truck. William was awake and wriggling in her arms.

'You took your time,' Kesiah complained, as William began to cry tetchily. 'Is Jono safe?'

'He's fine,' Silas reassured her. 'Is everything all right here?'

Kesiah visibly relaxed and gave a small nod. 'We got bored in there, didn't we?' she cooed to William, whose response was to cry even louder. 'And I think he's missing Jono.'

'Give me a minute to get some of these boxes,' Zoe said, opening the back of the truck, 'and then we'll take you straight to Maxie and Val's.'

'Pass my Soulsight, would you please?' Silas asked, as Zoe loaded him up with a hefty container of Jono's belongings. She precariously balanced the box of Soulsight Silas had collected on top of that.

'Please, William, try to be quiet now,' Kesiah muttered anxiously, as the baby's cries grew even more fraught. She tried rocking him in her arms to soothe him, but that seemed to make him more distressed.

Zoe emerged from the back of the truck, wincing at the sound. 'Silas, you know the way now, so why don't you take Kesiah and William to the house? He's so unhappy, he just needs to see Jono. I'll sort through what we need to bring, and will follow you down in a moment.'

'Good idea,' Silas replied, and Kes nodded her agreement. The sooner they got the baby inside the better.

William seemed to calm down as Kesiah carried him along the street. There were so many interesting things for him to look at, and his head turned this way and that as they passed houses and shops and increasing numbers of people.

Initially, Silas enjoyed the wonder with which baby William greeted this strange new world. However, he grew uncomfortable as more Seen emerged from their nocturnal curfew. The baby aroused far more interest in the passers-by than Silas wanted. He could see the blatant curiosity flickering across their faces.

'I should have smuggled him in at sunrise, under my Unseen coverings. Someone's bound to ask us about him soon,' Silas said under his breath.

Any infant was enough of a novelty to attract attention, but William was dressed in strange off-cuts and wrapped in a grubby blanket. He did not look like the treasured child of a Seen. Any minute someone would ask who William was and where his parents were. The quicker they got him to Maxie and Val's house the better.

'Just around the corner,' Silas muttered to Kes. 'Oh, excuse me.' He smiled apologetically at two smartly dressed Seen women, as he deliberately manoeuvred his large boxes to effectively block William from their inquisitive glances. One of them had a decidedly malicious air and Silas wasn't going to let her get even a glimpse of the baby.

However, in his attempt to shield Kesiah and William, Silas failed to notice what was going on outside Maxie and Val's house.

'Oh no! Go back, go back!' he said, rapidly retracing his steps and treading heavily on Kesiah's foot as he pushed her back the way they had just come.

'What are you doing?' Kes complained. 'Careful, you nearly knocked us over!'

'Sorry,' Silas said, glancing anxiously down the street again. 'Look!'

'What is it?' she said as she peered past him. 'Oh!' she gasped, as her eyes took in the obvious problem.

The gleaming hull of a Health Emergency-Life Preservation transport filled the road directly outside Maxie and Val's house.

'What are HE-LP doing there?' Kesiah asked. 'They can't have found Jono already.'

'It's probably coincidental,' Silas said, trying to soothe her. 'I expect they are here with medicines for Val or something. If they had found Jono, they would have already called for the Health Advisors. I'll check what's happening. You had better stay here with William. I don't want to have to explain him to the HE-LP.'

Despite his reassuring words, Silas felt nervous as he approached. The door to Maxie and Val's house was wide open.

Partially covering the boxes with the trailing lengths of one of the Unseen robes hanging behind the door, Silas quietly moved along the hall to the front room.

All seemed quiet. Perhaps the HE-LP were at a neighbouring house, Silas wondered, and began to push open the inner door.

'What are you doing?' asked a deep voice, and Silas swung around to be confronted by the broad chest of a uniformed HE-LP.

'Sorry, I was just…' Stuttering an apology, he backed away, nearly falling into Maxie and Val's front room.

The HE-LP reached out an arm, and Silas flinched until he realised the man was offering a steadying hand. 'Careful, kid,' the man said, patience and concern filling his large frame. 'This is an Unseen residence. You shouldn't be in here. We get kids like you all the time. Trying to get a look at what horror lies beneath the Unseen robes. Well, I can tell you, the Unseen aren't monsters… they are just people.'

'That's not why I'm here, but please will you let me stay? I… I've been wondering if I should train as a HE-LP when I leave clinic.'

Silas registered the ease with which he had lied, but he knew he had said the only thing that would appeal to the man's simple and steady heart.

'I still can't really allow you to come in,' answered the HE-LP, with the measured calm of someone who was merely performing the necessities of his job. 'We are re-screening for contagion in here.'

'Why would you need to do that?' Silas asked, stepping quickly into the front room and glancing around to see if Jono was there.

A woman in a HE-LP uniform had her back to them and was watching a data stream that projected from the Biocubicle.

'There was unusual activity at this address just before the overlap of curfew. That could indicate a fresh outbreak of contagion.' The HE-LP towered over Silas and spoke with steady deliberation. 'We are simply doing what needs to be done.'

Silas swallowed nervously. He hadn't realised the Unseen premises were so carefully watched.

'We either do a complete assessment here,' the HE-LP explained, watching Silas' expression curiously, 'or all the Unseen at this address will be taken to the quarantine facility in Prima.'

Silas could see the man was telling the truth; Soulsight showed him that much. It was a routine check and, as yet, they were unaware that Jono wasn't simply just another Unseen.

Just then the woman turned from the data stream. 'This one's contagion free,' she called to her colleague. 'She's as healthy as she'll ever be. I'll bring the tall one through while you get that kid out of here.'

'He wants to become a HE-LP,' the man explained.

'There's protocol for taking on trainees,' the woman responded brusquely, turning to Silas. 'Your clinic manager will be able to advise you.'

The Biocubicle doors hissed faintly as they slid open, and Maxie stumbled out, her eyes dark with swirling fear shadows.

'Jono?' Silas mouthed at her, hoping that somehow his friend had had time to hide, but Maxie shook her head, mutely following the female HE-LP who ushered her through the door into the separate back room.

'Last one,' the HE-LP beckoned impatiently as, stooping to clear the doorframe, Jono stepped into the room.

Insecurity and anxiety rippled across his features as he approached the Biocubicle.

Silas longed to say something to reassure him. Things hadn't gone as they had planned. Jono had been picked up by the Health Authorities too soon, but maybe he could be transferred to Prima after his classification.

The Biocubicle door slid closed.

'You've had a good look at them now. Being a HE-LP means you have to be able to work with all kinds of people, Seen and

Unseen.' The HE-LP took a firm grip of Silas' shoulder to guide him forcefully from the house. 'Maybe you don't have what it takes.'

'But please, can't I wait until he finishes his assessment?' Silas asked, trying to think of another reason why he should stay.

'You need to see this!' The woman suddenly called out to her colleague, her eyes fixed to the stream of data now pouring out of the Biocubicle.

'What's the matter?' he asked, letting go of Silas.

The two HE-LP were huddled around the data as they discussed the results, and Silas' presence was temporarily forgotten. He inched nearer to hear what they were saying.

'... no record locally or nationally... so he must be an Unclassified.'

'From that place they cleared out a few months back?'

Silas guessed that they were talking about the Community, and internally he seethed. How dare they speak of 'clearing out' the Community, like you would clear out the rubbish?

The woman nodded. 'I guess. But how did they miss this one? He's not exactly small. I've sent an alert. The Advisors are on their way.'

Silas' blood ran cold. The Health Advisors had already been informed. It was all happening too fast.

'What else are the results showing?'

'Um... unusual phenotype... well, you saw him. Uh-oh...' The HE-LP shook her head. 'We've got a positive for the contagion. When the Health Advisors get here they can take him straight to quarantine and classify him later.'

'I don't understand,' Silas muttered, shaking his head. This made no sense. Jono couldn't have picked up a virus in the few minutes he had been in the town. Apart from Maxie and Val, he hadn't had contact with any other Unseen.

The data suddenly dispersed and was replaced by the words, 'Prepare for transfer.'

'Good,' the HE-LP said. 'Let's get this one into the transport and wait for the Advisors. That should limit any spread.'

'No! You can't,' interjected Silas.

'We can,' the man insisted. 'And we must. It's best for the Unclassified. As a Seen you are not at risk from infection, but stay out of the way as we escort the Unclassified outside.' The Biocubicle opened and Jono shakily stepped out. He looked like he was about to collapse. Fear shadows were spilling from him, thick and fast, twisting his features and distorting his appearance.

'Let me go with him,' Silas said, desperate not to leave Jono alone. If one small scan in the Biocubicle produced this response in Jono, how would he cope with being in a quarantine facility? And what would happen when the Soulsight wore off? If he were scared now, he would be terrified then.

'Absolutely not!' The female HE-LP sounded appalled. 'We have to hand this Unclassified over to the Health Advisors. It's the correct emergency procedure. Now, you should be at clinic, so why don't you go before I report you to your manager? This Unclassified is not your problem. Do you understand?'

Silas understood all too clearly. He agreed with the HE-LP, Jono was certainly not his 'problem'. He was his friend and his responsibility, and Silas was not going to let him out of his sight.

'Please listen.' Silas turned to the more sympathetic of the two HE-LP. 'I haven't been honest with you. I know who this Unclassified is. There must be a way for you to let me travel with him?' Silas asked again.

The man shrugged, but a high-pitched whine of a transport landing outside forestalled any reply.

'The Health Advisors are here already. Now follow me,' the woman commanded Jono, who looked helplessly at Silas as he fell into line behind her. His fear had diminished him, making him appear smaller. Silas couldn't bear it. To see Jono looking so... so fragile.

A fire of frustrated rage burned within him. Why wouldn't they listen? 'Take me with him, now!' Silas shouted, balling his hand into a fist, and as the tall male HE-LP passed him, he did the only thing guaranteed to get attention.

Silas had never struck another person, but he let his anger fuel his punch, and swung.

It was a weak blow, and taken from an awkward angle, but it hit home under the man's chin, catching him by surprise. He staggered and fell back against the wall.

'What the…?' he bellowed in confusion. 'You attacked me!'

The HE-LP pushed himself upright, glowering at Silas and rubbing his chin before cautiously running his hand over the back of his head. His visible anger immediately turned to fear as his fingers came away red with blood.

'999!' he shouted to his colleague as, unaware, she continued to lead Jono towards the front door. 'We have a triple 9!'

The response to the 999 call was rapid and terrifying, and before he knew it, a squad of four white-suited Government Health Advisors had pushed Jono back into Maxie and Val's front room, and Silas was staring down the wrong end of a disruptor.

'It looks like we got here just at the right time. You need to get your colleague checked up, then he can file his accusation,' one of the Advisors barked at the female HE-LP as he pointed a disruptor at Jono. 'We'll take over.'

The HE-LP seemed all too ready to hand over responsibility to the Health Advisors and hurried to the safety of their transport.

The Advisor turned to Silas. 'Let's get a background check on you. Get in the Biocubicle. No sudden moves, no trying to run!'

He tried not to shake as he moved towards the Biocubicle. His plan had gone drastically wrong. All he'd wanted to do was stay with Jono. He hadn't meant to cause injury. They were classifying it as a 999… a grievous assault on a government worker.

Obeying the threatening wave of the disruptor, Silas slowly stepped inside.

He'd never been in one of the new Biocubicles, and as the door shut behind him he experienced a feeling of claustrophobia. The dull white interior seemed to close in on him. He rubbed his eyes to reduce the optical illusion.

Then the walls began to glow.

Instead of the usual mesh of red scanning beams, a cold, blue light surrounded him. His skin prickled and the hairs on the back of his neck rose. With a sudden chill, the light passed through the outer layer of his skin, and Silas was conscious of its icy touch as it permeated his muscles and bones. It was like freezing water passing *through* his body.

He felt strangely violated by the illumination as the penetrating light reached his inner organs, causing his gut to clench in revulsion. Just as he thought he couldn't take any more, the glow was extinguished and the door slid open.

'Stay where you are, Silas Corelle.' With the disruptor still pointed at him, he remained standing in the doorway of the Biocubicle, staring at the scene before him. All four Health Advisors were brimming with fear. Their professional training kept their voices and commands clear, but Soulsight showed the bubbling anxiety that was rolling out from each of them.

Jono was on his knees, his good arm on his head and a disruptor trained at the back of his skull.

One of the Advisors was talking into a com-link, and Silas heard his name mentioned, and then he heard the accusations… '999, grievous assault', followed by a far more chilling statement. 'Bio-assessment forgery.'

Silas' heart sank as it dawned on him. He was in serious amounts of trouble. He had forgotten about the recorded results being pumped out from his Biocubicle at home. He'd been caught red-handed; simultaneous results from two different Biocubicles hundreds of miles apart. How could he have been so stupid?

A simple two-dimensional projection filled the far wall. A wave of heat coursed through Silas' body, for there, staring at him from across the room, the disapproval in the projected image as overwhelming as it would be in person, was his father.

Chapter 20

He vomited.

The combination of the invasive bio-assessment, the looming threat of the disruptor, the utter failure of his attempt to help Jono, and now his father's disapproving glower caused his guts to react in the only way they knew.

Silas looked with disbelief at the sticky pile of brownish watery nutrition that now lay on the floor of Maxie and Val's house. He couldn't remember ever having been sick before. It was disgusting, and as the bitter taste of acid burned his throat, he began to dry-heave.

'Get him into isolation,' the Advisor instructed as Silas continued to retch, 'before he's sick again.'

Still feeling shaky, Silas meekly followed the Advisor out of Maxie and Val's house and towards the waiting transport.

'Sit,' the Health Advisor instructed, pointing to a long, raised, flat sill beside a clear partition.

Silas did as he was told and the partition glided closed, sealing him behind a transparent wall.

Moments later, the tall, stooped figure of Jono, now covered head to knee in a grey Unseen robe, was ushered in to an identical isolation unit.

As the clear barrier closed on him, Jono wrenched the covering from his body and threw it against the wall. Rage, fear and frustration merged to produce something dark and terrifying, and the Jono that Silas had seen in the Soulsight caverns was lost under rolling waves of fury.

'Jono!' Silas shouted, but his friend wouldn't even look at him. 'I'm sorry. I tried to help...' Silas pleaded, but then Jono's appearance twisted dramatically as he threw back his head, opened his mouth wide and screamed.

Silas heard nothing.

The isolation units were completely soundproof. Jono began to kick and beat against the transparent wall that contained him.

'Stay calm,' Silas shouted, but Jono didn't even glance his way. He seemed completely lost in his fear and anger.

'Look at me!' Silas shouted again, and started waving his arms frantically around to try to get his attention. That seemed to work, as Jono stopped his fruitless attack on the isolation unit and sat unsteadily on the raised shelf. His anger receded, and finally he looked at Silas.

There was a moment of connection. A millisecond of clarity. 'I'm sorry...' Silas mouthed, then Jono's eyes clouded and he yawned, lay down and closed his eyes.

'You've sedated him?' Silas shouted with furious disbelief to the Advisor who watched impassively as Jono began to breathe deeply and steadily.

'Stop ignoring me! I know you can hear me. Look, I'm sorry for what I've done. I only wanted to help my friend. Won't you even look at me?'

Eventually the Advisor cast Silas a frustrated glance and typed something on his screen. Silas felt his anger subside, and he felt foolish for shouting at the glass screen. There was a shelf running the length of his cubicle... he should lie down on it. If he rested, just for a moment, he might think of a better way to help himself... and... Jono...

Waking up happened as gradually as had falling asleep, and Silas' thoughts become coherent once again, seamlessly restarting from when they had been interrupted.

'Jono! Why have you...?' he started to say, then, with a sudden jolt, he saw that the isolation unit opposite his own was empty. The Advisor had his back to Silas, and he banged furiously on the glass again. 'Where is he? Where have you taken him?' Silas shouted.

Eventually the Advisor turned to face him, and Silas took a surprised step back. While he had slept, his Soulsight had worn off, and before him stood an immaculate Government Health Advisor. He was tall and powerfully built, and his face was an unreadable mask. His true self was once again hidden behind a perfect physical shell.

Immediately, Silas' thoughts returned to Jono.

'The Unclassified... where is he?' Silas asked, trying to keep his voice calm to avoid being sedated again.

The Advisor lightly touched the other side of the transparent partition. There was a barely audible click and the soundproofing was temporarily removed.

'Where did the Unclassified go?' Silas repeated.

'Your concern should not be for the Unclassified,' he said gravely, a frown wrinkling his otherwise smooth forehead. 'He will be treated and will then be allocated Unseen duties. You should be worrying more about your own situation. I am to take you straight to the Health and Safety court to be judged.'

In the windowless, soundproofed isolation unit, Silas wasn't even aware of their landing until the rear doors of the transport slid open. This time the Advisor was holding a disruptor in his hand as he released the partition and scowled at Silas.

'Come,' the Advisor barked abruptly.

Obediently, Silas followed him onto the landing area.

A surprisingly large number of people had gathered by the entrance to the Health and Safety courts, and Silas wondered what they were waiting for. Then a shout went up and the crowd started to surge towards him. Drone cameras hovered in his face as questions were fired at him from all directions.

'Silas Corelle, is it true you have been charged with a triple nine?'

'Did you forge your bio-assessment?'

Silas looked behind him to see the source of that question.

'Is your father aware of the charges against you?'

How did they know these things about him?

'Keep moving,' the Health Advisor commanded, shielding Silas as he pushed through the crowd.

'Why were you in the Outerlands?'

'Have you been exposed to the Unseen virus?'

Try as he might to ignore the barrage of questions, Silas couldn't help but want to explain his reasons and defend himself. Then it occurred to him that there was nothing to defend. He had broken the rules – broken the law – and now he would face the consequences.

The Advisor steered him through the tall glass entrance of the Health and Safety courts, and Silas was initially glad when the doors closed behind them, cutting off the noise from the crowds outside. However, the thick blanketing silence offered an unpleasant contrast, and the air of hush and dread that filled the vast antechamber sent a shiver down his spine.

'Judgement Point 74H,' the Advisor read off an information panel. 'This way.' He set off down a side corridor, evidently expecting Silas to follow.

For a fleeting moment he considered running, until he looked back and saw the pack of eager reporters waiting for a hint of a story, and his heart sank. There was no escape for him. He was at the mercy of the courts now.

Then, from behind the scandal-hungry crowd, he saw a familiar figure approaching.

'Dad.' Silas felt his throat constrict. He desperately wanted his father's support, but he knew it was unlikely to be forthcoming. His father would demand an explanation, and Silas didn't even know where to begin.

He hadn't been the only person to see his father. The crowd immediately recognised Anton Corelle as well, and, despite his physical strength, his father seemed hemmed in and was having difficulty getting to the door of the court.

'Follow!' the Advisor instructed, noticing Silas' hesitation.

Reluctant to go, Silas stood his ground. 'My father – Anton Corelle…' he began to say.

'… will be directed to your Judgement Point,' the Advisor finished for him.

Then Silas saw another figure barrelling through the crowd, clearing the way. Head and shoulders above the reporters, his brother, Marc, forced a path to the door and ushered their father through.

Silas' spirits sank. Why was Marc here as well? Maybe he couldn't resist the spectacle of Silas being in trouble. Suddenly, Silas didn't want his father or Marc to see him and, using the bulk of the Health Advisor as a shield, he let himself be led away.

'Do you realise the embarrassment you have caused me? The damage you have done to the Bio-health laboratory… to all that I have been working towards? Did you see the crowd out there? What have I done to deserve this?' His father glared at him.

Silas leaned against the wall and stared unblinkingly at the ground. He daren't open his mouth. Anything he said would just be fuel to the fire of his father's anger.

'You struck a HE-LP and are charged with a 999! And assessment forgery! What were you doing in the Outerlands in the first place? In the home of an Unseen? There's a contagion! Have you forgotten? Do you want to end up like your mother?'

Shocked, Silas looked up. 'This is how it starts, Silas.' His father's voice was measured, but the throbbing vein on his temple belied his barely contained rage.

'No, Dad, no! It's not like that.' Silas was horrified. 'Mum didn't know she was sick.' He tried to defend her memory. Nana had said that his mother had given so much of her time to helping the Unseen that she had neglected her own health and stopped her bio-assessments. Without the regular scans, a tiny aneurysm had grown unnoticed on her cranial artery, and when it had suddenly ruptured it was too late for the HE-LP to intervene, and she had died.

For years Silas had believed that her death fully deserved the shameful label of being self-inflicted, and he had resented her for it. However, his time with the Community had taught him the incredible breadth of his mother's compassion for the Unseen. Even without Soulsight she had loved and cared for the unlovable.

'Silas, you remind me of her in so many ways. You look like her, you have her character, her manner... but you are also my son, and I don't want to lose you too.' His father's expression grew severe. 'Yet your behaviour has been unbelievably foolish. I am hoping that whatever punishment you receive will serve to remind you of what is truly important. I can try to help you, to present your side to the judge before sentencing, but for that you have to tell me exactly what you were doing in the Outerlands.'

'I... I...' Silas didn't know what to say. The truth would expose Zoe, Nana, Maxie and Val, and although there was an inevitability to Kesiah's involvement being uncovered, he didn't want to hasten it. It was just a matter of time before either her recording square was discovered or his Biocubicle records would betray her. Then the whole story would unravel. His father would want to know why she had been staying at the house when Silas had been in the Outerlands, and whether she had been covering for him. He could see it all now. Kes would no longer be Gold Standard. Maybe she'd have to move away from Prima altogether. How would he explain that to Jono?

'Well, Silas?' His father frowned at him impatiently.

'Um...' Silas looked around the room desperately for some kind of inspiration. Then his gaze fell on Marc, who had been standing silently in the corner. Marc winked. Silas frowned, and Marc winked again.

He's enjoying this, Silas thought, and clamped his mouth firmly closed. He definitely wasn't going to say anything with Marc in the room.

'He was running away,' Marc said, his voice harsh and loud.

Silas stared at his brother with confusion and dislike. Why was Marc getting involved, anyway?

'What do mean, Marc?' his father asked. 'What do you know?'

'It's because of Kesiah,' Marc said.

'No!' Silas cried, trying to stop his brother from revealing more. 'Keep your mouth shut!'

'Kes finished with him. She chose me, and he couldn't handle that, so he ran away. He became so angry he did the only thing a pathetic kid like him would do. He tried to get lost in the Outerlands rather than deal with it! Didn't you, Silas?'

Silas couldn't believe what he was hearing. 'What are you talking about? Kes never... I didn't...' His anger turned to uncertainty as Marc widened his eyes and angled his head briefly to one side. Then Silas saw it. Glinting in the palm of Marc's hand was a gold recording square. Kesiah's recording square.

Suddenly he understood. Marc had created an excuse that would explain the bio-assessment records. He was covering for them. With this dawning realisation, Silas stopped contradicting him.

'Is that what this is about?' Stunned fury had replaced any compassion in their father's voice.

Risking another glance at Marc, who nodded his head once, Silas found he was nodding too.

'Are you mad? You put your health, your future, both of our reputations on the line... because of a girl?' The outraged incredulity in his father's voice made Silas want to protest his innocence, but then it occurred to him that he *had* risked everything for a girl... except the girl wasn't Kes; it was Zoe.

'What's going to happen to me, Dad?' Silas asked sheepishly.

Anton sighed heavily. 'A normal punishment would be a residency in Re-education, but you are still a minor, so perhaps the judge will be lenient. I'll see what I can do.' Shaking his head in disbelief, he turned away. 'I am very disappointed in you.'

The sting at finally hearing his father's true opinion of him expressed aloud was surprisingly intense. 'I'm sorry that I let you down,' Silas murmured, trying to swallow back his tears.

But his father either didn't hear or chose to ignore him.

'Judgement Point 74H. Request exit, Anton Corelle and Marc Corelle,' Anton announced. The door opened, and he and Marc left without looking back.

Silas sank down the wall with his head in his hands. Never before had he felt so helpless and so hopeless. This was all Zoe's fault, he thought self-pityingly. If only she had listened to reason. Then he caught himself. It wasn't Zoe who had done this to him; it was the Biocubicles, the Health system that controlled everyone and everything. And Jono had exchanged the freedom of the Soulsight caverns for this.

Suddenly his situation seemed to pale into insignificance as he thought about what Jono must be going through.

Where had he been taken, and how was he feeling? The contagion diagnosis had been such a complete surprise that Silas had hardly begun to process it. What was the illness like? What if Jono didn't get better? The HE-LP had mentioned treatment and a quarantine facility, but Silas had no idea where that was. He needed to get out of the Health and Safety courts and tell Zoe and Nana what had happened. They would know what to do.

'The judge will be with us in a moment,' his father announced tersely as he and Marc swept back into the judgement room.

Almost immediately, the stark white wall at the end began to change colour, and through it walked the projection of a Health and Safety judge. Her grey hair and ramrod posture reminded Silas of Nana, but when she spoke there was none of Nana's warmth in her words.

'Silas Corelle, step forward,' she instructed.

With shaking legs, Silas stood and walked towards the projection.

'The evidence against you has been presented and weighed. Do you have any personal statements you wish to add at this time?'

Silas mutely shook his head. A numbing panic had set in, so he couldn't have said anything even if he had wanted to.

'You are charged with a 999 and a bio-assessment forgery. Your actions have threatened your health, and the health of those around you.

'This is the first incident on an otherwise unblemished record, and your father has clearly explained the childish ignorance behind your unwise conduct. However, to permit such damaging behaviour to go uncorrected would be detrimental to you as an individual, as well as to society as a whole. Therefore, Silas Corelle, you will be suspended from clinic attendance and be subject to an unspecified period of Re-education. Your father assures me that you *will* attend without needing to be resident at one of our facilities.'

'I get to go home?' Silas asked in a faltering voice.

The projection of the judge gave him a withering stare, and Silas quailed under her glower.

'If you fail to attend the sessions, you will be made a resident.'

'Thank you, Judge,' Anton stepped forward and put his hand on Silas' shoulder. 'I'll make sure he attends Re-education.'

As the wall reverted to bright white, Silas gave a sigh of relief. He was heading home, and although Re-education sounded gruelling, at least he could meet up with Zoe and Kes in the evenings and together they would be able to find Jono.

Chapter 21

'Are you awake?' Silas whispered, as he knocked quietly on Marc's door.

All evening he had been desperate to talk to Marc, but his father had watched Silas' every move since they had arrived home.

'I still can't believe you did something so reckless,' his father kept saying. 'Running away. I mean, why? Things are going well for you at clinic. And Kesiah, well, she was always out of your league... she's Gold Standard.'

'You don't need to remind me, Dad,' Silas said, privately thinking that it was just as well he wasn't heartbroken over his supposed break-up with Kes; he wouldn't have got any sympathy from his father.

'There must be someone else, someone in Silver or Bronze, perhaps?'

Silas had let the conversation slide. He hadn't thought it was a good time to mention Zoe. Instead he had spent longer than usual in the health suite and then taken a lengthy shower. His dad had even checked up on him while he was getting cleaned up.

'I won't do it again, Dad. I'm sorry! It was a mistake. You don't have to follow me around. I'm not going anywhere!' he called out as he saw the shower room door open a crack.

At last Silas had his final Biocubicle assessment of the evening and heard his father and Marc move to their respective bedrooms. Fighting fatigue, he forced himself to wait before going to Marc's room.

He was about to knock again when the door opened and Marc, with his finger to his lips, ushered him inside.

'House, low light.'

A soft glow radiated from the walls and ceiling, glinting off of the many medals and trophies that adorned the room, all proclaiming the triumphs of Marc Corelle.

A projection of the finishing line from Marc's final race at Vitality Clinic was on permanent rerun on the far wall. It displayed a miniature 3D Marc, his chest thrust forward as he crossed the line, the other sprinters trailing behind him. Then came the moment his fans poured onto the track to congratulate him on setting the new clinic record.

Silas looked away as it started to replay. He didn't need to be reminded which of them was the golden child, the success... and yet that was what had made Marc's deception even more surprising.

Silas swallowed nervously and decided he would have to be the first to speak. 'Why did you...' he hesitated, trying to think of a better word than 'lie'. 'Why didn't you tell Dad the truth about the recording square with Kesiah's results on?' he finally asked.

Marc regarded him with unblinking eyes. Silas longed to have Soulsight. He could really do with understanding Marc a bit better. They had led separate lives for so long that they were more like strangers than brothers.

Eventually Marc spoke, but he didn't answer the question. Instead, he asked a question of his own. 'Who was the Unclassified you were with?'

Silas looked up in surprise. 'Unclassified?'

'Don't play dumb. I was with Dad when the com-link came through. I saw you in the house of that Unseen, and there was an Unclassified in the background and... I don't know why, but he seems familiar. Who was he?'

Silas gulped. How had Marc recognised Jono? When they had met previously, Marc was so heavily affected by Soulsight he had thought Jono was the perfect Seen and had tried to protect him from Helen Steele and the Health Advisors.

'Tell me, or I'll have to let Dad know about my discovery and Kes can join you in Re-education,' Marc threatened, holding out the gold square with the proof of Kesiah's forged Biocubicle results on it.

Silas finally understood. That was why Marc had hidden the truth from their father. It wasn't to protect either him or Kesiah… it was so he could use it to get information. He stared anxiously at Marc, weighing his options. Perhaps this would be the moment to tell his brother everything? The truth would be difficult for Marc to hear, and even more difficult for him to believe…

'Tell me what you know,' demanded Marc, adding an element of threat to his voice, while slipping the square into his pocket.

Silas shrugged. He was too exhausted to come up with a believable alternative. If Marc wanted the truth, he would get the truth. What was the worst that could happen? Kes would simply have to join him in Re-ed. With Jono stuck in some quarantine facility, facing imminent classification as an Unseen, Kesiah's predicament suddenly seemed less pressing.

'He's called Jono,' Silas said.

'And how do you know him?' Marc pressed, narrowing his eyes as if he could detect the truth of Silas' responses.

'I met him when I went away last season-break,' Silas said, assessing Marc's reactions in turn.

'Last season-break?' Marc sounded surprised. 'I didn't know you'd been away. Where did you go?'

This was it, Silas thought. This was the moment. 'A place known as the Community, in the Northern Outerlands. Jono lived with a group of Unclassified without monitoring or Bio-assessments. Then, one day, the Government Health Advisors came and took all the people for classification. They destroyed their homes so they could never return.'

Marc looked puzzled. It was like watching a faulty projection flicker as he veered from comprehension back to confusion.

'I don't... How do you...? I was...' he stuttered.

'Yes,' Silas nodded. 'You were there too. I know what you did. I saw what happened.'

This was almost a step too far, and Silas watched with a sense of satisfaction as Marc's mouth opened and closed like a trap. 'You were... there?'

'I saw everything,' Silas confirmed.

'Then tell me what happened! I've spent six months trying to remember and all I get are half-fragments. Some kind of cave, maybe... an Unclassified... a disgusting Unseen without the proper coverings on,' he shuddered. 'And then the Flawless Leader suspended me from the Advisors. Apparently I was "unfit for active duty"! When have I ever been unfit?' he protested, growing increasingly agitated.

'Shh!' Silas motioned, nervously, looking at the door. He really didn't want to wake their father. Keeping his voice as calm as possible, he began to explain about the Community and about Soulsight. Silas was impressed with how well Marc listened, only becoming agitated again when Silas began to describe the Flawless Leader.

'No. That can't be right. I cannot believe it. That was *not* Helen Steele. I still get nightmares!'

'Me too. But out of everyone there, only we could see the Flawless Leader for who she really is... something abhorrent... evil... I don't know if you remember, but you attacked her.'

Marc frowned. 'I attacked the Flawless Leader?'

'You put your hands around her neck,' Silas agreed quietly.

'I did what?' he exclaimed loudly, making Silas glance nervously at the door again. 'You are saying that I tried to strangle her? But that would be a 999, against Helen Steele!' His face paled. 'What have I done?'

'You were trying to protect Jono.'

'And this whole time you knew?' Marc asked accusingly. 'You knew what had happened and didn't tell me?'

'I'm sorry, Marc. I didn't know how to explain it. How to even begin.'

'And why were you back there this time?'

'I went back to help a friend. Kesiah wanted to come too. I didn't force her or anything. She persuaded me, really. Can I have her recording now?'

Marc didn't respond immediately. He looked stunned, as his world was being slowly turned upside down. 'How did I look with Soulsight?' he asked hesitantly, as if fearing the answer. 'Did I look like... her?'

Silas considered how best to respond. In all honesty, Marc had looked childlike and underdeveloped, but he couldn't say that. 'You weren't perfect,' he said eventually. 'I can get some more Soulsight if you want to try it again. I collected a box load, if Kesiah has managed to bring it back with her.'

'Yes,' Marc said decisively. 'And I want to meet him, this Jono. It feels important. Like we are connected in some way.' Uncertainty clouded Marc's expression. 'I can't explain, but that's why I went to your room. I wanted to try to find out how you knew him. Then I saw the two recording squares. I knew you'd tell me what I wanted to know if I had something on Kesiah.'

'When you first came home, after being dismissed from the Health Advisor Squad, you spoke of owing a debt, do you remember?' Silas asked.

Marc nodded slightly. 'Yes, that was what I felt.'

'After you attacked Helen Steele, she was going to have you killed. Jono defended you so she punished him instead. That's why you recognise him and why you feel this connection. He saved your life, Marc.'

'Why would he do that?!' Marc exclaimed, wrestling with this new bombshell.

Silas shrugged. 'We can ask him if we can find him,' he offered, looking thoughtfully at Marc. 'He's receiving treatment before his classification. What do you know about this quarantine facility?'

'Nothing… yet. Though I can try to find out,' Marc replied. 'Tomorrow when you're at Re-education, I'll make some enquiries at work.'

'Really? You are going to help?' Silas managed a tired smile.

'I'll do what I can.'

Silas tiptoed back to his room, allowing himself to feel a glimmer of hope. As unlikely as it seemed, Marc had become an ally.

The house woke him with the usual instruction for a bio-assessment.

Remembering the cold blue light of the new cubicles, Silas was glad he still had an old-fashioned model. His results were unchanged by his time away, and he went through his allocated exercise in the health suite. Unusually, both his father and Marc were there, and his father seemed torn between encouraging Marc and warily eyeing Silas.

'I'm going to take you to your Re-education session this morning,' his father announced abruptly. 'The only reason you have avoided residency is because I have vouched for you, Silas. You went off the rails, lost your focus. It happens. I'm not going to add to your punishment. Your suspension and Re-education should be enough, but I am not risking you dodging out of this.'

'Of course, Dad.' Silas sounded as contrite as he could.

'Marc will meet you after your session and escort you home. You have a long way to go to rebuild my trust in you.'

Silas nodded meekly, although he was glad that he would get to spend some time alone with Marc. Hopefully he would have news of Jono's whereabouts.

They took an autocar into the city centre, and Silas fidgeted as they sped through the streets. They were heading for Prima city centre, and he wondered which of the vast central buildings housed the Re-education facility.

'Here we are,' Anton said as the vehicle eventually slowed and stopped. Stepping out, Silas gazed up in open-mouthed wonder. Soaring above him to brush the clouds with its slender tip was the Spire. He'd only seen it from afar as he sat in the tree house back in the Uninhabited district. The building had looked beautiful then, but up close it was a marvel of creative genius. The glass walls mirrored the sky in a shimmering grey and silver waterfall.

'This is where Re-education happens?' Silas asked breathily. He couldn't believe this was his punishment. To come to the Spire – the heart of Prima city.

'Through here.' His father motioned to a side entrance of the magnificent building. A discreet sign with the words 'Re-education' and the golden torch logo marked an inconspicuous doorway.

Anton spoke into the door interface. 'Silas Corelle for Re-education.'

A male voice enquired. 'Is that for day case or residential?'

'Day case,' Silas' father affirmed, while anxiously looking over his shoulder. Remembering the pack of eager reporters outside the courtrooms, Silas also lowered his head. He could sense his father's shame and it made him feel doubly guilty.

'Welcome to Re-education,' a gentle voice suddenly interjected, causing Silas to jump. He hadn't heard the small door open. A pleasant-faced young man dressed conservatively in a pale-green silk shirt and trousers smiled at Silas and his father. The man looked peaceful, and Silas immediately felt his anxiety melt away.

'I am Reeph,' the man said. 'You must be Silas. Come inside.'

Silas nodded. He felt oddly tongue-tied around Reeph, but at the same time drawn to him. There was something about the way he spoke… every word had a melodic ring as if he were singing rather than just speaking.

'Silas…?' his father started to say as he hovered anxiously outside the door.

'Silas will be safe with us,' the man reassured him with the same gentle tone.

'Of course, yes. Marc will collect you,' his father reminded him.

'I know, Dad,' Silas replied, and without looking back, he followed Reeph into the Re-education facility.

Chapter 22

'This is amazing,' Silas said, as he gazed around in awestruck reverie.

He didn't know what he had been expecting, but it certainly wasn't the lush green forest that lay before him. He stepped through the doorway from the preparation room to stand on the edge of a large, grassy clearing. A light breeze rustled through the branches of the surrounding wood, and the treetops swayed gently against a perfect blue sky.

To one side of the clearing a gurgling stream ran into a pool. The water looked clean and deep and refreshing, and Silas longed to dive in and let his lingering anxieties be washed away.

He almost laughed. If this place was considered a punishment, then Silas couldn't imagine what a reward would be like.

A movement caught Silas' eye and he could make out figures, other Re-education residents, running or walking among the paths that wound through the trees. They were all wearing the same orange uniform with a tight black hood, and when Silas looked down he saw that he was wearing it too.

'I don't remember getting changed,' he said, raising a hand to feel the encasing hood over his own hair and ears.

Reeph smiled at him, and Silas immediately felt at ease. 'What you are wearing is necessary. Come with me, this way.'

I must have put this on in the other room… when Reeph was talking to me, Silas thought. But any concern about his clothing completely disappeared as he followed Reeph along a wide path fringed with fragrant flowering shrubs that cut through the middle of the forest.

'How is all this possible, Reeph?' Silas asked, trying to see as much of the facility as he could as they passed increasingly exotic plants. 'How do you get sunlight down here? How does all this fit under the Spire? I am assuming it's underground... but the sky looks so real... Why didn't I know about this place?'

'It is quite complicated, Silas, and you do not need to worry about such questions. This is your time to concentrate on *you*. You are special, Silas,' Reeph said. 'Quite exceptional.'

'Oh, well, I don't know about that. I'm not really special. You should see my brother,' Silas said, flattered by Reeph's attention.

'I think you may have forgotten how important you are,' Reeph continued with utmost sincerity. Silas looked for sarcasm, or asense that Reeph was trying to lure him into a false sense of security, before cruelly putting him firmly back in his place. 'I know that you are unique,' Reeph said, and Silas found himself desperately wanting to believe it.

'Thank you,' he stuttered.

'Without you among us, we would all be so much less. You bring something significant to me and to all of us.'

Silas smiled. Reeph seemed to mean every word he said. This was the kind of acceptance he had experienced at the Community. He couldn't believe he had found it here in the city too.

'This is the beginning of you recognising your value, your worth. Think over my words while you enjoy the Re-education facilities,' Reeph said. 'What would you like to do first?'

'Can I swim in the lake?' Silas said enthusiastically, thinking how wonderful it was to be given such an opportunity.

'The lake it is,' Reeph said with a light laugh.

There were fish in the clear water, darting slivers of blue and gold, sparkling jewels that, despite Silas' best efforts, were too fast to be caught. Giving up on the fish, he turned on to his back and floated in the middle of the lake while gazing up at the unblemished sky. It was idyllic. The water was warm and soothing and he lay, weightless... not thinking, not striving...

just being. He had never felt so peaceful and content, so it was disappointing when he saw that Reeph was waiting by the side of the pool.

'Your session is over for today,' Reeph said, in his calm and measured voice.

'Already?' Silas was disappointed. 'But I haven't been for a run or explored properly yet.'

Reeph gave a delighted smile. 'There will be time enough when you come tomorrow.'

'Can't I stay in as a resident?' Silas asked hopefully. 'Just for today?'

'You will not require residency. I can predict that you will do exceptionally well in Re-education. I am pleased with you.'

Glowing with pride at Reeph's words, Silas readily followed him out of the underground forest and into the bland side room.

Once more, Silas was dressed in his own clothes, and Reeph was waiting for him. 'Your brother is here for you. It is time to go.'

'How was it?' Marc asked curiously.

The Autocar was travelling through the most beautiful part of Prima's central inhabited district, but it all seemed shabby compared to what Silas had seen under the Spire.

'Amazing,' Silas answered enthusiastically, eager to relive his experience. 'A man called Reeph showed me around, and then I swam in an underground lake; the water was so clear... it was unbelievable...' He tailed off, suddenly distracted by Marc's physique. Then he glanced down at his own skinny frame. 'I need to take better care of myself. Will you help me on the weights machine when we get home?'

Marc eyed him curiously. 'Silas... hello? Extra workout? Didn't Re-education work you hard enough?'

'I can always do more. I need to improve. I've been lazy and selfish but I want to be ready when I go back to clinic. I've got more than a season left at Vitality. Maybe I could reach Gold, like you.'

'Hmm… I guess.' Marc sounded puzzled. They travelled in silence for a while and then Marc said, 'Do you want to know what I found out at work?'

'What do you mean?' Silas asked, giving his brother a blank look.

'About your friend?'

Silas frowned. What friend? He didn't have any friends, except for Kesiah. That would change, though. As soon as he got back to clinic he would do everything he could to be the best. The other students would start to take notice of him and he would make his father proud.

'Jono,' Marc said abruptly, interrupting Silas' daydream.

With a jolt, he remembered. 'Jono! Of course!' How had he forgotten? He tried to organise his thoughts as they tumbled chaotically through his mind. How had his priorities become so altered? All day he'd been enjoying himself in Re-education, and Jono was stuck in some quarantine facility somewhere.

'I think I know where he might be,' Marc said, with a conspiratorial grin.

'Really? That was quick work,' Silas said, feeling even more ashamed of his forgetfulness in the face of Marc's dedication.

'I checked on recent Biocubicle distribution and there has been a particularly large delivery to one specific location, but the strange thing is, it's in the heart of one of the Uninhabited districts. I'll show you on a map when we get home.'

The Autocar pulled up outside their house. Silas followed Marc inside and immediately headed for the health suite until Marc stopped him. 'Didn't you want to look at the projection?'

'Yes…' Silas frowned, and reluctantly turned away. The urge to go straight to the weights machine was powerful, and he tried to control it as Marc pulled up a map of the city.

'It's here.' Marc singled out a block surrounded by the usual devastation which characterised the Uninhabited area. 'This is the old financial quarter… derelict office blocks and towers.'

'Can we get a street view?' Silas asked, trying to manipulate the map.

'Not of this district,' Marc said, zooming out to the full city overview again. 'You want to check it out?' he asked.

'Now?' Silas said, looking over his shoulder longingly at the health suite.

'Yes, now! While we've got a chance. We've got time before Dad gets home at curfew,' Marc said, sounding irritated. 'What is it with you and that health suite?'

'I don't know,' Silas said crossly. 'It's just that it's important…' he tailed off feebly, 'but finding Jono is more important. I'm with you, let's go.'

It took them just under an hour to run across town to the edge of the Uninhabited area that Marc had singled out. The weather was a wintery grey, and Silas found himself longing for the subtropical warmth of the Re-education facility.

'Let's stick to the back alleys,' Marc said suddenly. 'I don't want to be picked up by any patrols. We've got no business being here.'

'Definitely,' Silas nodded. He, too, felt uncomfortable, as if he were trespassing, which was strange given how happy he was to explore the Uninhabited district nearer his home.

They clung to the shadows and narrow passageways between the tall, broken buildings, nervously looking over their shoulders at every tiny noise.

'Get down!' Marc instructed, and at the same time Silas heard the familiar sound of a HE-LP transport. He crouched in the shelter of a derelict wall, and Marc huddled beside him. They could see the belly of the ship as it glided over their heads, and Silas realised it was coming in to land.

'I think we may be on to something,' Marc said. Their eyes followed the transport until it disappeared behind the jagged top of one of the tall buildings in front of them. 'We should stay under better cover from now on though,' he added, leading Silas through a large hole in the wall and inside one of the old buildings.

The ancient tower block was full of gaping ceilings and broken floors, and, looking up through the dizzying levels, Silas could make out slices of grey sky above them. It felt as though the whole structure might topple down around their ears at any moment.

'Marc,' he called softly, 'it's not safe…'

Marc scowled at him. 'Look, Silas, I don't know what your problem is, but we are out here trying to find your friend. You need to pull yourself together. These buildings have been derelict for decades. They're not going to suddenly collapse today. We'll tread carefully and take it slow, OK?'

Silas bit his lip; he didn't know what was wrong with him either. All his old fears of being injured and of becoming an Unseen were beginning to resurface. All he really wanted to do was to go to the safety of the health suite and stay there until curfew. And yet he also wanted to find Jono, and that meant following Marc.

They clambered over piles of rubble and slabs of reinforced concrete, trying to maintain a straight path through the maze of sagging partition walls and abandoned office spaces, until they had nearly crossed through the entire building. As they approached the furthest wall, Marc pointed through an empty window frame.

'That must be it. The contagion quarantine facility.' He stepped closer as the bulk of the slowly descending transport ship momentarily blocked out the light.

Keeping Marc safely between him and the window, Silas stood on tiptoe to look over his shoulder.

The transport filled the entire space between the derelict building they were hiding in and the gleaming black wall of the spotless, smooth, windowless building opposite.

Measured alongside its giant crumbling neighbours, the black structure barely reached five storeys and, surrounded by shards of skyscrapers and tower blocks, no one would ever have known of its existence. It was completely hidden.

Silas felt oddly unsettled. His eyes traced the structure's clean, sharp outline. It's just a building, he thought, trying to rationalise his discomfort; just a huge, ugly, black box. It's somewhere for the Unseen carriers of the virus to go, a small disgusted voice inside his head reminded him; it's sealed, there's no way out… it's a tomb.

'Marc, we need to go… now!' Silas said, feeling panicky. More than ever he wanted to be back home, or in Re-ed, or even at clinic. Anywhere but here.

'Wait a moment,' Marc said crossly. 'I want to see what happens next. How do you get inside? There's no entrance…'

The HE-LP transport doors began to slide open and Marc leaned closer to the empty casement, trying to see inside the ship.

Silas stepped back. He could clearly imagine the stumbling figure of an Unseen being escorted out, and had little desire to see it.

Impatiently, he stared around the derelict innards of the office block, looking for the quickest way back out. Suddenly something caught his eye. A flicker of grey just disappearing around the edge of one of the remaining walls.

Probably a rat, he thought, feeling his skin crawl. He wished Marc would hurry up. He turned to look at his brother, silhouetted in the empty window when, to his horror, he saw the billowing grey robes of an Unseen rushing at Marc from behind the broken wall.

Silas didn't have time to cry out a warning before the assailant grabbed at Marc and roughly pulled him back into the gloom of the ruined building.

'What…?' Marc struggled, and tried to get a grip on his attacker, but he merely found his hands full of the cloth of an Unseen robe.

'Get off me!' Marc cried with revulsion. 'Ugh! Don't touch me!'

'Thhhh,' the Unseen hissed, thrusting a hand across Marc's mouth.

'Leave him alone!' Covering the distance between them in a few bounds, Silas intervened, grabbing at the Unseen's head and wrenching back on the hood. With a cry of alarm, the Unseen released his grip on Marc to snatch at the hood, and re-cover his face. But Silas had seen enough. The twisted features and small puckered mouth were instantly recognisable.

'Derry?' Silas stepped back in surprise.

Grimacing, Marc straightened his clothes and, wiping his face where Derry's hand had touched him, he rounded on the Unseen. 'What are you thinking, touching me, a Seen? And, you are in serious breach of curfew. I should report you. There's a HE-LP transport just outside, you know!'

With this threat, Derry started shaking his head vigorously. Putting his finger to where his twisted lips were under the hood he made a hideous hissing 'thhh' noise, then pointed frantically towards the street outside.

'Guarth,' he said in his strange speech.

Silas thought for a second, then he understood. 'Guards – Derry says there are *guards* out there.'

Marc glanced from the hooded Unseen back to Silas, and frowned. 'How do you even know who this is?'

Silas shrugged and looked guilty. He didn't want to explain how he had first met Derry. The risks he had taken on the night that the contagion was announced were foolish. How had he behaved so stupidly?

'Silas, stay here, and if the Unseen makes a move then shout loud enough to bring all the HE-LP in here,' Marc said quietly, then cautiously returned to the window. With his back pressed against the wall, he peered out.

Derry seemed agitated, shuffling on the spot and making quiet clicking noises with his mouth.

Silas grimaced. 'Stand still,' he grumbled, impatient for Marc to finish so they could leave Derry in his dirty and dangerous ruin and go to the safety of the inhabited district.

The rumble of the HE-LP transport engines drew Silas and Derry's gaze back to the window. As the ship took off, casting its long shadow into the room, Marc rejoined them, but his expression was grim.

'Can we go now?' Silas asked hopefully, but Marc ignored him and turned to Derry.

'Why would a treatment facility need a whole squad of Government Health Advisors armed with disruptors?' he asked.

'Guarth awl awoun',' Derry said slowly, as if trying to speak as clearly as possible.

'So guards are permanently stationed around the facility?' Marc confirmed, and Derry nodded.

'Untheen go i', none ow,' Derry added, miming a closed door with his hands. 'I wai' for a frien'.'

'Someone we know is in there,' Marc explained. 'We wanted to get in to see him...'

Silas almost protested. Yes, he wanted to see Jono, but he had no desire to find a way *into* the quarantine facility.

'So, could you help us find an alternative entrance?' Marc asked, but Derry began to make a strangled coughing noise and Silas realised he was laughing.

'What's so funny?' Silas asked crossly. How dare an Unseen laugh at them?

'No get in.' Derry shook his head, sending ripples down the length of his crumpled Unseen robe. 'Guarth dithrup,' he mimed holding a disruptor and pointed it at Silas' head.

'Even a Seen?' Marc said disbelievingly, and Derry shrugged.

'Af'er yoo?' He gestured at the empty window as if inviting Marc to try his luck.

For an awful moment, Silas thought his brother was actually considering his chances against the disruptors, but then Marc sighed. 'I'm sorry, Silas. I know we are close, but we can't risk it. Perhaps we can find Jono after he's been treated and he's out of this place.'

Silas couldn't have agreed more. The looming presence of the quarantine facility and Derry's warning were more than enough to keep him as far away from this Uninhabited area as possible.

Chapter 23

He had nearly completed his fifth set on the weights machine when the house announced, 'Silas, you have visitors.'

'Who is it?' demanded Silas, more out of irritation than interest. He had wasted enough time on the fruitless trip to the Uninhabited district, and now he simply wanted to complete his routine, and maybe even push on to do a bit extra.

'Zoe Veron and Kesiah Lightman,' the house responded.

He sighed. 'Fine, they can come in,' he instructed, continuing with his workout until he heard them calling out in the hallway.

'Silas?'

'Health suite,' he called back. 'Just let me finish this and I'll have a short break,' he said as they wandered in.

'Hi,' said Zoe, her smile faltering at Silas' brusque manner.

'A few more minutes, Zoe. You can wait in the Image room if you want,' he said, without trying to disguise his annoyance.

'Oh, OK, sure…' Zoe and Kesiah shared a confused look and backed out of the health suite. With renewed effort, Silas managed another programmed set, then paused the machine.

'I'll be back in a moment,' he said, patting the machine fondly. He walked into the Image room to find Kes and Zoe deep in a hushed conversation.

'What's up?'

'Are you all right?' Kesiah asked abruptly.

'Of course. Why?' he answered.

'You're acting strangely.' She looked at him with narrowed eyes.

'In what way?' he asked with confusion.

'In *every* way! Come on, Silas... you left us in the Outerlands. You were taken away in a HE-LP transport in some heroic attempt to stay with Jono. No one hears anything from you, then today, when we were on the Subterranean heading home, we saw a news projection of you arriving at court accused of assessment forgery.

'You haven't said hello, or asked about William, and you haven't even hugged Zoe...' Kes left the sentence unfinished, but by her exasperated expression there was plenty more she wanted to say.

Silas gazed sheepishly at his feet. 'Oh, right, yes, sorry. I... I guess I'm tired.' He walked up to Zoe and gave her a half-hearted embrace. Her body felt too soft under his hands and he pulled away, trying not to grimace.

'So, what else have you been up to?' he asked, feigning interest. 'How's the baby?'

'Back with Bonnie, and as you can imagine she was thrilled to have her child home,' Zoe answered, her voice tight and clipped. He knew that she had picked up on the lack of warmth in his touch.

'Great, that's... great,' Silas said with false enthusiasm. All the problems that had so recently consumed him no longer seemed important.

He remembered feeling incredibly protective towards Bonnie's baby, but that drive simply wasn't there any more. And then there was Zoe. From the way she was staring at him he knew she wanted something more from him. With embarrassment he recalled that he had actually kissed her and told her that he loved her. What had he been thinking? Looking at her now he saw too much fat and too little muscle. He glanced at Kesiah and couldn't help but compare them. Kes was practically perfect. She had such exceptional muscle tone in her calves and thighs and...

'Hello? Silas?' Zoe said.

'Sorry, what? Were you talking? I was miles away,' Silas wrenched his eyes away from Kesiah's legs and turned politely to Zoe.

'I asked what has happened to Jono, and what did they say at court?'

'Jono's fine,' Silas said glibly. 'Well, not fine, exactly... he's got the FGSV contagion, but he's in the quarantine facility and I'm sure he'll receive whatever treatment he needs. It's the best place for him. As for Health and Safety courts, they were easy,' Silas shrugged, suddenly smiling. 'I've been sentenced to Re-education, which I was nervous about at first, but it's fantastic. It's in this enormous forest that is under the Spire. I wish you could see it. If you thought the crater was beautiful, you would think this was paradise!'

Zoe frowned at him. 'I don't understand. If the Health Advisors know about your forgery, why haven't they come for Kes yet? They must have found her recorded results when they removed yours.' she asked.

'Marc helped,' Silas said, as if that explained everything.

'Your brother? Why would he help you?'

'He removed Kesiah's recording square. He wanted some information from me and thought he could do a deal...' Silas said distractedly, staring once more at Zoe's excessive curves. 'Look, Zoe, would you like to use the health suite? I'm sure the house can work up an exercise schedule for you.'

'What?' She looked stunned.

'The health suite... I bet with a bit of consistent training you could lose the excess fat. You've got to look after yourself, you know.'

There was a moment of shocked silence, then Zoe straightened her shoulders, turned her back on Silas and, without another word, walked out of the image room.

'Zoe!' Kes chased after her. 'Wait! Curfew's nearly started.'

'I'd rather risk my chances out there than stay in here with him!' Zoe said, loud enough for Silas to hear.

'But something's not right...' Kes protested.

'You can say that again!' Zoe replied furiously, then Silas heard the front door slam.

Kesiah looked warily at Silas as she returned to the Image room. 'You were cruel to Zoe.'

'I wasn't being cruel. Someone has to tell her the truth. It's for her own good,' Silas said defensively. He didn't feel guilty about upsetting Zoe – she needed to hear the facts – however, he didn't like being on the receiving end of Kesiah's disapproval.

'You've changed.' Kes looked closely at him.

'Not enough,' Silas said, glancing forlornly down at his thin arms. 'I've got a lot of catching up to do.'

'I brought your Soulsight over,' she said abruptly. 'Why don't we have some now? You went to a lot of trouble to get this.'

'I suppose I did,' Silas agreed, but looking at the grubby box he couldn't understand why.

'Let me make you some Soulsight tea. It looks like I can't get home before curfew now, so maybe you can tell me more about Re-education.' Kesiah sounded genuinely interested.

'Sure,' Silas agreed enthusiastically, pleased that Kes would be staying around. She was incredible to look at, and his gaze was drawn once more to her legs…

'Silas!' Kes said, and hearing the warning in her voice, he guiltily looked up.

'What?' he asked, attempting innocence.

'Maybe you should stay in here. I'll get the tea sorted.'

'Fine.' Silas tried to appear nonchalant and resisted the urge to watch her as she left the room. 'Play sporting highlights,' he instructed the house. He scanned through the various specialities, catching glimpses of runners, wrestlers, swimmers and gymnasts, until he came to the climbing news. He expanded the projection, and by the time Kes returned with a glass of warm tea, he was completely absorbed in a piece on endurance climbing.

'Drink it,' she said in a no-nonsense tone. Keen to please her, Silas swallowed the mixture in three rapid gulps. It sloshed in his gullet as it went down, and a leaf fragment tickled inside his throat.

'There,' he coughed, returning the cup to Kesiah.

'Good,' she said, watching him through narrowed eyes. 'Let's go to the health suite, then, as that seems to be your new preoccupation.'

'How about some stretches?' She stood in front of the mirrored wall holding her arm taut across her chest. 'Climbers need to stay flexible, don't they?"

Silas nodded eagerly and copied her movements.

'Watch your *own* reflection rather than mine, Silas. See how you are holding your body to increase your core tone.'

Silas did as she asked, then blinked and stood upright, surprised by what he saw. He moved closer to the mirror and ran his hands along it. It was flat and smooth and undistorted.

'Kes, I look weird, awful... What's the Soulsight done to me? I think I must have picked a bad batch.'

Glancing at Kes, he was struck by the clear, pure depths of her soul, but his own reflection looked hollow and lifeless.

'There's nothing wrong with the Soulsight, Silas. The problem is with you. I don't understand how you have become so altered. Can you see it?'

'Of course I can!' he snapped. 'I look so... ugh... empty. What's happened to me?'

'I think the word is "shallow",' Kesiah agreed, smiling as she stepped closer to Silas.

'It's not funny.' He winced as he compared their reflections. Suddenly he didn't want her near him. He felt overshadowed by the richness of her soul, and as he backed away he saw a faint accumulation of fear shadows dulling his eyes.

'Where's Zoe?' he asked, looking around in panic. 'She'll know what's going on.'

'She left,' Kes said bluntly.

'I didn't mean to upset her. I was trying to help. I don't know why I behaved like that. I need to com-link her,' Silas said with desperation in his voice.

'What do you want?' Zoe asked abruptly as she answered his com.

'To say sorry. Zoe, please forgive me.' Silas spoke quickly, fearing she would cut the connection.

Soulsight wasn't quite as effective on her projected image, but nonetheless, her goodness and kindness were clearly visible, as was the hurt that Silas knew he had been the cause of. It stained her beauty like a bruise, and he longed to find the words to undo the damage. 'I behaved like an idiot. I was obnoxious and stupid and I am truly sorry.

'I've taken some Soulsight and what I saw of myself was really bad. It's like my soul is fading away. I don't understand what's going on, but I'm scared.'

'OK,' Zoe said warily. 'I'll take some Soulsight myself and then com you in ten minutes.' She didn't even smile as she cut the connection, and Silas covered his face with his hands. He now remembered that Zoe had been the one genuinely perfect thing in his life, and he had hurt her.

Kesiah padded in behind him and gently rested a hand on his shoulder. 'It'll be all right. When she sees you she'll understand,' she said, trying to console him.

'I thought I heard voices.' Marc sauntered into the image room. 'What's going on?'

Silas raised his head. 'Marc, you have to help me. There's something wrong with me. I'm fading!'

'OK...' said Marc hesitantly, 'What are you talking about? You look the same to me. Do you need a bio-assessment?'

'No, you don't understand,' Silas said despairingly. 'It's inside here.' He slapped his hand against his chest. 'Even you look more real than I do, and that's impressive considering what you were like six months ago.'

Marc's eyes widened as he looked from Silas to Kesiah. 'You brought that Soulsight stuff over, didn't you?'

'Silas told you about it?' asked Kesiah, curious as to the sudden closeness between them.

In response, Marc reached into his pocket and produced the gold recording square with Kes' results on. He held it up between his finger and thumb. 'Silas told me everything in exchange for this.' He casually flicked it towards her. 'You might want to destroy that if you don't want to end up in Re-education with this loser.'

'Of course!' Silas cried. 'It's Reeph and the Re-education facility! They've done something to me. I was fine before, but now...' He began anxiously pacing around the room. 'When will Zoe call back? She's the clever one. Surely she can work out how this has happened and how to fix me.'

'Silas, you need to calm down,' Kesiah said. 'I'll get you some more Soulsight to drink, OK?'

'Have you got any spare?' Marc asked. He looked eagerly at them both.

'Sure,' Kesiah answered when Silas didn't. 'You understand that it will alter how you see?'

'Yes, I know. Apparently this won't be my first experience of it,' he said wryly. 'At least this time I'll be expecting it.'

'Come with me, then.' Kesiah led Marc into the nutrition area just as the com-link sounded.

'Hi, Zoe,' Silas said nervously answering the com. 'Can you see me? Can you see what's happened to me?'

Zoe stared at him for a moment, and Silas was relieved when her appearance softened.

'I have never seen anyone look this empty.' He heard pity in her voice but it was overshadowed by her blatant curiosity. 'Tell me when it started.'

'It must have happened at some point during Re-education. Look what it's done to me. Do you think it can be reversed?' He looked pleadingly at Zoe. 'And I am really sorry for how I acted earlier. It was as if I had forgotten who you are,' he said sheepishly.

The warmth of seeing her forgiveness was enough to make Silas want to break curfew and rush to her house. Her projected image wasn't enough. He wanted to hold her again.

'I understand. It's not your fault, and whatever happened in Re-education is already lessening. I think the Soulsight is starting to undo the effects. You already look far more substantial.'

'I wish you were here,' Silas said mournfully. 'I've got another session of Re-ed tomorrow. What if this happens again?'

'Can you dose up before you go?' she suggested, and Silas nodded. Perhaps he could even take some cooled Soulsight water in with him.

'Can I see you tomorrow, then? After Re-ed?' he asked, still needing reassurance of her forgiveness.

'See you tomorrow,' she confirmed with a genuine smile, before signing out.

'You are looking better,' Kes said, passing him a fresh cup of Soulsight tea as he joined her and Marc in the nutrition room.

'Better?' Marc queried. 'He looks like a faulty projection.'

Silas rolled his eyes. 'Thanks, Marc, as encouraging as ever.'

'What did Zoe say?' Kes asked.

'She'll come over tomorrow.' Silas grinned, feeling relieved. 'She's forgiven me.'

'OK, now you're improving.' Marc moved closer to Silas. 'So, Kes, what am I looking at here?' he asked. 'Why does Silas look so... good?'

Kes scratched her head. 'I've never really thought about it,' she admitted. 'I think it's kindness... oh, and he's truthful... that's beginning to play a big part.'

'Hey!' Silas held his hand up in protest. 'This is not meant to be my initiation! Let's talk about Marc.'

Marc smiled, but fell quiet as he allowed Silas and Kes to study him. The undeveloped parts of Marc's soul that Silas had previously noticed had matured. He was far from perfect – fear shadows clouded his eyes, and self-doubt added a heaviness to his appearance – but there was beauty too. Compassion and courage were two new and surprising elements, and as Silas interpreted what Soulsight was showing him, he felt a lump form at the back of his throat.

'I see you, Marc,' he said, stretching his hand from his eyes to his brother's face.

'And I see you, little brother,' Marc responded with a laugh, and pulled Silas into a rough hug.

Chapter 24

'I cannot physically drink another mouthful!' Silas said, pushing away the third cup of Soulsight tea that Kes had made for him that morning.

'You don't want to fade out again,' she warned, moving it back towards him.

'I'll take some in a bottle, OK?' he said.

'Silas?' Marc called from the health suite. 'You need to get your morning session logged. Dad will be checking up from work.'

'All right! I'm on it,' he called back.

'Soulsight,' Kes insisted. Pulling a face, Silas took another swig of the tepid tea.

'Incoming message from Anton Corelle,' the house chimed merrily.

'Answer,' Silas sighed. 'Hi, Dad, I'm just heading to the health suite now,' he said, before his father could complain.

'Hi, Silas.' His father's voice filled the hallway. 'Is Marc home, still?'

'Yep, he's on the treadmill.'

'Could you ask him to see me in the image room?'

'Sure, Dad. Is anything the matter?' Silas asked.

'I just need to speak to Marc,' his father said distractedly.

Silas wandered into the health suite. Marc was concentrating on his pace as the treadmill took him into a sprint. Silas stood in front of the machine to get his attention.

'It's Dad,' he shouted, over the noise of Marc's pounding feet. 'He wants to see you in the Image room.'

Grunting his acknowledgement, Marc began to slow his pace. 'Tell him I'll be there in a minute.'

Shrugging, Silas went to the Image room and saw a projection of a gaunt old man pacing the floor.

'Dad?' he gasped.

'Where's Marc?' the projection responded, staring up at Silas with rheumy eyes.

'Just coming,' Silas answered slowly. 'What's happened, Dad? You look really... um... worried.'

'Hi, I'm here. What's up?' Still breathing heavily from his sprint, Marc walked in. Silas was glad his brother hadn't topped up his Soulsight that morning; he didn't think Marc could handle such a shocking view of their father.

'Marc, I need you here at Bio-health as soon as possible,' the ancient figure said.

'I've got to get Silas to Re-ed,' Marc reminded him.

'Book an Autocar for him. He'll have to make his own way. I've sent a transport for you. We have had an emergency here.'

'What kind of emergency?' Marc asked, for the first time grasping the seriousness of their father's call.

'It's Dr Veron. She's taken her research. During last night's curfew she returned to the lab and completely cleared her workstation. I don't understand why she would do such a thing.'

A security recording began to run alongside the projected image of their father. It showed a woman, her head bowed over one of Bio-health's workstations. Her hair was a neat cap of close-cut black curls. She seemed to be intent on her work, pulling data streams and information packets into a recording square, until the workstation had been emptied. As she turned from the desk, Silas caught a glimpse of her face. Fear overlaid on fear.

Shocked, Silas took a sharp breath. Shadows pulled at the woman and he had to squint to make out any of her other features through the distorting effect.

'She's taken everything.' Anton was also watching the replay of her incredibly thorough data sweep, and seemed to age even more as worry developed into despair. 'We were nearly ready for launch. The Biocubicles were finished; her work was almost complete. She's betrayed Bio-health; she betrayed me. What am I going to do? We were supposed to be ready for Helen Steele's Future Health ceremony. If I can't get the data back, then the Flawless Leader will pull her support. The company will collapse...'

'I'll be there as soon as I can,' Marc tried to reassure their father. 'A back-up copy of her work must be kept somewhere.'

The Bio-health transport arrived just as Marc had finished showering and dressing.

'Make sure you get to Re-ed, Silas. This is serious. Dad doesn't need the extra stress of you going off somewhere,' said Marc, as he hurriedly opened the front door.

'I know,' agreed Silas remembering how frail his father had appeared. 'I saw him... I'll be at Re-ed.'

A knot of anxiety formed in his gut as he watched Marc board the Bio-health company transport. What was going on with Dr Veron? Where could she have gone?

He rushed into the Image room to find Kesiah waiting for him. She'd stayed out of the way as Marc had hurried to get ready, but she was obviously thinking the same thing that Silas was.

'You are going to call Zoe, right?'

'Of course. Even if Zoe doesn't know where her mother is, then maybe Nana does. House, com-link Zoe Veron,' he instructed, and stood waiting for her to answer.

'There is no one available to answer your com. Would you like to leave a message?' the recorded voice responded.

'Hi, Zoe, it's Silas,' he began, 'could you com me when you get this? I've got something important I need to ask you.'

The message recording ended with a chime.

'Perhaps she's already on her way over,' he speculated. 'You don't think she's avoiding me, do you... because of yesterday?'

Kes shook her head. 'I doubt it. Try calling again.'

Four fruitless coms later, Silas was starting to get worried.

He glanced at Kes. Even the clear depths of her soul were beginning to look troubled. 'I could go to her house now. If she's on her way over, I'll bump into her.' But as soon as the words came out of his mouth, he knew it would be impossible. He had promised Marc that he would go to Re-ed.

'I'll keep com-linking her,' Kes volunteered. 'You go and get ready. I'll call you if I get any response.'

After a quick wash, just as Silas was running back downstairs, the house began to speak, but it wasn't a returning call from Zoe. 'An Autocar has arrived for Silas Corelle,' it announced, and Silas groaned. Surely it couldn't be time to go already?

Kes handed him a bottle of green-tinged water. 'Don't worry,' she attempted to reassure him. 'I'll wait here for Zoe, and if she doesn't turn up, I'll go to her house.'

'Thanks,' Silas said, wishing it could be him meeting up with Zoe instead.

The Autocar was waiting at the end of the path. Silas gripped his water bottle. He felt like he was going into battle and that Soulsight was the only defence he had. He just hoped it would be enough to keep him from turning into that awful, vacant and shallow version of himself.

'Hello, Silas. It's nice to see you again,' Reeph said, as the door to the Re-education facility slid open.

Silas did a double take. It had occurred to him that Reeph would look different, but he hadn't been expecting this. Reeph was two-dimensional. Merely an image. Completely empty, without even the depth of a projection and utterly devoid of a soul. Finally it dawned on him that Reeph was entirely artificial. Yesterday Silas had felt proud when Reeph had praised him, yet he wasn't even a real person.

'You seem anxious, Silas.' The simulation smiled reassuringly as the image intensity increased and a faint pulsing vibration filled the air. Immediately, Silas felt the weight of worry that he had carried all morning begin to lighten and be replaced by a pleasant numbness.

'That's better,' Reeph smiled again. 'You don't need to feel troubled. You are safe here.' The brightness of the simulation returned to normal and the thrumming pulsation died away. Silas felt his thoughts and emotions begin to restart and he ran through an internal checklist to see what Reeph had done to him.

He felt the same. His concerns over his father and Dr Veron were still uppermost in his mind, closely followed by his disappointment at not seeing Zoe. Whatever Reeph had tried to do, it didn't seem to have had the same lasting effects as yesterday. The Soulsight must be counteracting it, Silas thought. Hiding his relief, he adopted a vacant expression and repeated Reeph's last comment. 'I'm safe here…'

'Follow me,' instructed Reeph, leading Silas down a long corridor lined with doors on one side. Eventually he halted and one of the doors slid open. 'In here, please. Leave your outer clothes in the preparation room and then move through to the Re-education chamber.'

Slowly Silas walked into a small cubicle. It was twice the width of the doorway, and facing him was a second exit. Along the short stretch of wall between the two doors ran a bench on which an orange and black uniform was neatly arranged.

'Room in use,' Reeph announced from the corridor, and the door slid closed with a soft clunk, shutting Silas inside. For a claustrophobic moment, he feared he had been locked in. Pressing his ear to the door, he listened for sounds from the corridor, but there was nothing.

'Open,' he whispered, and the door slid back to reveal the corridor devoid of anybody, real or simulated.

He briefly considered making a break for it. He could go to Zoe's for the day. They could work together to find Dr Veron and then let his father know. However, if he were caught, he would be made a resident. And that would mean running out of

Soulsight and becoming vulnerable once more to the soul-altering effects of Re-education.

Continue with the play-act, Silas, he persuaded himself as he gingerly held up the multipurpose smartfabric exercise uniform.

Self-consciously, he changed. The suit had a tight-fitting hood, and as Silas slipped it over his head he heard Reeph's voice. Yet it wasn't exactly hearing. The gentle murmur seemed to be *inside* his head... almost as if Reeph's voice had merged with Silas' thoughts. The sensation was unpleasantly invasive, and even with the barrier of Soulsight his brain once more felt numbed by the calming tones of Reeph telling him how important he was.

'You are vital, and maintaining your health is your priority,' Reeph burbled.

Easing the hood back off his forehead, Silas turned to face the other door. This must lead to the underground forest, he thought, taking a fortifying sip from his bottle of Soulsight water. Despite the terribly damaging effects of Re-ed, a part of him was excited that he would get to see the beautiful woods and lake again. Today he would explore properly and see what other amazing features were hidden in the chamber under the Spire.

Chapter 25

Silas was confused. He looked behind him as the preparation room door slowly slid closed. He had expected to see the forest stretching out in front of him, but instead he was standing in a large, low-ceilinged area lined with doors. Light bands ran across the ceiling casting a stark, white glare on dozens of people each dressed in matching hooded exercise suits. Some were running on the spot while others jogged around the periphery. A small rectangular pool was set to one side and another figure suited in black and orange was swimming steady, repetitive lengths.

In his mind, Reeph's voice persisted, and Silas realised it was describing the setting that he had seen yesterday. 'A lush forest surrounds you. Before you is a sparkling blue lake. This is the most beautiful place you have ever seen. Today you will take a run through the forest and later you will want to swim. You are a special person, and looking after yourself is your priority.'

A man jogged towards him, and Silas could clearly see the same emptiness that had afflicted his own soul the previous night. A hollow man, he thought with a shudder as, without a hint of acknowledgement, the man sidestepped Silas and continued on his imagined path around the room.

This is bizarre, Silas thought, feeling unsettled by the vacant people that surrounded him. If it weren't for Soulsight, he would already be just like them. Now he was more determined than ever to avoid becoming a resident. He just needed to stay focused, keep sipping Soulsight and try his utmost to suppress Reeph's monologue inside his head.

Thinking it might be best to blend in, he began to slowly jog around the room, mimicking the glazed, dreamlike state of the other residents. Re-education was just another term for reprogramming, Silas thought. They were all being reprogrammed and losing their individuality. While the voice in his mind told him how special he was, Re-education was trying its best to strip him of that.

As he passed the row of doors to the individual preparation rooms, one of them opened and another uniformed resident stepped into the main hall. Silas was about to step around her but there was something about the newcomer that brought him to a stumbling halt. He recognised her!

Only that morning he had watched footage of her sabotaging his father's work at Bio-health, and now here she was. The fear shadows that earlier had distorted her features were replaced by the hollowing effect of Re-ed, but there was no doubt that this was Dr Veron.

Her mouth curved into a broad smile as, ignoring Silas, she began to explore the empty room, shielding her eyes from the glare of an absent sun and gazing up into a non-existent forest canopy.

Although he wouldn't wish Re-education on anyone, Silas felt a sense of satisfaction that the Health and Safety courts had got it right this time. Dr Veron had been found and was being punished, and Silas could imagine how relieved his father must be at the news.

But why had she done it? Silas mused. And what about Zoe? His sense of righteous indignation shrivelled. What must Zoe be feeling? She may not be particularly close to her mother, but Silas knew that she loved and admired her. Did she already know what had happened?

Frustrated, he stared around the stark facility and the empty residents. He didn't want to be stuck in here. He should be with Zoe. He felt trapped and anxious...

'You are experiencing emotional fluctuations. Do not be worried. You are safe; you are valued.' The voice spoke loudly into his mind,

startling him. Taking a deep breath he forced himself to relax. The Re-ed suits must be monitoring bio-feedback, Silas thought, slowly breathing out and in once more. He had to be more vigilant, he couldn't afford to give himself away. *Tell me, Silas, what can you see?*'

'I can see a wonderful forest,' Silas answered in a dreamy monotone, looking at a blank piece of ceiling.

The time dragged.

Trying to jog around an empty room while concentrating on blocking Reeph's hypnotic murmurings, yet still trying to maintain a realistic somnolent appearance, was surprisingly draining. After a while, Silas took a moment to rest and pretended to observe the imaginary woodland. Cautiously he allowed Reeph's voice to fill his mind once more.

'By investing in yourself you are investing in the future. Care for yourself, love yourself. Your life is precious.'

'Reeph?' Silas whispered experimentally.

The flow of words continued unabated. Silas glanced at the other residents as they mindlessly wandered around the fictional forest. There seemed to be a uniformity of speed and behaviour and Silas guessed that, once they were firmly under the Re-education programme, they were set on a maintenance level. Just like he should be, he thought with a sigh, and resumed his slow jog.

Out of the corner of his eye he saw Dr Veron climb into the pool. She began to dive in and out of the water, grasping forward with her hands.

She's trying to catch the little fish, Silas thought, cringing inwardly at his own deluded behaviour the previous day.

'Re-education is over for today, Silas. Please make your way to your preparation room.'

Hoping he wasn't overdoing the acting, Silas pulled his face back into a blank expression and drifted slowly towards the same door through which he had entered the Re-ed chamber.

When he was in his normal clothes, the door to the corridor quietly slid open and the simulated version of Reeph stood patiently waiting for him.

'Congratulations on completing day two of your Re-education. Do not forget what you have learned.'

'I won't forget,' Silas readily promised, carefully keeping any trace of sarcasm out of his voice. His bottle of Soulsight water was empty and he didn't want to risk staying in the facility for a moment longer.

'Your father has arranged an Autocar to transport you home,' said Reeph, pointing towards the exit.

'Thank you.' Silas tried to sound enthusiastic. 'I'll see you tomorrow?'

'See you tomorrow,' Reeph smiled warmly as the door to the facility opened and, without looking back, Silas walked out towards the waiting Autocar.

The lingering effects of Soulsight made Silas' journey home far more interesting than usual. The central Inhabited district around the Spire was particularly busy, and as the Autocar manoeuvred through the crowds of Seen, Silas could do little but stare. The twisted faces and bodies, the dark heavy-shadowed eyes, the unsightly bulges and lumps protruding from under lurid and clinging fabric made for a fascinating view.

By the time the Autocar reached the Uninhabited district his Soulsight had almost completely worn off. However, there was something he wanted to do before his vision returned completely to normal.

'Com-link Anton Corelle, Bio-health Laboratories,' he said, and the Autocar projector screen sprang into life. The dreadfully frail version of his father that he had seen that morning had been bothering him all day. But now Dr Veron had been caught, hopefully his father's anxiety-laden appearance would have improved.

'Connection established. Confirming, Anton Corelle,' the Autocar burbled.

A cropped head and shoulder projection of his father appeared on the com-link. The fading Soulsight had a disconcerting effect on his father's appearance so that his physical strength was overlaid with the same ageing concern that had been so shocking that morning.

'Dad,' Silas said, forgetting to conceal his surprise. 'What's the matter? Has something else happened?'

'Silas, it's *all* happened,' his father said, with an exhausted facial spasm that Silas took to be a brave smile. 'How was Re-education?'

'Re-ed was OK, but what's going on? Didn't Dr Veron return the data?'

'What can I say?' His father sounded utterly despondent. 'The project is in tatters. The Flawless Leader is offering extra technical support, but no one can replace Dr Veron. She has the unique expertise, as well as all her notes, and the Health Authorities can't seem to locate her.'

Only a hint of Soulsight remained so Silas saw the burden of his father's concerns sap what residual life was left before the ghostly Soulsight image shrivelled, puckered and faded away. Now Silas had only one view of his father – the vibrant, capable leader of Bio-health Laboratories.

'But Dad, I've seen her at the Re-education facility. She's been caught.'

His father shook his head. 'I don't think so, Silas. Helen Steele assured me that efforts to locate Dr Veron have been redoubled, but there is no sign yet. You must be mistaken.'

'I'm certain it was her,' Silas said slowly, then immediately began to doubt himself. After all, he was comparing a hollow shell of a Re-education resident with this morning's fear-filled recording of Dr Veron… yet he had felt so sure.

'I have to go, Silas. I have a lot of work still to try to do here. I won't be home again tonight. Make sure you log your health suite workout.'

'Of course, Dad,' Silas nodded, and his father cut the link.

Lost in thought, Silas stared out of the window as the Autocar emerged into another Inhabited zone. It *had* been Dr Veron in Re-ed. There had been something in her, some lingering element of a whole person that had reminded him of Zoe.

'Autocar re-route,' he announced, making a sudden decision. Rattling off Zoe's address, he leaned against the window.

Chapter 26

Once again, Silas found himself standing on the familiar step, peering through the thick glass set in the sturdy front door. Eventually he saw movement, but the excited cry of 'Zoe!' died on his lips as Nana opened the door.

'Silas,' she said, with a frown, sparing him a brief glance before scanning the street behind him as if she were looking for someone else.

'N... Nana,' he stuttered, caught off-guard by her cold greeting. She seemed angry. Her face, framed by her iron-grey hair, was set in a severe scowl.

'Where's Zoe?' she asked bluntly.

Confused, Silas stared at her. No 'I see you' greeting, or even a 'How are you?', but maybe that was to be expected, he thought bitterly. She had forgotten all about him for the last six months, so why would she suddenly care now?

'Silas?' she prompted, sounding impatient.

'How would I know?' he answered defensively.

Nana's shoulders sagged. 'I hoped she would be with you. Your friend Kesiah hasn't seen her, either.'

'I've come straight from Re-education,' he explained, as it slowly dawned on him that Nana wasn't angry, she was worried. 'I spoke to her last night, though, after curfew,' he added, trying to be helpful.

'What time was that?' Nana fixed him with an interrogative stare.

'Um, nine...' he answered nervously, 'or a bit earlier. Why? What's the matter?'

Nana clenched her hand on the door frame until white bone showed through the skin on her knuckles. 'Something has happened here,' she said, her expression growing increasingly stern.

'What? What's the matter?' Silas asked, not needing Soulsight to recognise the fear that Nana was trying to conceal.

'You say that yesterday evening she was here and spoke with you. I stayed with Bonnie last night and today Zoe wanted to help with the twins, but she didn't turn up, or com. She hasn't left a message. Her bed hasn't even been slept in. The nutrition area is in chaos. Chairs overturned, smashed glass... as if...' she took a deep breath and held Silas' gaze for a moment, and he could imagine shadows building in her eyes. 'And no trace of Zoe. No one's seen her.'

'Do you think it's because of what's happened with Dr Veron?' Silas said suddenly as, with a sinking feeling, he started to put the facts together. 'I know it's a shock, but surely Zoe wouldn't simply leave Prima again without telling me, would she? No one's going to blame her for what her mother has done.'

Nana's frown deepened. 'What do you mean, Silas?'

'Because Dr Veron's been sent for Re-education. I saw her there,' he started to explain, before recognising a look of incomprehension spreading across Nana's face. 'You didn't know?'

'Esther, my daughter? Why has she been sent there?' Nana's expression hardened as she looked past him and inspected the street. 'Perhaps you had better come in and tell me what you know.'

Horrified, he stared around the nutrition area. Nana had downplayed the devastation. The chairs were scattered, the table had been up-ended and shards of glass mixed with pungent herbs and spices covered the floor.

'What happened here?' he gasped. 'Did Zoe do this?'

Nana shook her head. 'I think not,' she said grimly, righting a chair each for Silas and herself. Then, ignoring the rest of the chaos, Nana gave him her full attention. 'Now, sit down and tell me where you saw my daughter.'

Briefly, Silas described the facility under the Spire, and how he had used Soulsight to counter the peculiar soul-draining effects of Re-education. 'Then, today, halfway through the session, Dr Veron came in.'

'But are you certain it was her?' Nana asked.

'I think so... no, I am sure.' The more he thought of the woman in the orange and black Re-education suit, the more convinced he became. 'It would make sense. After all, she had broken curfew, and when she took her research it was all caught on the security monitors. I don't know why the Health Authorities have kept it from you and my father, but it was definitely her.'

'What I am struggling to understand is why Esther would do such a thing. She is dedicated, driven, often ruled by her work, but to do something so out of character...'

'I'm not making it up,' Silas said, hearing the disbelief in her voice.

Nana raised a placating hand. 'I don't doubt you, Silas, but what would cause her to...' Nana's gaze ran over the devastated nutrition area. 'Unless... I've got a bad feeling about all of this. Silas, could you talk to her tomorrow? Find out what happened. Ask about Zoe.'

'I can try,' Silas agreed, thinking about the unresponsive, shallow Re-ed residents.

'I need to make some coms.' Nana suddenly stood up. 'One of my contacts may be able to access the Citizen Safety Monitor records. Someone must know something.'

'Wait. I care about Zoe, too. I want to help, Nana,' he pleaded, recognising that he was being dismissed. 'I can look for her. Maybe she's gone to the Uninhabited district; there's this place we have. Just don't leave me out again.'

'Leave you out?' Nana queried. The intense scrutiny of her gaze made Silas feel too open, too vulnerable, and he found he didn't want to look at her.

'Is that what you thought?' she asked gently.

'Where were you?' His voice wobbled, and he hung his head, fixing his eyes on a shard of glass near his foot, trying not to let the full extent of his hurt show.

Nana sighed. 'The last few months have been difficult for all of us. Zoe needed time to recover and I was busy looking after Bonnie. I thought you were doing all right. I asked Thomas Atkins to keep an eye on you. He said that you had made a friend, and I took that to mean you had moved on.'

Silas gave a strangled snort of surprise. 'Coach Atkins hasn't said a word to me. How would he know how I've been? And I haven't moved on.' Anger began to build in him and he took a steadying breath. 'I wanted to help.'

At last he looked up and met Nana's searching gaze.

'I see you, Silas,' she said, moving her hand towards his eyes. 'It was never my intention to shut you out. I should have checked on you myself. So much happened with the Community. Friends and families were scattered. I've been looking for a way to rebuild, but I'm afraid it may be too little, too late.'

'You're trying to make a new Community?' Silas asked hesitantly.

Nana shrugged. 'We can never recreate exactly what we had, but we just wanted something.'

'I can help,' he repeated enthusiastically.

Nana shook her head. 'The situation with the contagion and the curfew makes any free movement impossible. And now with Esther in trouble and Zoe missing, I am afraid that everything is spiralling out of control. My daughter and my granddaughter are my priority,' she said, leading him to the front door.

He reluctantly followed. 'Nana, I am serious. I will do everything I can to find Zoe, and if you are planning a new Community, I want to be involved.'

She turned towards him and gave a half-smile. 'So like your mother,' she murmured, then gave a firm nod, as if she had reached a decision on something. 'Wait here. There's something

I want to give to you.' She stepped into the room at the front of the house and returned moments later holding a tightly wrapped parcel. 'I do not fully trust the com-links. We must be cautious in what we say and to whom. So if you want to be part of what is going on, you will need this.' She handed him the package and he started to open it, but Nana stopped him. 'Best do that at home, when you are on your own.'

Silas jogged towards the Uninhabited area with the parcel awkwardly slung under his arm. There was enough time before curfew and he had to make sure.

The old cottage was becoming more derelict each time Silas visited. One of the walls had finally collapsed inwards, covering the shrubs and weeds that had grown freely inside the ancient building. But all that Silas was interested in was the tree.

'Zoe?' he called up into the branches. The alarm-cry of a startled bird made Silas jump as it took flight from the canopy.

The presence of the bird meant that Zoe was unlikely to be there. Undeterred, Silas swiftly clambered up until he reached the small platform and walls that formed the start of the tree house. Usually he felt pride in his and Kesiah's achievement. It may not be as grand as Jono's old home, but it was sturdy and strong, and also completely undisturbed from their last visit. With a heavy heart he sat on the pile of salvaged planks and gazed over the vast, sprawling city.

Where was she, and what had happened at Nana's house last night? If Dr Veron had been trying to hide her stolen data and the Health Advisors had tracked her to Nana's house… He thought of the black disruptors that were a standard part of the Advisor uniform. How far would the Health Advisors go against a Seen?

The Spire glowed distant and cold in the late afternoon sunlight. This time it didn't fill him with any admiration or wonder, just a sinking feeling of dread.

The house was silent and empty when Silas arrived home.

'House, are there any messages? Has anyone called?' he asked, hoping for some news of Zoe.

'You have two messages,' the house responded cheerily. 'One from Manager Gilroy,' Silas grimaced, 'and one from Kesiah Lightman. Please visit the Image room.'

The projection of Manager Gilroy informed him that Vitality Clinic was 100 per cent contagion-free and normal schedules would resume in the morning. Silas paid little attention to the additional instructions from the clinic manager. He would be in Re-education in the morning and concerns about clinic and levels seemed insignificant compared to what was going on with Dr Veron, Zoe and Nana.

His eyes fell to the parcel in his hands. He unwrapped it, and out slipped the smooth grey fabric of an Unseen robe. Silas flinched and the material slid from his hands to land in a pile on the floor. It was one thing to wear one in the Outerlands, but to have one in the house felt like an uncomfortable intrusion.

'You have a second message,' the house reminded him as he rapidly stuffed the fabric back into its packaging.

'Yes, house. Play next message,' Silas said, thinking about where the best place would be to hide the Unseen robe. Manager Gilroy faded out and Kes came into view.

'Hi, Silas. Hope you withstood Re-ed this time. If not, then get some tea and call me back.'

'House, com-link Kesiah Lightman,' he instructed, before Kesiah's message had finished.

'About time!' Kes said as she answered the com. 'Are you all right?' She narrowed her eyes at him.

'Yes,' Silas nodded.

'Yes, I can see you are. Good. Listen, I tried to get hold of Zoe, but she's not been home...'

'I know,' Silas interrupted, remembering Nana's warning. 'There's loads I need to tell you but I'd rather it be face to face,' he spoke slowly, willing her to understand.

She stared at him thoughtfully. 'I think I know why. Now tell me the *truth* – do you like Re-education?'

Silas nodded. 'You know how much I love Re-education,' he smiled, aware that Kesiah must be using Soulsight and was seeing a shadowy flare from his simple lie.

'That's what I thought,' she slowly nodded.

'I feel very safe there, and I won't let anyone hear me say otherwise,' he added.

Kes frowned. 'The problem is that I can't come tomorrow. I've got an Inter-clinic competition. I'll be over as soon as I can, though. Remember, it's very important to stay well hydrated.'

'I will,' he said, then cut the connection. Talking in code was very frustrating, although Kes had just given him an idea. Suddenly he knew how he was going to get Dr Veron to talk to him.

Chapter 27

Sweat dribbled down his back and Silas shifted his shoulders to allow the fabric to absorb and expel the excess water. He was too nervous; he would give himself away if he didn't relax.

Cautiously he tuned into Reeph's voice, allowing it to fill his head.

'... must seize this opportunity to fulfil your destiny. Perfection is within your reach...'

He took a protective sip of Soulsight and concentrated on blocking the voice once more. Where was she? he thought impatiently.

The other Re-ed residents were steadily jogging their way around the bare hall. Hollow, empty people admiring a hollow, empty room. It would have been funny if it hadn't been so tragic.

At last a side door slid open and Dr Veron walked in. The nerves that Silas had been trying to suppress returned in force.

'Dr Veron,' Silas whispered.

He had taken a circuitous route around the room, weaving past other residents until it looked like it was pure chance that caused him to finally move alongside her. 'Dr Veron, it's Anton Corelle's son, Silas,' he said a little louder, watching carefully for some alteration to her shallow appearance.

Completely ignoring him, Dr Veron gazed at something in the far corner of the room and began walking towards it. He fell into step beside her, but she remained completely unaware of him.

'Dr Veron?' he said. 'A drink for you.' He pushed his nearly full bottle of Soulsight water into her hands. 'You are thirsty,

176

drink it all up,' he said in his best imitation of Reeph's melodic tones.

That seemed to get through to her, and she lifted the bottle and took a sip.

'That's not enough. Drink more,' Silas tried again. 'Your body needs to stay hydrated, you need to look after yourself.'

This time she drained the bottle, obedient to the slightest suggestion of personal benefit. Then all Silas had to do was wait.

He jogged around the edge of the room, passing the other vacant exercisers, all the while trying to screen out the relentless monologue in his mind: '... *you are important. Your health is paramount. Maintain your levels, exceed your targets...*'

Circling back to Dr Veron, he guessed that the Soulsight had begun to have an effect. She looked startled, and stared around her in confusion as the wonderful forest she thought she had been exploring was replaced with the stark reality of the facility. Her appearance became more substantial. Fear shadows began to dull her eyes and mask her features, but at least she was looking more solid now.

Silas managed to catch her eye. He put his finger to his lips to make sure she didn't draw attention to herself.

'What is going on? Where am I and who are you?' she asked with barely contained anger as Silas approached.

'Quietly, Dr Veron. You are in Re-education. I need to ask you some questions about what happened at Bio-health,' Silas muttered. 'I'm Silas Corelle, Anton Corelle's son... and I'm a friend of your daughter.'

'Zoe.' Dr Veron's fear shadows suddenly increased, blotting out her eyes completely. 'Is she here?'

Silas' face fell. 'You mean you don't know where she is?'

She frowned with concentration. 'They said she'd be safe but I don't know what they've done with her!' Panic sent her fear levels rocketing.

'Dr Veron, try to stay calm. Tell me what you know.'

'It was the Health Advisors... they had her...' Dr Veron's eyes flooded over with a terrifying wave of grey. 'They wanted my research. All of it. She was sedated and they held a disruptor to her head! So I did what they said.'

'What?' Silas cried, no longer caring about subtlety. Zoe had been threatened. He had to get out of Re-ed and find her. Surely they wouldn't dare to hurt…

Reeph's voice cut through his mind. What had been an annoying background hum reached a new intensity as a smothering numbness began to dull his thoughts. *You are one of a kind and you must invest in yourself… believe in yourself…'*

Silas reached for his bottle of Soulsight to counteract the Re-education, but it was empty. Dr Veron had drunk it all.

'You can see that I am being honest with you. I want to find Zoe,' Silas said, doing his best to think clearly. 'You took the research from Bio-health to keep Zoe safe, but what do the Health Advisors want with it? I thought the Viva party and the Flawless Leader supported my father's work?'

She was still disorientated and obviously frightened, but she held Silas' gaze. 'It's the virus… it's not real, it's a sham, a fake. You have to tell people, tell Anton, let everyone know.'

'What do you mean, a fake? The infected Unseen are all in a quarantine facility… I've seen it.'

Dr Veron's eyes darted frantically from side to side. 'She wants control of my research,' she said, suddenly remembering. 'I have discovered a vaccine, but it's much more than that. It will change everything. So many of the Unseen will be cured and much sickness will be prevented.'

'No more Unseen…' Silas murmured.

'Almost, but the vaccine needs careful handling and targeted administration. That's where the new Biocubicles were supposed to help. For some Unseen the unregulated vaccine would prove fatal. Those carrying certain genetic imperfections are most at risk. The vaccine would cause widespread cytolysis, complete cell death, a horrible and painful end… We always knew this,' she added looking at Silas' shocked face. 'The new Biocubicles were to be used in conjunction with the vaccine to screen for and protect those with the highest risk of the cytolysis reaction.'

'... *you are surrounded by trees. In the distance the forest reaches the foothills of a mountain. The path follows a clear sparkling stream. You want to run...*' Reeph's voice filled every space in his mind. It was becoming increasingly difficult to ignore, and the faint impression of trees began to appear around him. They were intangible, like ghostly flickerings at the periphery of his vision. Silas struggled to concentrate on what Dr Veron was saying.

'But the Biocubicles have been tampered with... reconfigured...'

Silas frowned and loosened his hood. 'Reconfigured?'

'Yes. I discovered that there is an exact correlation between those who are most at risk of harm by the vaccine and those who have been labelled as having the contagion. This so-called quarantine is not designed to limit the spread of a real disease. It is a prison, and I fear for the lives of the Unseen who have been moved there.'

He immediately thought of Jono. That is why he had a positive result for the contagion... it wasn't a virus he had caught. Jono was one of those Unseen who would not survive vaccination.

'Why didn't you tell my father?' Silas asked. 'He would have shut down the Biocubicles if he knew they were going to be used to do harm.'

'I... I... didn't know who I could trust.'

'You suspected him!' Silas accused.

She nodded. 'But I was wrong. Your father knows nothing about what is planned for our work. I have to get out of here. I have to find where they have taken Zoe and warn everyone! When the vaccination begins, no Unseen should use the Biocubicles.'

Her panicked shout was cut short as an expression of excruciating agony twisted her face. She fell to her knees, cradling her head and gasping for breath. Alarmed, Silas looked around for someone to help her, but his concern faded to distracted wonder at his surroundings. Enthralled by the rich colours of the forest, he lifted his face to feel the same gentle breeze that moved through the swaying treetops. The sharp pinch of a hand grabbing his arm brought his focus back to Dr Veron. 'Helen Steele wants perfect health for all… but it will be at an unspeakable cost. To her the Unseen are either curable or expendable.' She shuddered and let go of his arm.

Silas smiled vacantly at the woman curled up on the grass in front of him. Why wasn't she enjoying the forest? He spun around as warm sunlight spread across his shoulders and back. He was free. Around him the trees spread for miles, and in the distance a single mountain was splendidly framed by the deep blue of the open sky, its peak fringed with tendrils of cloud. He could run there now. Setting off along the track that followed a burbling brook, he had never felt so alive, so in tune with his body and in perfect harmony with his surroundings. The feeling was wonderful.

Chapter 28

Undoing the effects of Re-education seemed far more uncomfortable this time, and Silas almost stopped drinking the fresh batch of Soulsight tea he had made. It was effortless to live in the fantasyland of Re-ed, where all he had to do was focus on himself. The reality of the threats facing Jono, Zoe and now Dr Veron was a painful emotional wake-up call.

He paced anxiously in the nutrition area, sipping Soulsight and resisting the urge to run to the health suite. Where was Marc or Kes? Surely one of them should be here by now.

Eventually Soulsight began to take full effect and his thoughts immediately turned to Nana. It was too near curfew to attempt to get to her house and back, but he could com-link.

Frustratingly, there was no answer, and Silas left a brief and cautious message.

He was beginning to think he would have to spend the night by himself when he heard the front door open.

'Silas?' Marc called, 'are you home?'

'Marc! At long last. Where have you been? I've got loads to tell you,' Silas answered anxiously.

'Good, you're here. Dad was worried. You didn't log your workout.' He sounded exhausted, but Silas was pleased to see a core of internal strength beginning to develop in Marc.

'How are things at Bio-health?' Silas asked.

'It's a mess,' Marc sighed. 'She wiped the records clean... took everything. Dad's got everyone working flat out to try to rebuild the project. But I don't see how it's possible without Dr Veron.'

Silas took another swig of Soulsight. 'I know where she is,' he said. 'I told Dad and he didn't believe me.'

'What are you talking about?' Marc growled. 'I don't have the energy for games. Did Re-education… you know… get to you again?' Marc twirled his hands in the air around Silas' temples.

'It's not funny.' Silas batted his brother's hand away. 'Dr Veron is a resident at the Re-ed facility. I spoke to her today.'

Marc lowered his arms and gave Silas his full attention.

'She said that the vaccine she produced is only safe for some of the Unseen, but is lethal for others. The Flawless Leader knows this but wants full control and intends to push forward with the vaccination. Dr Veron was about to go public, to expose Helen Steele, but Zoe was threatened so Dr Veron did what she had to do. She took the research and gave it to Steele. Now Dr Veron is being re-educated and we don't know where Zoe is and Jono is locked up facing a terrible execution!'

Hearing himself say it out loud seemed to clear the last of the Re-ed from his mind, and the full impact of what they were involved in hit home. Marc held up a hand in protest.

'Steady! Those are serious accusations. If they are true, if Helen Steele is behind all this, then you need to talk to Dad.'

'I tried yesterday. He won't listen to me,' Silas said, shaking his head.

The house burbled into life, interrupting them. 'There is a com-link from Eva Veron. Will you accept?'

'Image room!' Silas instructed, and leaving Marc in the nutrition area, ran through to greet Nana. Her projection shone with the reassuring love-light that he was so familiar with, but this time it was overlaid with the debilitating worry that he had seen draining life from his father; it was a shock to see it in Nana.

'I see you, Nana,' he said hurriedly. 'Please tell me you have good news about Zoe?'

'I have some news, Silas, but first, do you have anything you can tell me?'

'Yes. I spoke to... the person...'

Nana held up a hand to silence him. 'That's good. If your offer of help still stands then you need to use what I gave you. Wait at the corner and someone will meet you. Do you understand?'

'Er... I...' Silas stuttered. 'I think so.'

'Good.' Nana cut the connection and Silas was left staring at the centre of the empty projection room.

'What was that all about?' Marc asked, standing by the doorway. 'Who was the old lady? And what did she give you?'

'That's Dr Veron's mother. She gave me... um... something...' Silas hesitated.

'We are way past secrets,' Marc sighed, sounding tired and irritated by Silas' reticence.

'Fine. It's upstairs, under my bed. Go and take a look if you're interested, but you won't like it.'

'Not the most imaginative hiding place,' Marc observed wryly, unwrapping the plain packaging as he came back downstairs. The long grey robe unravelled onto the floor and he sprang back in revulsion. 'An Unseen robe? Is this a threat or some kind of sick joke?'

'No, Nana doesn't threaten people.' Silas almost laughed at the idea before growing more thoughtful. 'But she doesn't trust the com-links. She wants to speak to me in person.'

'No way!' Marc said as realisation dawned. 'She wants you to go out after curfew dressed in that? That's madness. You'll be noticed. You'll end up a full-time resident in Re-ed,' he warned, barely able to bring himself to look at the robe. 'You wouldn't be able to go anyway. You're terrified of the dark. Do you remember when you were younger and got left in the garden after sunset? You were wetting yourself.'

'You locked me outside!' Silas recalled the incident all too clearly... the awful terror... he had actually lost control of his bladder.

'That's not the point.' Marc sounded annoyed. 'You cannot be wandering around at night. If this woman refuses to talk to you over the com, then you'll have to wait until tomorrow when curfew is over.' Marc kicked the robe to one side. 'This is getting out of control. You need to tell Dad what you know and get this thing out of the house before he comes back. And log your workout.'

'All right, calm down,' Silas raised his hands in submission, but as Marc angrily turned away, Silas picked up the Unseen robe and slowly folded it.

The dark certainly no longer frightened him, and he'd got away with pretending to be an Unseen twice before without getting caught. Also, he needed to see Nana. He had begged to be involved and to help where he could, and now he had information that was too urgent to wait.

It was well past curfew and Marc had gone to his room. After logging a perfunctory workout and enduring his evening Biocubicle assessment, Silas headed for the nutrition area. As quietly as possible he made up a fresh bottle of Soulsight water and silently slipped out of the back door. Under the cover of the bushes at the edge of the large rear garden, he pulled the grey cloak over his head, then cautiously stepped over the low boundary wall into the side street.

A few Unseen were about, and, although Silas felt no fear of them, he was wary of giving himself away. Keeping to deep shadows and deserted alleyways, he cautiously made his way towards the edge of the Inhabited district.

He slowed as he neared Nana's street. She had said to wait at the corner and someone would meet him. It didn't seem necessary since he knew which house was hers, but the instructions had been clear.

The Citizen Safety Monitor glinted above him. Was it watching him? Feeling highly conspicuous, he leaned closer into the tangles of thick ivy that covered the wall of the end house.

'Eh-lo.'

Silas swung around, expecting to see another Unseen, but the dark street behind him was deserted.

'Who's there?' he whispered into the gloom, trying to keep the tremor from his voice.

With an alarming rustle, the ivy beside him began to move and the grey cloth-covered head of an Unseen suddenly appeared.

'Thith 'ay,' the Unseen spoke again.

'Derry? Is that you?' Silas asked cautiously, stepping closer and pushing his hood a fraction off his face. 'What are you doing here?'

'Thileth!' The Unseen made a derisive snorting cough of recognition, and Silas could imagine Derry's twisted mouth struggling to pronounce his name. 'Wha' *oo* doin' hee'ya?'

'I need to meet someone.' Silas answered warily.

'Na-na?' Derry asked.

'How do you know Nana?' Silas asked, still puzzled by Derry's unexpected appearance.

Derry shrugged. 'Ev'y wun nowth Na-na. She wanth ev'y wun come thith way. Fo'ow me.'

'What? Sorry I can't... could you speak slower?' Silas shook his head with incomprehension. With an impatient sigh, Derry reached out an arm, grabbed the edge of Silas' cloak, and pulled him through the tangled layer.

'Great hiding place,' Silas said appreciatively, impressed by the space under the ivy curtain.

'Thtairth,' Derry hissed.

'Stairs?' Silas guessed, and felt cautiously forward with his feet. Sure enough, a narrow set of steps led downwards. Dried leaves crunched underfoot and the smell of damp brickwork filled Silas' nostrils. The stairway led to a solid door. There was a jangling of metal and a grating clunk, then a rectangle of dark upon dark opened up before them. Derry went first, swallowed by the pitch black, then Silas shuffled unsteadily forward. He expected another step down into the underground room, but his cautious footsteps merely encountered the gritty sensation of dirt on concrete. The door closed behind them, deepening the darkness to suffocating levels, until at last, Derry opened a sunstorer. The slither of light to revealed an old and dirty cellar. A stack of cobweb-covered crates festered in one corner and a pile of rusting scrap metal filled another.

Now they were inside, Derry removed his hood and scowled at Silas. There was a bright boldness to him, a strange blend of arrogance and self-confidence mixed with a compelling vulnerability.

Silas also slid his hood back. 'What now?' he asked warily.

Derry grunted and turned his back on Silas. 'Thith 'ay,' he said crossly, and Silas followed the glow from the sunstorer through four more dusty and cluttered rooms, each connected by a thick door, and each opened by an old-fashioned manual key.

'I am expected at Nana's house. That is where you are taking me, isn't it?' Silas asked, watching him lock another door behind them. The jangle of metal was setting his nerves on edge.

What do I know about this Unseen? he thought. Nothing, except that he really doesn't like me.

Derry picked up a long, thick pipe that had been leaning against the wall, and turned to face Silas.

'What are you doing with that?' Silas asked, hearing the wobble in his voice but trying not to cower away from the threatening figure.

Derry made the strange choking noise that Silas recognised as laughter as he raised the pipe above his head. Silas flinched and covered his head with his arms, but the blow never came. Instead Derry laughed again and thrust the pipe upwards to bang loudly on the cellar ceiling. Three sharp raps.

With a drawn-out creak, a square section of the ceiling opened, flooding the gloomy cellar with light. As he shaded his eyes from the glare, Silas could just make out first rung of a slender ladder being lowered towards them.

'Af'er 'oo,' Derry said, still spluttering with laughter as he waved the pipe in a pretend threatening manner.

Silas hesitated for a second, trying to think of something to say that would put Derry in his place, but then he heard Nana's voice.

'Good, Silas is here. We can make a start.'

Keen to escape the dark cellar and Derry's mocking laughter, Silas raced up the ladder and, blinking from the light, emerged in the front room of Nana's house. Grabbing her outstretched hand to steady himself, he studied Nana's face and finally began to appreciate the crushing weight of her worry.

'I see you, Nana,' Silas said softly. 'I'm glad I'm here. You know I want to help you.'

'Thank you. I see you too.' She stretched her hand to his eyes.

'Hel' m'ee?' Derry grumbled, rudely interrupting, and Silas turned to see he had closed the trapdoor and was struggling to push the piano back into its place against the wall.

I wonder if Zoe knows about the secret entrance to Nana's house? Silas thought, as he leaned a shoulder against the box and helped manoeuvre it to cover the hinged floorboards.

Chapter 29

The nutrition area was in better shape than when Silas had last seen it. The broken glass had been swept up and the table and chairs were in their usual place. However, this time there were nearly a dozen people crowded into the small space.

'Silas, you know most people here,' Nana said as she ushered him through the door. Silas stared at the group, grateful once more for the powerful effects of Soulsight. There were four strangers, all wearing Unseen robes. He wondered how many were true Unseen and how many were like him, using the robes as a useful disguise.

Then there were the more familiar faces. Bonnie, rich and golden, her self-sacrificial radiance blending beautifully with a deep joy. Cradled in her arms was baby William, contentedly sleeping. Scanning the group, Silas saw Bubba Gee, seated on a chair, with Bonnie's second twin also asleep and filling most of his lap. Coach Atkins stood behind them, his appearance weighted by the thick air of sorrow he always carried with him. It took Silas a moment to recognise Mags, her shining soul obscuring her twisted exterior.

Raising his hand in a shy wave, Silas was met with a chorus of 'I see you' greetings from his old friends and nods of welcome from the others. Nana stood, leaning against the stove, and made room for Derry to limp in beside her.

'Thank you, everyone, for coming here tonight. I never imagined that the situation would become so hostile that we would need to use the route through the cellars again, but we must be cautious and vigilant. As you all know, Esther and Zoe are now both missing, along with many of our Unseen friends and family who have been diagnosed as having the contagion. We need to know what is going on and how best to act. Derry has been monitoring the quarantine facility and has some new information.' Nana nodded at Derry.

'I wath neer qwa'ree' an a Theen wath ta'en inthi'e.'

Silas barely understand a word, but everyone else seemed particularly interested.

'Was it Zoe?' Bonnie asked.

'May'ee.' Derry shrugged.

Nana manoeuvred through to the table, holding a miniature projector. A small version of Zoe sprang to life. She was sitting on the edge of a boat, her feet dangling into a crystal-clear sea. She was waving and smiling. Silas felt a lump form at the back of his throat. If anyone had harmed a hair on her head…

'Is that who you saw?' Nana asked.

'Yeth… may'ee.' Derry sounded uncertain. 'Lon' way ofth.' He spluttered, miming peering into the distance.

'Wait a minute,' Silas interrupted. 'You saw Zoe being taken into the quarantine facility?'

Derry nodded.

'That would fit with what Dr Veron said.'

Now everyone's attention was on Silas, and he looked uncertainly at Nana. 'I gave her my Soulsight to drink and it broke through the Re-education. She said that Zoe was taken away by Health Advisors and…' he was reluctant to mention the disruptor for fear of adding to Nana's worries, '… and they wouldn't say where she was unless Dr Veron collected all the research on the vaccine and gave it to them.'

'That makes sense of Esther's behaviour, but why would they want the research? Her work is designed to help everybody.'

Silas took a deep breath and recounted his conversation with Dr Veron. They stared at him open-mouthed as he told them about the fabricated contagion, the vaccine, the sinister role of the new Biocubicles and Helen Steele's ruthless plans. By the time he had finished speaking, the atmosphere in the room had completely shifted. His friends were vibrant with the fiery heat of injustice, and he felt himself being swept up in their outrage.

Derry was trying his best to communicate his horror to Nana, Mags had begun to cry, no doubt thinking of her brother still locked in quarantine. Only Coach Atkins remained unflustered, letting the storm of emotion swirl around him.

Eventually he spoke, his passionless voice cutting through the anger. 'What is planned is appalling,' he said tonelessly, 'but I expected it would come to this. Helen Steele cannot tolerate imperfection. The question is, what to do now?'

'Brae in'o quara'inee,' Derry said emphatically. 'Rethcue frien'!'

A rumble of agreement and nodding heads ensued.

'The Advisors have disruptors,' Nana reminded him.

'Ge' all U'thee'.' He waved a fist in the air, but Nana gently lowered his arm.

'Too many would be hurt.'

'It seems to me that Dr Veron is the key.' Coach Atkins spoke again. 'If Helen Steele simply wanted the research, then she would have taken it. She must still need Dr Veron's full cooperation for some reason.'

A thoughtful hush descended over the group.

'We need her out of Re-education. At the very least it will buy us some time to get our family and friends out of quarantine and then expose what Helen Steele is truly up to,' Mags said, wiping the tears from her eyes.

'But she's a resident. She won't be allowed to leave,' Silas said.

'Can we interfere with the power supply to the facility? Perhaps the hooded Re-education suits that Silas described could be disconnected or shut down,' Bubba Gee suggested.

'Geren, you've worked at the Spire.' Nana spoke to one of the Unseen that Silas didn't know.

He shook his head. 'The Spire has many power processors. It would take days to locate and neutralise them all.'

A despondency spread over the group. It was impossible. They were far too few to stand up against Helen Steele and the Health Advisors.

'It's a shame we can't give all the residents Soulsight,' Silas murmured, thinking aloud. 'In the confusion, Dr Veron could maybe sneak out... but I can't walk into Re-education with a couple of hundred bottles of water!'

'Now, there is an interesting idea,' Geren said, leaning forward, a faint spark of hope kindling deep in his eyes.

Chapter 30

'What? Silas!'

Marc's furious shout carried all the way through the house, waking Silas with a jolt. The next thing he knew, his door was flung open and Marc was towering over him. Feeling vulnerable in the face of his brother's wrath, he pulled his thin sheet up to his chin.

'What's going on?' he muttered, before his gaze fell to the bundle of cloth gripped in Marc's fist.

'Tell me you didn't?' Marc shouted.

'Err...' Silas looked from the cloth back to Marc's face, piecing together the events of the previous night. It had been raining heavily when he had eventually left Nana's house, and in his exhaustion he remembered stumbling into the house and shoving the sodden robes into a cupboard in the nutrition area.

'The house detected abnormal moisture around the nutrition dispenser. It's been trying to locate a leak in the system!' Marc said angrily.

'I can explain,' Silas sheepishly ventured.

Marc's anger hardly lessened as Silas outlined the events and plan from the previous night.

'That sounds like madness.' Marc frowned. 'Why are you involved in this?'

'It is my choice. Nana, Zoe and Jono are important to me. They are like family. I will not abandon them.'

'You have your real family too,' Marc said. 'What about Dad and me? The Advisors are not to be messed with. If it's true that they have taken Zoe, then what is there to stop them coming for you too?'

'I'll be careful. I promise,' Silas said, but Marc shook his head despairingly and dropped the Unseen robe in a wet heap on the floor.

'Get rid of that,' he said crossly.

Wearily, Silas climbed out of bed and stepped into the Biocubicle. He mulled over the conversation from the previous evening. All the planning and discussion had been condensed by Bubba Gee into a single maxim: Freedom is won through the truth.

Last night it sounded so simple, but now it seemed impossible. It was far more likely that the truth would produce chaos and danger.

'Muscle...' The Biocubicle began to reel off Silas' results. They were remaining static but were definitely not improving. If his father hadn't been so distracted, he would have had Silas doing overtime in the health suite. There was no time for an extra workout this morning, however, not with so much preparation to be done.

Reeph was waiting in the entrance hall of Re-ed, smiling and handsome, and to Silas' Soulsight vision, completely hollow.

'Good morning, Reeph,' Silas said, faking a grin.

'Good morning, Silas. What have you got there?' Reeph asked, looking at Silas' bag.

Silas took a deep breath. Slowly he lowered the bag to the floor and unzipped it. 'Just some spare kit, for climbing. Please say you've got a climbing wall. I don't want to let my levels fall by the time I return to clinic. I want to aim for Gold.'

'Of course, we can arrange something for you. You won't need your climbing equipment; we have adequate clothing. Your bag will remain here.' It wasn't a suggestion; it was a command, disguised beneath Reeph's calm and persuasive tone. The strange pulsing light accompanied his words and began to numb Silas' thoughts.

Silas concentrated, trying not to lose his focus. He really needed the bag, or rather, the contents of the bag.

'Can I please take my utility belt,? My father gave it to me. I always use this one.' He tried to sound anxious and childish, hoping that Reeph's programming would respond accordingly. He wasn't disappointed.

'Of course,' Reeph said. 'It is important that you feel comfortable here. You are valuable to us.' The projection waited as Silas rummaged through his belongings, then led him into one of the changing rooms.

So far so good, thought Silas, as the preparation room door slid closed. Hurriedly, he changed into the Re-ed uniform and fastened the belt around his waist. It was standard climbing equipment with the usual rope locks and loops; however, although his father had given it to Silas, it held no sentimental value. What it did hold was his chalk bag. The small bag usually contained fine powdered climbers' chalk, but this time it was full of dried and crushed Soulsight. It looked like green dust. Silas tried to stop his hands from shaking as he carefully repositioned it.

He closed his eyes and breathed deeply in and out. Leaving the uniform hood down, he opened the preparation room door back into the corridor, rather than the stark Re-education hall. Nervously, he peered out. The projection of Reeph was nowhere to be seen, so, quietly, Silas headed away from the entrance and deeper into the building.

'Service level,' he muttered to himself, looking desperately for a route to the upper levels. At last he reached a doorway, but it was marked 'residential level'. It slid open as he approached, revealing a brightly lit stairway, heading downwards. He paused. Nana's friend Geren had definitely said up.

Silently he closed the door. There was still no one else in the corridor, but it wouldn't be long before his absence was noted. He wondered if Reeph's voice had already begun the cycle of re-education through the hood, trying to fill his head with soothing, empty platitudes.

Silas hurried on and was nearly at the end of the row of preparation rooms when he found the staircase leading upwards. Trying to move as quickly and as quietly as possible, he took the stairs two at a time.

Silas stopped again. He could just see into the upper level, and it was exactly how Geren had described it.

Two transparent doors faced him. The one on the left had the words *Service Area* etched across its surface, while the door to his right bore the title *Re-education Programming Hub*.

Easy enough, Silas thought, except for one complication that the Unseen hadn't factored in. His duties in the Spire all took place at night. But now it was day, and standing with their backs to him, intent on their work, were four Seen Re-education technicians. Silas tensed, ready to escape down the stairs if one of them even began to turn his way.

The Programming Hub was a wide room with one long, rose-pink tinted glass window that overlooked the rain-spattered street outside.

The interior walls were filled with streams of data, arranged in columns, and it was this, rather than the outside view, that held the attention of the four technicians. The columns of numbers scrolled steadily upwards, and although it was an indecipherable code to Silas, he could clearly see a name at the top of each column. From his position in the stairwell, he couldn't see Dr Veron's name, but his own was there. The column under his name was empty and he guessed that without his hood on, he wasn't plugged into the Re-education system. How long would they allow before Reeph was sent to find out why? He knew he had to act now.

Before he could talk himself out of it, he crept up the last few steps. He would be completely visible to the technicians, but they remained focused on the lists of numbers as Silas slipped into the Service Area. Easing the door closed behind him, he scurried behind the first tall bank of machinery until he came to a hatch on the floor.

This was it. If Geren had remembered correctly, then this was the environmental regulator for the entire Re-education facility. Swiftly removing the cover, he looked down into the gloom of the underfloor area.

As his eyes adjusted, he found he was staring at a long, flat tank. A small inlet valve protruded from the top. With trembling fingers Silas eased the lid off. Reaching behind him, he unclipped the chalk bag from his climbing belt and carefully began to tip the powdered Soulsight dust into the tank. The fine dust settled in a layer over the surface, slowly becoming waterlogged before sinking.

Brushing the remaining powder from his hands, Silas returned the lid and hatch to their correct position then stood up.

The regulator would do the job of distributing the Soulsight throughout the facility, and in the ensuing confusion, Silas would lead Dr Veron out. Perhaps she might be able to persuade his father of the threat to the Unseen, and together they would stand against Helen Steele.

Now, if he could just get back to his changing room before anyone in the Hub noticed he was missing...

Silas slipped through the Service Area door and glanced once more into the Programming Hub. This time the four technicians were standing around one empty column. It was the one with his name at the top.

Moving downstairs with far less caution than he had climbed up, Silas reached the main corridor. He had to get to the Re-ed hall. Reaching for the hood of his suit, he pulled it into place.

Immediately an agonisingly icy chill encased his scalp, penetrating deep into his brain. Reeph's voice pierced through the frozen fog of his thoughts. It felt as if his mind was fracturing into tiny shards and he staggered under the intense pain in his skull, folding into an uncoordinated heap of limbs. He knew it was the hood causing this awful icy paralysis, but he couldn't control his arms to remove it.

'Where are you, Silas? Why are you not in the main hall?' Reeph asked in his beautifully modulated voice, but the sound grated and creaked through Silas' conscious.

'It hurts!' Silas gasped, desperately trying to soften the splintering effects of the hood. 'Reeph... it hurts!'

'Pain is temporary. Where are you?'

Silas managed to drag his knees up into a foetal position, trying ineffectively to shield himself from the terrible mental agony. He had to get the hood off; it was going to kill him.

'You promised me a climbing wall. I couldn't find it,' Silas managed to whisper as a last-ditch attempt to get Reeph out of his head.

Abruptly the pain subsided, and Reeph's calm voice continued. *'You went the incorrect way for the climbing wall, Silas. I cannot help you if you are not inside the main body of the facility. You can return there now.'*

At once a soothing lightness filled his head. The icy grip completely vanished and Silas could feel the memories of the last few seconds begin to disperse. Soulsight was still working to counter the hypnotic suggestions of the Re-education and, with effort, Silas held on to his fragmenting memory. He refused to simply forget what Reeph was doing to him, this awful invasion of his mind.

'Aim to be the best you can be. You are worth investing in...' Reeph's voice resumed and, finding strength returning to his trembling legs, Silas stood. Supported by the wall, he stumbled along the corridor until he found the room with his belongings just as he had left them. Easing the hood away from his head, he breathed deeply and, with trembling hands, drained the Soulsight water from the bottle.

All he wanted to do now was hide. He simply wasn't brave enough to continue with the plan. His brush with the terrible power behind the Re-education Programming Hub, and the realisation that Reeph could inflict such pain and destroy the fabric of his memories, chilled him.

What if Re-ed took away other memories? What if they erased his memory of Zoe and the Community?

But the plan was too far in motion to back out now. Soon everyone in the whole facility would be exposed to Soulsight, and Silas needed to be ready.

Bracing himself, he walked through the door into the main hall. It was hard to watch the other residents around him, their expressions vacant and their souls empty. Hollow shells of people. He wondered who they were and what their crimes had been to get them into Re-education. Whoever they were, there was no turning back now. They were all about to experience an abrupt awakening.

Chapter 31

Looking carefully at the face of every resident, Silas once more circled the room. But it was to no avail. Dr Veron was not in the main hall.

Where else could she be? If he were going to get her away from the Spire, he needed to be with her when the Soulsight began to work. Silas could have kicked himself; he should have checked she was in the main hall before he had contaminated the environmental regulator.

Time was running out. There was already an alteration in the behaviour of the other Re-ed residents. A man looked his way and actually made eye contact. A shiver of apprehension ran down Silas' spine. This was really happening. Soulsight was breaking through Reeph's hold, but there was still no sign of Dr Veron. Where was she?

Perhaps she was still in the residents' rooms, he thought, remembering the downwards staircase. If he was going to find her, he would have to go now.

'Where am I?' The man who had looked at Silas moments ago was now staring around the room in utter confusion. Silas felt for him. To be dragged from the beautiful oblivion of the Re-ed hypnotic state and to be confronted with the brutal reality of the empty main hall was utterly disorientating.

'This is Re-education. The forest and the lake were not real. This is the truth.'

'It can't be,' the man insisted. 'I was happy. I need to get back to the forest. Where's Reeph?' he asked, desperately looking around for the comforting presence of the projection. 'And what's wrong with everyone?' Fear began to manifest its shadowy presence in the man's eyes. Although unpleasant to see, at least it was a genuine emotion and not the awful emptiness of Re-ed. 'Look, I don't know who you are, but you need to help me. I know you can.' Admiration filled the man's voice.

Unused to any form of appreciation, Silas was taken aback. Under the influence of Soulsight, he must seem like the only person of any substance..

'Look at me,' Silas ordered, and as they maintained eye contact, the fear began to recede from the man's shadow filled face. 'Now is your chance to get out of here. For the time being, Reeph can't control you.'

By the confusion that now flitted across the man's features, Silas guessed he wouldn't attempt to leave. The desire to be in the beautiful forest, with Reeph's soothing voice telling you how valuable you are… who would choose to be anywhere else?

Around them, people were beginning to fully emerge from their hypnotic state. The unsettled mutterings were becoming louder, and more people were beginning to turn their attention on him.

Silas couldn't stay in the main hall. He had to find Dr Veron before the technicians in the Programming Hub realised that they had lost control.

As he hurried towards his preparation room door, he heard a cry and saw a woman fall to her knees. She clutched her head, obviously in extreme pain. Uncovering his own head, he backtracked a few steps and wrenched the woman's encasing hood off.

She gasped with sudden relief and tried to focus on Silas.

'Help the others. Take their hoods off,' he instructed as he saw more people silently dropping to the floor, their faces set in a rictus of agony. She stood up and began groggily following Silas' instruction. Feeling guilty for abandoning them, but knowing he needed to find Dr Veron, Silas left the main hall.

Hastily he stripped off the Re-education uniform and kicked it under the bench. Then, flinging on his own clothes and bundling his belt under his arm, he headed into the corridor.

The door to the residential level closed firmly behind him, muting the sounds of chaos that spilled out from the main hall. He raced down the staircase, and upon reaching the bottom was confronted by another transparent door, similar to the ones on the upper level. This time however, there was a female technician staring directly at him, her mouth open in surprise.

Silas stood staring back at her, mirroring her expression, until she made the first move and walked towards the door. It slid open as she approached.

'You startled me!' She laughed. Her appearance was light and untroubled, and she was seemingly unaware of the breakdown of Re-education control in the main hall. 'Come in. How can I help you today?'

Silas tried to stay calm as he stepped into a small anteroom. The door slid shut behind him and he listened for the tell-tale click of a lock being engaged. The woman was waiting expectantly, and Silas realised that she genuinely wanted to help him. 'I've been sent here to collect someone,' he said, deciding that honesty was the only policy here. This woman would also have been exposed to Soulsight, and the faintest hint of fear or the smallest of lies would distort his soul and frighten her.

'Who might that be?' the woman asked helpfully.

'Esther Veron,' Silas answered. 'Do you know her?'

'Esther has been discharged from here.' The woman smiled.

'She's been discharged home?' Silas asked with surprise. All the subterfuge had been completely unnecessary.

'I would expect so. Positive outcome from Re-education can happen quickly with some residents.' The woman walked around a central workstation. 'Reeph, details on Esther Veron.'

'Reeph?' Silas asked feeling a little weak, recalling the agonising pain Reeph had so recently inflicted on him.

'Our name for the Re-education Programming Hub. It's an acronym, ReEPH,' she spelt out for him with another smile.

'The holographic projection gives a reassuring face to the programme. It's very convincing. Have you met him?'

'Yes, at reception.' Silas gave a feeble smile in response. No wonder the projection was so compelling. It had the whole power of the Re-ed Hub behind it.

'Of course,' she nodded, then pointed at a list of information as it scrolled across the workstation. 'Here it is. Oh, that's not so good. Esther Veron. Unusual reaction to the Re-ed hood yesterday so she underwent an intensive session with follow-up care under the Health Advisors at...' she paused, reading the information silently.

'Where?' Silas prompted her.

'She's been transferred to an address I've not come across before. Right over in the middle of the Uninhabited district. Anyway, there it is.' She smiled and waved a hand to Silas, encouraging him to step closer. He edged towards her and looked where she indicated. The workstation rippled and morphed into a flickering aerial projection. Silas immediately recognised the brand-new contagion quarantine building.

'Do you know why she's been taken there?' Silas asked, trying to squash the fear that the black, sleek structure produced in him.

'Maybe there's a new Re-education facility there,' the technician smiled, eager to help. 'Anyway, the transfer was approved by one of your colleagues from Viva head office.'

Silas did a double take. 'My colleagues?' he queried, wondering how exactly the woman was seeing him. Maybe, in such a small anteroom, she'd had a Soulsight overdose. She must think he looked absolutely perfect.

'Tell me,' she suddenly gushed, leaning towards him over the workstation, 'do you work with Helen Steele herself? I've always longed to visit the offices at the top of the Spire. But here I am, stuck in the basement. Maybe you could put in a good word for me?'

'I don't work at the top,' Silas said, backing towards the door. He needed to get out now. The whole of the facility would be on the brink of meltdown and, with or without Dr Veron, Silas couldn't stay a moment longer.

'That's a shame, with your obvious advantages.' Her smile was just a little too wide, almost predatory, and Silas suddenly understood her friendliness in a new light.

'Better go,' he blustered.

The door slid open behind him and the sound of shouting and screaming echoed down the stairwell. It sounded like Reeph was working overtime to try and contain the residents.

'What's that noise? What's going on?' The technician asked, her eyes immediately filling with fear shadows.

'I'm not sure,' Silas replied, before remembering too late that he mustn't lie.

'Ugh!' The technician stepped away suddenly. 'What's wrong with your face? It looked all twisted up.'

'I don't know,' he responded automatically. The technician's disgust deepened and he realised that another lie had slipped out. 'I have to go now,' he said, backing away. Abandoning the residents' level, he leapt up the stairs two at a time, the sound of shouting and panic adding extra speed.

Orange-suited figures were stumbling around the corridor. Those who were still wearing the hood were clutching at their heads in pain, as Reeph attempted to re-exert control. Others had removed their hoods and were desperately trying to find their way out of the facility.

Heading away from the turmoil, Silas ran the length of the corridor. Geren had described an alternative service exit. Turning a corner, Silas was relieved to see a solid-looking external door. Clearing his throat, he spoke into the lock: '5172.' With a faint hiss the door slid open and Silas stepped outside.

The damp coolness of the falling rain was a welcome change from the sterile environment of Re-education, and he drew in great lungfuls of air.

He was in a service alleyway for the Spire. Sheer crystalline walls rose imposingly beside him, dwarfing all the surrounding buildings. At the far end of the narrow alley, he saw a waiting

Autocar. That had to be Coach Atkins, Silas thought, sprinting towards it. A high-pitched whine made him look up, and he caught a glimpse of an Emergency Health transport, no doubt responding to the unfolding chaos in the Re-education facility.

'She wasn't there,' Silas said, as the door of the Autocar closed behind him and the vehicle began to silently glide away from the Spire. 'She's been transferred.'

Coach Atkins simply nodded, as if he hadn't expected Silas' rescue attempt to be anything other than a failure.

'It wasn't my fault,' Silas said, irritated by the lack of response.

'That makes it far more difficult,' Coach Atkins replied in his slow monotone. Silas was taken aback. He would have appreciated a little encouragement. An 'at least you tried', or 'it was a gamble' would have sufficed. However, nothing was forthcoming, so by the time they reached Nana's street the cloud of all-pervading gloom that Coach Atkins exuded had begun to affect Silas too.

Chapter 32

Even though it was daytime, Coach Atkins had insisted that the safest option was to use the cellars to get into Nana's house. With Dr Veron and Zoe missing, he was convinced that it would be under surveillance.

'Your unusual behaviour at Re-ed will have been logged, and your absence noticed. It won't be long before the HE-LP and possibly the Advisors are looking for you. They cannot be allowed to suspect a wider involvement, or we will all be Re-educated,' Coach Atkins said leading Silas down the hidden cellar staircase.

Silas nodded wearily, further disheartened by Coach Atkins' relentless pessimism.

'I see you, Silas, and you, Thomas,' Nana said, as they climbed up the ladder and into the room.

'I see you, Eva,' Coach Atkins responded. 'The plan was unsuccessful.'

Silas was almost too afraid to look up, but when he did, he was shocked to see how frail she seemed. 'Nana, I'm so sorry,' he said, unable to keep the concern for her out of his voice. Her soul had been strong, and to see her so weakened was awful. It made Silas feel even worse.

'I am anxious,' Nana said, explaining her appearance with a wave of her hand. 'Worry causes more problems than it solves and has the horrible effect of tainting everything else,' she sighed. 'Now, can you tell me what happened?'

As Silas recounted his desperate attempt to find Dr Veron and the news of where she had been transferred to, Nana's appearance began to shift. The weakening effect of worry was replaced with burning anger. Silas had seen glimpses of anger in Zoe before, but Nana's reached such a frightening intensity that Silas wanted to hide from her. She must have seen his fear, as before he'd finished talking, she cut across him.

'Silas, thank you for trying. You have helped so much. Stay there a moment, would you please? Thomas, before you go, could I speak with you in the nutrition room?'

Puzzled by his sudden exclusion, Silas remained standing by the trapdoor entrance, feeling rather foolish as Nana and Coach Atkins walked from the room. Clear logic told him that nothing that had happened was his fault, so why did he feel like it was?

'What are we going to do, Thomas?' Nana's words were muffled, but her fierce anger was adding an edge and volume to her voice so that Silas could make out everything she said. Immediately feeling guilty, he started looking at the collection of books on the shelves. The spines were mostly torn or faded, but Silas attempted to read a few rather than listen in on Nana's conversation.

'Silas should not have been involved,' Coach Atkins said. Silas couldn't ignore hearing his own name.

'You are right,' Nana agreed, causing Silas flush to with annoyance. He expected her to defend him, not discount him. They were both seemingly holding him responsible. 'We will have to find another way now. Will you contact Bubba Gee and Mags to see if Derry has any new information about the quarantine facility? This is all spiralling out of control. We need to act now! We cannot afford another mistake.'

Nana's apparent blame fuelled Silas' indignation. It wasn't his fault that the plan had failed; he had done his part perfectly. Maybe he hadn't explained clearly enough. And now it sounded like they wanted him out of the way. He had messed up and now he had nothing more to offer them. He didn't want to stay somewhere he wasn't needed, but there must still be something he could do to help Zoe, Jono and Dr Veron. If only he could get his dad to believe him… That was it. Nana and Coach

Atkins may want him gone, but his father had the right to know what was going on.

Looking at the open trapdoor, Silas suddenly knew what to do. He would find his father and give him Soulsight. Then he too would know the truth.

Hurrying through the cellars, Silas was soon outside and heading home. He would collect some Soulsight and go straight to Bio-health.

A group of Seen were standing on the street outside his house. There was a hungry air of expectancy in the crowd that reminded Silas of the reporters who had gathered by the Health and Safety courts before his sentencing.

His step faltered. Two Health Advisors were guarding his front door, and instantly he knew that they must have come for him. They would take him back to Re-education, and this time they would make him a resident.

Both Advisors were looking his way, but neither moved to challenge him. One of the Advisors seemed familiar, and Silas squinted, trying to filter out his residual Soulsight.

'Oh, no!' Silas muttered, suddenly feeling faint. 'Taylor Price.'

Opening his eyes fully, he allowed Soulsight to show him the true heart of Vitality Clinic's previous Gold Standard.

Physically, she was the epitome of health. Together with Marc, she had joined the Health Advisors as soon as she had left Vitality Clinic. Yet to look at her now, with the frightening truth of Soulsight, made Silas feel a strange mixture of disgust and compassion.

She looked grey and sickly. Her skin was thin and her sunken eyes had an opaque white cast to them. She was blind, or rather, her heart was. She had stared down the viewfinder of a disruptor with the full intent to take a life – to take Jono's life. Never mind that he had survived, the moment her thumb had pressed the Disrupt button, her twisted soul had withered and died.

Unnervingly, her sightless eyes locked on to his, and any pity Silas had for her evaporated. He should turn and run. Why was he just standing there?

'What are you staring at?' she barked aggressively, making Silas jump. 'Get lost! This is private property!' She took a menacing step forward.

Silas was confused. 'You're not looking for me?' he asked, surprise making his voice sound squeaky.

'Why would anyone be looking for you, little boy?' she sneered, running her blind eyes up and down his body, trying to make him feel small and insignificant. At any other time he would have felt exactly that, but knowing who she was and what she had become emboldened him.

'I see you, Taylor Price,' he said, moving towards the front door. 'And this is my house. I'm going inside.'

Standing up to Taylor felt fantastic, and she was so surprised that, had she been alone, Silas didn't doubt that he could have walked right past her. However, the other Health Advisor lifted his arm to block the door.

'You'll have to wait,' he said firmly.

Just as Silas was about to protest, the door to his house opened from the inside, and he was standing face to face with the Flawless Leader, Helen Steele.

Taylor and the other Advisor immediately bowed their heads, and cheers and applause came from the crowds who had been waiting on the street.

Silas' jaw dropped open in shock. Helen Steele was as terrible as he remembered. Her writhing flesh seemed barely restrained by her clothing, and her eyes were dark pits of loathing and fear.

'Silas!' His father's voice broke through the haze of dread. 'Move out of the way!'

'It's all right, Anton,' a silken voice oozed from her warped mouth. 'The boy is smitten. It often happens.'

'Of course, Flawless Leader,' he gushed, his old and frail soul brimming with admiration.

Silas gulped as courage and defiance rose within him. 'What are you doing here?' he challenged.

'Silas!' His father's surprise turned to anger and his expression darkened.

'Silas Corelle.' Helen Steele stepped closer to him. Her skin bubbled and she stared at him with death-filled eyes. 'You remind me of your brother,' she said with a light laugh. 'The things he would say sometimes... quite inappropriate.

'Whatever is the matter with your sons, Anton?' Helen Steele pushed past Silas. 'So different from their father,' she purred. 'There must be a weakness from the mother's side.'

A flicker of pain crossed his father's face.

Defend my mother! Silas wanted to shout. Defend your wife! But Anton's hurt was quickly eclipsed by slavish devotion.

'Why are you here? You are supposed to be in Re-education,' his father hissed, grabbing Silas' arm as the Flawless Leader walked on. 'Why are you so determined to humiliate us, and now in front of the Flawless Leader, herself?'

'Anton,' Helen Steele beckoned.

'Go inside and wait in your room. This behaviour has gone far enough. You and I are overdue a serious talk!' His father glowered and roughly steered Silas towards the house before scurrying after Helen Steele.

Taylor Price grinned viciously at him. 'Wait in your room, little boy,' she mimicked, before she and the other Health Advisor also followed after the Flawless Leader.

Taylor's taunt didn't sting half as much as his father's comments. He wants a 'serious talk', does he? So be it. I'll tell him exactly what's going on. It's about time he heard the truth.

He watched his father trot alongside Helen Steele like a faithful pet. The hold she had over him made his blood boil.

A faint buzz caught Silas' attention, and two circular drones glided smoothly over the heads of the waiting crowd and came to a halt in front of Helen Steele.

His father appeared hesitant, but the Flawless Leader seemed to be expecting it, and posed, smiling. One of the drones landed next to Helen Steele and immediately sent up a projection. The image flickered and then sharpened, and the waiting crowd cheered once more as a projection of the famous *Prima Life* reporter, Terin Poltz, turned to wave at them.

She was dressed from head to toe in pale pink, and a translucent rose train shimmered around her. To everyone else, she would have looked breathtaking, but to Silas, there was something bloated about her. Her body and face looked swollen and overfull, causing her features to appear too small. Lifting a puffy hand, she smoothed her hair and twitched her miniscule mouth into a pout before turning towards Helen Steele.

'Good afternoon, Flawless Leader. Thank you for inviting me to interview you. I cannot apologise enough for not being with you in person.' Even though she was merely a projection, Silas could see the same element of slavish adoration across Terin's distended face as his father's, except that hers was mixed with an ugly streak of envy.

'No need to apologise,' Helen Steele said sweetly, and only Silas saw the ripple of irritation that ran over her body. 'I know this interview was short notice for you. Shall we begin?'

At a signal from Terin, the drone camera hovered closer.

'I have the great honour of joining our Flawless Leader outside the home of the founder and head of Bio-health Laboratories, Anton Corelle. Today is an important day for Viva and for Bio-health. Flawless Leader, would you like to tell us more?' The camera repositioned to focus on Helen Steele.

'To the city of Prima, to the whole nation, I want to say thank you.' She took a step forward, fake sincerity oozing from her voice, and poison pouring from her soul. 'Thank you for your courage during what has been an uncertain time. The contagion among the Unseen and the inconvenience of the curfew has been a test for us all, but your cooperation has meant that the progression of this illness has been halted. We at Viva are dedicated to fulfilling our obligations as set out in the "Future Health" edict, which will see a transformation in the lives of Seen and Unseen. Today we want to announce that the first phase of our pledge has been completed. Thanks to the dedication of Anton Corelle and the Bio-health team, we have fitted the latest model of Biocubicles in every home of every citizen. This morning, the final cubicle has been installed, and it is appropriate that this phase has finished at the point where it began, in the home of Anton Corelle.'

Helen Steele stepped back and waited for Silas' father to say something.

'You seem a little lost for words, Anton?' Terin prompted. 'We haven't forgotten how the Biocubicles have been so valuable in improving health levels. Not all of us can claim the title, "Saviour of the Nation", can we?' As the reporter leaned towards Silas' father and smiled encouragingly, Silas saw a thick layer of deep shadow develop around the Flawless Leader. 'But now,' Terin continued, 'am I correct in saying the new model will offer us something more?'

Finally Anton seemed to break out of his star-struck daze. 'Yes, Terin, that's right.' The camera hovered closer to Silas' father, and he smiled nervously into its watching eye.

'The new Biocubicle range uses what we have called "weighted light". I know that sounds like a contradiction in terms, but this technology manipulates light waves to assess at a molecular level.'

'Don't get too technical on us, Anton,' Terin teased.

Silas' father laughed nervously. 'Of course not; all it means is that health assessments will be far more thorough. For instance, blood tests will no longer be necessary. Infections, such as the contagion, will be detected at a pre-contagious phase.'

'And you have a vaccine, Anton,' Helen Steele purred, her predator's grin looming through the dark cloud that surrounded her.

'Er, the vaccine…?' His father seemed bewildered. 'I thought we were going to delay that announcement,' he muttered.

'That sounds interesting,' Terin grinned at the camera, and then back at Silas' father.

'Well,' Anton hesitated, looking to Helen Steele for guidance. 'Bio-health has been working on a vaccine that is administered using this weighted light, thus combining diagnosis with treatment. We believe it to be close to a panacea, a heal-all, as it not only stimulates specific immune response, but it can also be guided to trigger spontaneous cellular repair.'

'Which means?' Terin prompted again.

'That if there is a damaged cell, for instance a cell on an artery wall that will, in time, develop into an aneurysm…'

Silas swallowed painfully. It had been an undetected aneurysm that had ruptured and killed his mother. Suddenly he saw his father's obsession with work in a new light. He was trying to fix the past.

'… the weighted light will not only identify each problematic cell, it will also carry the new vaccine to specifically target that area. The body's immune system will destroy the damaged material and the remaining healthy cells will be stimulated to regenerate. This will be a breakthrough treatment for many Unseen. I am in full support of Viva party's campaign, and I had hoped to have the vaccine ready by the time of the Future Health ceremony, but…'

'It will be ready,' Helen Steele interrupted, and Terin and the camera returned their focus to her, missing Anton's deepening confusion. 'As a nation we want to step into a new and healthier future together, but we need to recognise the vital and unique role that Bio-health, and in particular, our own nation's saviour, Anton Corelle, have played in the research and development of this incredible gift.'

As Silas watched, the Flawless Leader's face contorted into a leer, and the pits of her eyes flickered deep within the frightening darkness that enveloped her. There were so many lies on top of twisting lies that he couldn't unravel her true meaning. All he could recognise was a building animosity that was directed towards his father.

'Without Dr Veron...' Silas' father began.

'We will have *you* to thank for this vaccine.'

Suddenly it became clear. Helen Steele was setting his father up. She knew the vaccine's potentially deadly nature, and was going to let Anton take the blame. She was playing with him, like a cat would with its powerless prey.

'No!' he shouted, refusing to let his father be manipulated like this. Terin's projection turned to stare, as did his father and Helen Steele. The camera remained trained on the Flawless Leader.

'The vaccine isn't safe. Why don't you ask Esther Veron? You know where she is.' Silas pointed accusingly at Helen Steele.

The stunned silence that greeted his outburst lasted milliseconds, then both Terin and Helen Steele gave conflicting instructions.

'Cut transmission,' said Helen Steele, fury sending her body into paroxysms.

'Film the boy!' shrieked Terin.

Silas' father bellowed his name, and the betrayal that was writ large across his face was enough to keep Silas rooted to the spot. He shot his father a pleading look. 'Dad, you cannot trust her!'

His father's other emotions began to be swallowed by blind anger. 'You are talking about your Flawless Leader!'

Then Silas realised his folly. He couldn't challenge Helen Steele. His own father didn't believe him; why would he expect anyone else to?

Out of the corner of his eye, he saw her signal to the Advisors. Taylor began to approach him warily, her hand hovering over the disruptor at her waist. So Silas did the only thing he could... he ran.

Chapter 33

Feeling cold, lonely and frightened, he leaned against the rough plank that formed one of the tree house walls, and tried to shelter.

Night had fallen, and gusts of wind laced with fine, drenching rain seemed to seek him out behind the flimsy wooden wall. He shivered and wrapped his arms tightly around his body. The clothes he had worn to Re-ed simply were not able to compensate as the temperature dropped further.

He had managed to evade Taylor. If she had been chasing him across open ground he wouldn't have stood a chance, but this was his territory. First he had led her away from the Uninhabited district and then had doubled back, boldly cutting through the overgrown edges of his own back garden before sprinting for the safety of the tree. But now he had no idea what to do. He couldn't go home, or even to Nana's house, without being picked up on the Citizen Safety Monitors. Yet he couldn't stay in the Uninhabited district either. Any moment he expected to hear the rumble of a scanning ship and to see the penetrating red beam break through the clouds to scour the derelict buildings, looking for him. And when they found him, what kind of punishment would await him? Permanent Re-education residency or worse, he imagined.

Silas squeezed his eyes shut and tried to breathe slowly and steadily, like they taught in clinic. It didn't last long. His breathing became increasingly ragged as panic built in his chest. His mind once more replayed Helen Steele's manipulation. She had deliberately arranged the interview with *Prima Life* so that everyone would know exactly who had made the vaccine. His father clearly hadn't been expecting it. She was orchestrating the whole thing, and that confirmed that Helen Steele was intent on using the vaccine in its untailored, selectively lethal form. And when Unseen began to die, the blame would fall firmly on Anton Corelle.

Suddenly Silas tensed. He heard a rustling in the grass below him. Through the bare branches he could make out a shadow moving past the edge of the broken-down cottage. There was nowhere else to run. He was trapped.

'Silas?' Kesiah's familiar voice called up from below the tree.

'Kes?' Silas croaked with relief. 'I thought you were a Health Advisor!'

'I'm coming up.'

Moments later she was sitting across from him on the platform, stuffing an Unseen robe into her bag.

'Useful things, these robes,' she grinned. 'I kept mine from our trip to Maxie and Val's house. I've got yours here too.'

'What... how did you know? I mean, what made you look here?'

Kes laughed.

'I thought about it and decided that, if I were you, and I had publicly challenged the Flawless Leader live on *Prima Life*, where would I be now?'

'I had to say something! She's setting up my father so that everyone will blame him when the vaccine starts killing Unseen. Did you see her with Soulsight?' Silas asked.

Kes shook her head. 'No, I watched it at clinic.'

'I know what she's doing. She's going to use the vaccine before it's been fully tested.' He filled her in on the disastrous rescue attempt from Re-ed and how Dr Veron was now being held in the quarantine building.

'But what does that mean for Jono?' Kes asked, anxiety furrowing her brow.

'He and every other Unseen in that place are in serious danger,' Silas admitted gravely.

Kesiah began pacing the small platform, making it wobble and creak. 'We need to do something.'

'What can we do?' Silas said, as she stepped back towards him. 'We can't go up against Helen Steele directly. I just tried that... and failed.'

'Then we stick to the original plan. We know where Dr. Veron is. We can go to the quarantine building and get her out of there. Without Dr Veron, the vaccination programme will be delayed so Jono and the other Unseen will have more time,' Kes insisted.

'You've not seen where they're being held. It's like a sealed box. And there are guards. We won't be able to just sneak in,' Silas explained.

'We have to try,' Kes implored. She stopped pacing and knelt in front of him. 'I need to do something to help Jono. He left the safety of the caverns for me – to be with me. I won't abandon him.'

Her distress silenced Silas' further objections. She was right.

'We've got the Unseen robes so I guess we can go and take a look,' he conceded. 'But don't get your hopes up. We won't simply be able to knock on the door and walk inside, and as for leaving with Dr Veron...'

'We'll think of a way when we get there,' Kesiah said, as a relieved smile spread across her features. 'Here.' She pulled a swathe of grey cloth from her bag. 'This one's yours. Also, I brought this.' She handed Silas a packet of finely ground Soulsight leaves and a bottle of water.

'An Unseen robe and a bottle of Soulsight water versus Health Advisors armed with disruptors – we must be mad,' Silas said.

'We'll be careful. Like shadows,' Kesiah replied, standing up and pulling her robe over her head.

'Big, grey fear shadows,' Silas muttered. He tipped the coarse leaves into the bottle and shook it thoroughly before taking a mouthful.

They walked slowly through the Inhabited district. Silas was aware of the Citizen Safety Monitors watching every move. Once he had been reassured by their presence, but now he felt unnerved by the eyes everywhere.

Street after street and monitor after monitor, all the while at a steady stumble of an Unseen. Several times they heard the whine of a transport, but their field of vision was restricted by the enshrouding robes. On one occasion Silas was certain he heard the distant rumble of a scanning ship, and he had to resist the urge to break into a run and escape.

Silas' nerves were worn thin by the time they reached the old financial district, and he hastened inside the first derelict building they came to and pulled his hood off.

'What's the matter?' Kes asked anxiously, following him in.

'What's the matter?' he repeated incredulously. 'Everything! I feel like a hunted animal!'

'Keep it together, Silas,' Kesiah said crossly. 'How much further to the quarantine facility?'

'It's not far,' he answered, wary of her sudden anger.

'Wait,' Kesiah said and, turning to face Silas, slipped the hood back on her robe. Fear clouded the usually untroubled pure depths of her heart.

He completely understood and raised his hand. 'I see you, Kes.'

She nodded. 'And I see you. And I need you. I'm frightened for Jono. I can't do this on my own.'

They zigzagged carefully from ruin to ruin until they came to the place where Derry had been hiding. Silas half-expected him to be there again and whispered his name into the gloomy shell of a room, but no grey-robed Unseen emerged from the shadows.Silently they crawled forward to peer out of the glassless window.

In the dark, the quarantine facility was far more forbidding than Silas remembered. A block of black granite; smooth, windowless and lifeless… completely impenetrable.

Silas crouched in the shadow... watching... waiting for some kind of inspiration.

Suddenly, light blazed down on the street and the surrounding buildings, and with an ear-splitting whine a transport came in to land.

Two Health Advisors emerged, followed by the shambling forms of eight Unseen. Two more Health Advisors brought up the rear of the group, this time holding disruptors loosely in their hands.

With a heavy clunk, a thick section of wall slid sideways to reveal a rectangle of light which glowed brightly against the black walls. The Unseen were herded forward, a pathetic huddled cluster of grey that was swallowed whole by the wide-open doorway. The Advisors followed after them, and Silas expected the wall to close, sealing the group in, but to his surprise it remained open.

'This is going to be easier than I expected. We *can* simply walk in,' Kesiah murmured. 'But we'd better go now. Before the Advisors come back.'

'Hang on, Kes,' Silas said. 'This doesn't feel right...' He leaned cautiously out of the empty window. The light from the facility doorway merged with the neat circle shining below the transport, but there wasn't a Health Advisor in sight. Remembering Derry's warning about armed guards, he leaned out a little further, trying to see into the dark shadows either side of the transport ship. Suddenly he pulled his head back and lay flat on the floor.

'What is it?' asked Kesiah, copying his movements.

'Advisor,' he whispered, before peering once more over the broken sill. A Health Advisor was approaching the facility on foot, however, not from either end of the street. To Silas it seemed as if they had come from the same ruined building that he and Kes were currently hiding in.

'That was close,' he whispered. 'We could have easily bumped into him.'

The new Health Advisor had his back to them and was escorting a smaller figure in robes that were clearly far too long for them across the uneven road.

'Oh, no,' Kes murmured, the pity in her hushed voice evidently clear. 'Is that a child?'

They watched sadly, but Silas began to notice something strange in the way the Health Advisor and the Unseen child were moving. They looked almost furtive, and both glanced up at the hull of the silent transport as they passed underneath it.

The Health Advisor bent to say something to the robed child, who seemed to answer with some form of instruction, and the Advisor nodded. They were nearly at the opening in the facility wall when the four Health Advisors emerged from the entrance. They seemed unnecessarily rough, pushing past the single Health Advisor and the Unseen child to form a tight pack around them. The disruptors that had been held so casually before were now angled, not at the Unseen, but firmly at the lone Advisor.

As the single Advisor slowly pivoted, seeming to assess his situation, the light from the transport ship fell across his face, and Silas gasped. Even from across the broken-down street, Silas could recognise the shape of the developing soul of his brother.

'Marc!' he exclaimed, and would have jumped to his feet if Kes hadn't gripped his arm. Silas looked at her with wide eyes. 'Why's Marc an Advisor again?'

'Shh!' Kes said urgently. 'I don't think he is.'

Confused, Silas huddled back on the cold rubble and watched helplessly as, framed in the light from the doorway, another white-suited Health Advisor appeared. Silas recognised that clouded heart anywhere.

'Taylor Price,' he hissed.

With a leer of self-importance, she began to circle the small group, shaking her distorted head slowly from side to side.

'Marc Corelle,' she mocked, her arrogance lending a shrillness to her voice, which carried clearly to where Silas and

Kesiah were hiding. 'How the mighty have fallen. What a disappointment you turned out to be!'

'Taylor,' Marc acknowledged calmly. 'I see you, and you are looking just as I remember you.'

Silas and Kes exchanged glances. It sounded as if Marc was using Soulsight.

'What you see is someone who is considered fit to be wearing the uniform, whereas you were suspended from active duty. So why the sudden urge to dress up as an Advisor again?'

Marc stayed silent, but kept his eyes on Taylor as she paraded in front of him.

'You don't want to talk to me? That's all right. The Flawless Leader anticipated some attempt on the facility, especially after your idiot brother spouted off on *Prima Life*. But to be honest, I was expecting something a little more elaborate than you and – what is it? An Unseen child? You are more feeble than I thought. What is it with your family? It's like the Flawless Leader said, there must be some weakness you carry from your mother's side. So maybe you should both follow her example and take the truly selfish way out.' She laughed at Marc, and Silas saw the same anger that he felt begin to build in his brother.

'Self-sacrificial, young lady. Ellen Corelle was not selfish.' A deep voice that seemed to come from the Unseen child caused Taylor to take a step back. Silas instantly recognised the voice. The small childlike figure was Bubba Gee.

'Be silent, Unseen!' Taylor commanded, furious at being contradicted. 'Bring them both inside. The Unseen will need a bio-assessment, and find an empty treatment room to hold the Seen traitor. And get that uniform off him!' She spun on her heel and walked into the quarantine facility as the other Advisors roughly restrained Marc and Bubba Gee.

Silas and Kesiah could do nothing except watch with growing dread as Marc and Bubba Gee were escorted inside. The black wall slid shut, sealing them in.

'What was that?' Silas asked, open-mouthed. 'Was that an attempt to reach Dr Veron? How has Marc got involved? And what were they thinking, trying to sneak into the quarantine facility... just the two of them?'

Silas glanced at his and Kes' own dusty Unseen robes. He supposed their plan hadn't been all that different.

'Now even more people need our help,' Kesiah said quietly, keeping her eyes fixed on the sheer wall of the building. 'We need to look for a different way in.'

Chapter 34

It was nearly dawn, and Silas and Kesiah had circled the whole facility looking for another entrance. Cautiously picking their way through collapsing office blocks and over piles of rubble had not been easy, especially as their search was frequently interrupted by descending transport ships, which cast their landing lights in wide circles across the surrounding ruins. Even when they did get a clear view, it was hard to make out any details on the featureless black walls. After a couple of hours of careful manoeuvring, they were back where they started, staring at the closed door of an inaccessible fortress.

'There has to be another way,' Silas muttered, unwilling to admit defeat. Maybe they should just go and knock on the front door. At least that way they would be inside.

'Perhaps we should try to sneak in with the next batch of Unseen.' Kes pointed up to where another transport hovered high in the sky, lighting up the ridge of the wall as it came into land.

Silas gazed thoughtfully upwards. 'I think I have an idea,' he whispered. 'I just want to check something out.'

Staying low, he backed away from their hiding place and looked up into the shell of the old building.

Grey light filtered down through a series of jagged holes in the ceiling.

'What are you doing?' Kesiah whispered as she followed him.

'I want to see if I can have a look at the roof. You never know…' He shrugged and began climbing up the crumbling remains of a staircase.

'That cannot be safe!' Kesiah hissed with alarm. 'The upper levels are falling in.'

'I just want to see. You stay there and keep an eye out for any Advisors,' Silas insisted as he climbed carefully up a central staircase to the first level.

The tattered remains of the floor bowed and sagged, exposing twisted entrails of broken wires and pipes. In the dim morning light he could make out the next staircase on the furthest side of the building.

The edges of the room seemed the most intact, and Silas began to cautiously shift his weight to his left leg. As he raised his right foot, he heard a loud crack. The section he was standing on juddered and then dropped away, disappearing with a crash. It was so sudden that Silas had barely registered that he was falling before he was pulled sharply backwards.

'Careful!' Kes warned, releasing his arm as he regained his balance.

'Thanks,' he said sheepishly, peering at the cloud of dust rising through the new hole in the floor.

'I told you it wasn't safe.'

And I told you to keep a lookout, Silas thought ungratefully.

'I don't like being left behind,' she said, accurately guessing his thoughts. 'So why don't I lead the way?'

'Why not,' Silas muttered, trying not to feel irritated as she began to pick her way across the damaged floor.

The second staircase had more gaps than steps, but they managed to reach the next level. It was covered with broken chunks of plaster and sections of partition wall that had long since toppled over. The ceiling curved downwards like the base of an enormous bowl, but as the third staircase was mostly intact, they continued up.

The next floor dipped away dramatically as it followed the contour of the ceiling belowy. A great pile of electrical oddities had been stored there. Ancient bulky projectors, desks, chairs and a tangled mass of wiring was weighing the floor down. They tiptoed silently to the next set of stairs, concerned that any sudden movement might send the whole lot crashing through to the floors below.

The fourth level was empty by comparison, and looking over a few rusting desks and thick snaking coils of mildewed tubing, they had a clear view through the gaping window opposite. However, they still weren't high enough to see over the top of the ominous wall of the quarantine facility.

'One more level,' Silas said, beginning to carefully climb upwards.

The fifth floor was pitted with holes and littered with debris that had fallen from the upper levels. Thankfully there were enough solid sections for them to make their way across. Clear morning light spilled in as the sun finally rose, giving them a complete view over the top of the facility wall. The roof space dipped away from the edge, but nestling in the centre was a rectangular shape, no bigger than a Biocubicle.

'There's a door!' Kes exclaimed, sounding surprised. 'A roof accessway!'

'That's our way in,' Silas grinned, thrilled that his instincts had been correct.

'Now we simply need to grow wings,' Kesiah said despondently, and Silas heard fatigue in her voice. It worried him. He had never known Kes to be tired.

'Hey, don't give up, there's bound to be something we can use.' Leaning out of the window, he looked on either side of the building. 'We just need a wire, a rope, a pipe… something… anything.'

'Silas, the door's opening,' she whispered sharply, pulling him back into the shelter of the building. He ducked beneath the windowsill.

'Who is it? An Advisor?'

'Don't know,' Kes muttered back. 'Could be an Unseen…' The hope in her voice made Silas immediately think of Jono, and he risked a quick glance.

The door to the roof access was held wide open by a figure that was neither Advisor nor Unseen.

'Zoe?' Silas said in a small uncomprehending voice, then suddenly, standing to his full height, he leaned out of the window and waved to get her attention.

'Zoe! It's me!'

She swung around as she heard her name and raised a hand hesitantly, as if unsure whether what she was seeing was real; then she began to wave enthusiastically.

'We need to get over there,' Silas said, looking with renewed desperation at the pieces of broken pipe around him. 'I just need something to bridge the gap. What about the tubing on the floor below? We could tie it here and throw it across to Zoe.'

'I'll go and look,' Kes offered.

She edged back towards the stairwell and Silas called to Zoe, 'We're coming across.'

Zoe seemed to be shaking her head and she began to shout a response, but her words were lost in the growl of an approaching transport.

'What? I can't hear you!' Cupping a hand around his ear, he took a step away from the window. The roar of the craft was loud as it slowed to begin the careful descent to ground level.

'Silas, it's no good,' Kesiah shouted as she carefully walked back towards him. In her hands she had a piece of tubing, and with one firm tug she snapped it in half. 'It's all rotten.'

Then a change spread across her features as the light was stolen by the descending ship. With two bounds she was by Silas' side, and as the edges of the transport became level with them, she gave his arm a tug.

'Here's your bridge. Let's go!'

Silas' eyes widened with alarm. 'What?'

'Now!' Grabbing his hand she stepped up onto the windowsill, dragging him with her.

'On the count of three!' she shouted over the noise of the transport. The edge of the wing tip was only a couple of metres away and Silas suddenly understood what she planned to do.

'No!' he cried out as she gripped his hand tighter.

'One, two...'

On 'three', they leapt onto the wing of the transport. It dipped and then straightened out as the stabilisers compensated for the additional weight, but Kesiah didn't stop. Pulling Silas behind her, they ran across the top of the ship and, without any hesitation, she launched herself at the rim of the quarantine facility. Their feet barely touched the top of the wall before they were tumbling down across the hard, cold roof.

When he had stopped rolling, Silas lay blinking up at the pale sky. His whole body was buzzing with so much adrenaline that he couldn't decide if he had been injured or not by his fall. Drawing a wobbly breath, he caught sight of Kes, already on her feet and dusting off her clothes. He didn't know whether to shout at her or hug her, but before he could decide, Zoe was by his side.

'Silas, are you all right?'

'I think so.' Silas gingerly sat up. 'Did you see what she made me do?' With trembling hands he patted down his chest and legs. He seemed to be in one piece. 'Kes… the transport… the roof…' He gave a strangled laugh.

Zoe nodded. 'I can't believe you're here,' she said, crouching down beside him. 'How did you find me? I've not been allowed to contact anyone. We're supposed to keep Mum's location a secret.'

She wasn't making sense, and for an awful moment Silas wondered if Zoe had been Re-educated too. He looked deep into her eyes.

'I thought they might have changed you,' he said, thinking how shallow his own soul had been. 'I see you, Zoe,' he said, pulling her into a tight embrace.

The sensation of her hair on his cheek and the feel of her face pressed into his neck lifted away every other thought, every concern, every fear. Silas didn't ever want to let go.

'We'd better get inside before that transport takes off,' Kesiah warned, breaking into the moment. 'Where does the staircase lead?'

'Into a living area. It's tiny, but you can come in. My mother's busy in the lab so it's just me,' Zoe said, helping Silas to stand.

'Can you take us to her?' Kes asked. 'And have you seen Jono?'

'Why would I have seen Jono?' Zoe asked, looking perplexed.

Kes and Silas exchanged glances.

'You don't know where you are, do you?' Silas pulled the door closed, shutting out the low rumble of the transport that had begun to take off. They walked single file down a narrow stairway and emerged in a small combined health suite and nutrition area.

'I guessed we must be in a Bio-health facility. My mother and I only arrived here yesterday. She said that some people were trying to destroy her research so we had to relocate, just for a few days, until her project was complete.' Zoe glanced around the basic room. 'I had no external com-link, Silas. I wanted to let you to know that I hadn't simply disappeared on you again.'

'I knew you hadn't,' he reassured, 'but this place is not part of Bio-health. Your mother no longer works for my father. You were threatened, and Dr Veron ended up in Re-education. She's working for Helen Steele now. They are going to use your mother's vaccine before it is entirely safe.'

He said it as gently as he could, but as the new information filtered through, a tight knot of fear begin to take root in Zoe.

'How can that have happened?' she frowned. 'I don't remember being threatened… we were moved here last night… my mother hasn't had any Re-education.'

'You must have been sedated,' Silas said. 'You went missing four days ago.'

'I don't understand,' Zoe said.

'I know it's a lot to take in, Zoe, but we need to see your mother. She is the only person who may be able to stop Helen Steele."

Zoe took a deep breath. 'The laboratory is next door, but she might not speak to you. I thought she was more anxious than usual. Re-education would explain it. She won't eat or rest… I don't know if you'll be able to get through to her.'

'Kes, is there any Soulsight water left? Silas asked. She passed him the half-full bottle of faintly green-tinged water. 'This worked on me, remember?' he said to Zoe. 'She just needs to see clearly, and then we have to get her away from here.'

Zoe made Silas and Kes stand out of view of the internal link before requesting a connection.

'Labs. Dr Veron.'

A few seconds later, Dr Veron answered. 'Zoe, what is it? I'm busy.' She sounded coherent but impatient.

'I know, Mum, but could you come through here? I have something urgent to tell you.'

'It will have to wait. Just another day… I will be finished then, and we can talk as much you like.'

Silas frowned. That sounded like a definite deadline. Helen Steele was going to act soon.

'Well, can I come through? It's about your work, the vaccine. It's really important.'

'Fine. Five minutes only, though. Come now and I'll let you in.' Dr Veron cut the connection.

Zoe looked at Silas and shrugged. 'We get five minutes,' she said.

Chapter 35

They followed Zoe through the back of the living quarters, past a small bedroom to a solid metal door.

'It won't respond to my voice,' she explained with a frown. 'I was told it was for security reasons.'

Zoe banged a closed fist against the door and they heard a muffled female voice give an indistinct command. With a clunk, the door unlocked and began to swing outwards. Leaning against it, Zoe pushed it fully open, and beckoned for Silas and Kesiah to follow her.

Silas' eyes opened wide. The layout of the room was almost identical to the laboratories he had seen where his father worked. No wonder Zoe had assumed they were in a Bio-health facility. Workstations, equipment and data processors were arranged in a large circle, and standing in the middle, feverishly manipulating virtual data strands, was Dr Veron.

Silas knew Zoe and her mother were not close and that Dr Veron's research had always been her primary concern, but Re-education had managed to drain her of every shred of compassion and care. Within that empty hollowness, however, was one sharp edge. A shard of focus that burned with an all-consuming intensity.

'Mum?' Zoe wound her way through the maze of equipment.

Esther Veron's keen concentration didn't waver from the feed of data.

'Mum?' Zoe tried again, waving her hand in front of her mother's face. 'It's me.'

'Not now, Zoe,' she responded impatiently.

'Mum, it's about the project.'

'I'm working,' came the reply. 'If you are not here to help, then please talk to me later. Where's Corelle? He should be here by now.'

Silas jumped at the mention of his name. 'I'm here, Dr Veron,' he said.

'You're not Anton,' she accused, briefly raising her head.

'I'm his son,' Silas said. The singular line of attention had wobbled at the sound of his voice, but was already reforming with a parasitic ferocity. 'I need to talk to you about the vaccine. You told me it was dangerous. Do you remember?'

She failed to answer.

'Re-education has done this,' Silas murmured to Zoe. 'I can see it. We can't leave her here.'

Proffering the water he tried speaking in the same tone the Reeph projection had used. It had worked once before. 'Have a drink, Dr Veron.'

She glanced in his direction, and Silas thought she was about to take the bottle from him.

'The test subjects are ready,' a voice interrupted, and Dr Veron's focus grew even more pronounced as she pushed past Silas and swiped through another data stream.

'Test subjects?' Zoe looked concerned.

'I'll have to begin without you, Anton,' Dr Veron muttered. 'Now, out of my way, Zoe. I need to concentrate.' She walked past her daughter as a projection filled the space in front of the central workstation.

Four cloaked figures were standing in four Biocubicles.

'Voice link. Esther Veron to test cubicles.'

'Connection established,' the laboratory computer responded.

'Remove your coverings,' Dr Veron commanded. The test subjects flinched when they heard her voice, but obediently all four slowly removed their cloaks.

Silas was fairly certain he didn't recognise any of them from his time at the Community, although he struggled to see past the raw fear that spun twisting shadows around their souls.

'They're terrified,' he said. 'Why are they so scared? What's going to happen to them?'

Dr Veron ignored him. 'Final testing, phase 1,' she announced. 'Laboratory confirm. Subject 1, 52-year-old female, spinal cord damage and partial paralysis. Subject 2, 34-year-old female, metastatic adenocarcinoma. Subject 3, 65-year-old male, cardiomyopathy. Subject 4, 21-year-old male, chromosome 15 partial deletion.'

'Confirmed,' the computer responded. 'Commencing final testing.'

Light encased the Unseen, and their fear increased.

'Add vaccine,' Dr Veron instructed, flicking her wrist to a data stream and feeding it into a growing mix of numbers in front of her.

'No, Mum!' Zoe shouted grabbing her mother's arm and pulling at it furiously. 'Not yet. You don't know what you are doing. This isn't Bio-health. This isn't your project! Silas, help me to stop her!'

Silas couldn't tear his eyes away from the projection. Escalating pain spilled from the four Unseen as the colour of the scanning light shifted from cold blue to dark purple. Within the bright haze, Silas could see that the agony for each Unseen was becoming unbearable.

'Lab, halt vaccination,' he cried, unable to watch any more, but the process continued. Three of the test subjects remained standing, enduring the torment, but one changed. His fear and pain receded until all that was left was a lifeless and soulless body that was held upright only by the tight confines of the Biocubicle.

'Subject 4, deceased,' the computer reported in unemotional tones.

Zoe began beating at her mother. 'You have to stop. You are killing them!' she shouted.

Silas ran his hands through various data inputs, trying to interrupt the programme.

Dr Veron cast a furious glare at him. At last he seemed to have her full attention; maybe he could get through to her now.

'Security, unauthorised persons in main laboratory. Assistance required,' she cried.

'We need to go,' Kes said, looking at the way they had come in.

'We can't just leave her, and them!' Silas objected, but the projection had dispersed and from a door on the other side of the laboratory, two Health Advisors appeared, each brandishing a disruptor.

Suddenly escape seemed the best option. Ducking behind a processing desk, he and Kes hurried back towards the living quarters.

'Mum, release the lock for them... please,' Zoe cried, but instead of a verbal command from Dr Veron, Silas heard a different voice.

'Targets acquired, ma'am. Awaiting orders.'

The words filled Silas with an icy dread. The only way out was sealed shut, and with his brainstem pattern acquired, there was no way to hide.

'No! Wait!' he pleaded. Slowly standing upright and raising his hands in a gesture of surrender, he turned to face the Advisors.

'You again?' Taylor Price's penetrating voice echoed around the lab. 'Keep them acquired, but don't disrupt unless you have to,' she instructed the Advisors. 'The Flawless Leader has been looking for the boy, and had I known he would come here we could have saved a lot of searching.' She sneered at him. 'But I didn't expect him to have a friend. That is a surprise.'

Silas tried to think of something to say, but any words withered as he looked at his impossible situation. What had he done? No one knew he was here. Not Nana nor his father nor Derry and Mags. He was completely at the mercy of Taylor Price! And what had he dragged Kesiah into?

'I made her come,' he said, pointing at Kes. 'You should leave her out of it. Any problem you have is with me and me alone.'

Taylor smiled, and Silas recoiled at the viciousness in her delight.

'I think not. The Flawless Leader will want to speak to all three of you; that includes the blob.' Taylor glanced at Zoe, and Silas saw a heightening of pure loathing emanate from her.

'That's my daughter...' Dr Veron spoke hesitantly, but her attention finally fixed on Zoe. 'She stays with me.'

'You are to prioritise your task, Dr Veron. The Flawless Leader expects you to complete your vital work.'

'She stays with me,' Dr Veron insisted, the sharpness of her consuming focus beginning to blur slightly as the threat to Zoe seemed to break through the distortion of Re-education. 'My work is important, but so is my daughter's safety. My enemies may try to get to my work through her.'

Your enemies already did that, Silas wanted to cry. Can't you see it? But he knew how powerful Re-education was. Without Soulsight, Dr Veron was as trapped as they were..

Taylor seemed to recognise that she was losing the argument, and made a swift decision. 'Have it your way, doctor. Just get the vaccine ready,' she growled. 'You!' She pointed to one of the Health Advisors. 'Escort the fat girl back to the living quarters and stay on guard. Make sure she doesn't leave.'

The Advisor nodded, reset his disruptor and trained it on Zoe, who wavered, and then hesitantly stepped towards Silas. 'I'm going with him,' she said, challenging Taylor with a defiant stare.

'I will not continue if my daughter is not with me!' Dr Veron threatened. Her concern for Zoe was now by far her most defined feature.

'The target has been acquired,' the Advisor announced, moving his finger towards the Disrupt button.

'Stop. It's OK,' Silas interjected, holding Zoe's gaze with his own. 'Stay here, Zoe... I'll be fine. Please.'

'Sickening,' Taylor sneered, looking with revulsion from Silas to Zoe. 'What a tragic pair you make.'

Silas bit back his anger but he couldn't stop the heat of a flush spreading across his cheeks. Taylor saw it and laughed maliciously. 'You make my stomach turn. But, just so you know, weakling, her safety will depend on your cooperation. Now, move.'

Chapter 36

'What now?' Kesiah whispered as they left the laboratory.

'I don't know,' Silas admitted, glancing back anxiously. Taylor and the remaining Advisor were several paces behind them with the disruptors raised, ready to use. There was no way to outrun them, Silas thought, despairingly.

'No talking. Face forward. Keep moving,' Taylor barked from the back.

A large door slid open. Row upon row of shiny Biocubicles stretched in front of them, and Silas hesitated.

Taylor pushed the disruptor into the back of his head and he stumbled forward down one of the rows.

'Why do you need so many Biocubicles?' Silas asked, half-turning around.

Out of the corner of his eye he saw Taylor move, and before he could flinch away, she had twisted her hand into his hair and forcefully slammed his temple against the door of the nearest Biocubicle. A dagger of bright light exploded behind his eyes.

With a yelp, he ineffectively curled his hands to his head, too late to protect himself from the sudden attack.

'Why...?' he began to ask, but Taylor pulled his hair around her fingers, forcing his head back. His Soulsight was starting to fade, but flashes of exhilaration and pleasure coursed through her misshapen body each time she caused him pain.

'I told you not to talk,' she said with a vicious smile.

She let go suddenly, causing Silas to fall back against the metal wall of the Biocubicle. He tried to stay calm. He wasn't going to allow his pain to be the source of Taylor's amusement. Straightening his shoulders and ignoring the throbbing sensation from the bump on his head, he walked unsteadily forward.

The rows of Biocubicles filled the whole level, and as they descended to the next floor, he expected to see the same layout, but instead there were lines of doors. Although the doors reminded him of the corridor at the Re-eduction facility, Silas was certain these were not preparation rooms. A term from Coach Atkins' history lesson came to mind: 'cells'. This building was not designed to quarantine the unwell; this was a prison.

The noise of their footsteps must have disturbed the occupants of the cells.

'Help!' someone cried from behind one of the closed doors. The shout was swiftly followed by more cries.

'Let me out!'

'Please!'

'Com my family…'

Soon the cries and calls blurred into an indecipherable racket. Shaken, Silas turned his head to look at Taylor and was horrified to see her grinning. He drew in an unsteady breath and glanced at Kes. Jono must be in one of those cells, he thought with a cold shiver.

At the end of the row was another circular room, similar in size to the laboratory but completely empty of equipment. The pitiful shouting and crying from the cells was silenced as Taylor pushed the door closed.

'Flawless Leader, Silas Corelle is here,' Taylor announced to the bare room.

Immediately the room began to change. Shapes formed around them, adding depth and texture to the space. An expansive view of Prima stretched out far into the distance, and Silas looked down to find he was standing on the edge of a pink-hued glass balcony. Beneath his feet, the shining wall of the Spire fell away in a dizzying sheer line.

'Such an ugly patchwork.' A soft voice behind him made him jump, and he wobbled on the balcony edge before remembering that this was a projection. He was still in the quarantine facility, not standing on the top of the Spire. Steadying himself, he turned as the Flawless Leader approached, padding barefoot across the translucent floor.

Everything about Helen Steele promised life. She radiated wholeness and health, and the exposed skin on her arms and shoulders gleamed gold with reflected light.

Automatically, Silas felt for his bottle of Soulsight, before remembering with alarm that he had left it in the laboratory with Dr Veron. Now more than ever he needed to see clearly. He knew what the Flawless Leader's true nature was, and yet her physical appearance was still able to confuse him. Blinking rapidly, he dropped his gaze.

Helen Steele seemed to take that as a compliment and chuckled at his averted eyes.

'Do you agree, Kesiah?' she asked, then laughed again at Kes' sharp intake of breath. 'Oh, yes, I know all about you. Such a promising Vitality student. You could be a Health Advisor one day, and yet you choose to waste your considerable talents. But I have a way to help you.' Helen Steele smiled. 'As I was saying, this is supposedly the best view in the whole of Prima, and yet all I see is an ugly patchwork. Health and decay. Life and death. Flawless and flawed.'

Lifting his eyes, Silas studied the city. The order and structure of the Inhabited districts were mixed and muddled through with ruin and chaos as buildings crumbled, and brambles, shrubs and trees reclaimed the land. In the distance he could make out Vitality Clinic's broad white tower, and his eyes followed the contours of the land until he saw the hill and a tree larger than all the rest, isolated, but still standing.

The Flawless Leader seemed to be waiting for some kind of response from Silas or Kesiah.

'So silent now, Silas Corelle, when you seemed so eager to speak out earlier?'

Goaded by her condescension, Silas couldn't help but respond.

'I know what you are doing.'

'You think you know, Silas, but you do not.'

'You've combined the vaccine with the new Biocubicle before it is ready,' he challenged. 'Before it is safe…'

She angled her head to one side and gazed thoughtfully at him. 'There is something about you that intrigues me, Silas. To be so young and yet so certain. Yet not all of life is so definite. There are choices, balances.' Her tone became gentle and persuasive. 'As your Flawless Leader I have to make difficult decisions that require careful implementation. Every day I look over a broken and divided city, and every night I witness true tragedy. We are suffering; our children are sick. An opportunity has arisen to bring change… a cure for our ailments, and an end to the division that splits our nation.'

'By "ailments" you mean the Fragile Gene virus?' Silas said, trying to resist being moved by her words. 'Except that it's made up.'

'In a manner of speaking,' Helen Steele smiled. 'There is sickness that needs a cure. And now we have a way to rid ourselves of *all* the illnesses that plague us, that linger from generation to generation. The contagion was a simple ruse to persuade the population for the need and validity of a vaccine.'

'But it's dangerous.' Kes moved alongside Silas, facing the Flawless Leader, united in their defiance. 'It killed a man!'

'Ah, yes, the unfortunate outcome for the few untreatables.' Helen Steele sighed. 'And now you understand how difficult my decision was. Think of our nation as a body, yet one limb is diseased.' She stretched out a graceful arm as if for inspection. 'We cure what we can, but for the sake of the whole body we must cut away the dead and dying flesh.' She closed her hand into a tight fist and let her arm drop to her side. 'To limit the impact to families and friends, I arranged a simple quarantine facility. The vaccine will not be able to cure everyone, but we do not want to cause unnecessary upset. However, our grief over the one death must not blind us to the three who have been cured. They no longer have to remain Unseen. They can be part of a healthy, functioning body. Is that not worth it? One death compared to the restoration of three lives.'

Silas and Kesiah exchanged a frightened glance. Did she honestly believe what she was saying?

'Imagine if the nation were whole again, not broken and scattered. Imagine if her people were one. If divisions and labels like "Unseen" and "Seen" were relegated to history. We would be leaner to start with, but we would be healthier, stronger. Cutting away sickness and suffering, we would be able to grow and expand and reach new levels of perfection. You can be a part of that future. Do you understand?'

Silas felt overwhelmed. The Flawless Leader was staring at him. Her words were strangely inspirational and he longed to nod in agreement, and to receive her acceptance, her praise, and yet he knew that she was wrong. The Community had been proof of that. Filled with the physically sick and broken, yet it had been possible for external suffering to be transcended through compassion and care. In the Community, the artificial divisions between Seen and Unseen had already been overcome... it had been a place of hope and joy and love; full of people with whole and undamaged hearts.

'You can't just get rid of people who don't fit into your idea of perfect!' he growled, rage bubbling inside him. 'There is value and life in the physically imperfect too.'

A cold smile spread across the Flawless Leader's face. 'Life in the imperfect? Is that what you think?'

Silas clenched his jaw. He thought of Jono and Bubba Gee and baby William. 'Yes, that is what I believe,' he said forcefully.

Her smile became rigid. 'And so we come to it, Silas, the root of your problems. Sometimes there is a sickness that masquerades as health. A self-destructive weakness that will never be eradicated by a vaccine or Re-education. Your mother, I believe, was afflicted with such a weakness.' She gazed at Silas, waiting for his reaction. He bit his lip, trying not to give her the satisfaction of seeing his anger. 'And you seem to be determined to follow her path... to ignore what is best for you. I have been watching you,' she continued, 'and I am intrigued by your desire to mimic the imperfect. You have every opportunity to succeed, and yet you seem drawn to unwise behaviour patterns.'

Suddenly the holographic projection altered, and Silas was watching himself surrounded by a shimmering grey aura.

'You were picked up by the Citizen Safety Monitor near your house, breaking curfew and dressed as an Unseen.'

'You saw me?'

'The robes are no barrier to the Citizen Safety Monitors. How else can we accurately monitor the Unseen?'

The projection cut to him hurrying through the corridors at the Re-education facility.

'Re-education would normally be sufficient to stamp out such peculiar desires, but you seemed somehow immune and able to evoke a widespread resistance to Re-education among others. However, all is not lost for you. There is one last way your Flawless Leader can help you.'

'I don't need your help,' Silas said warily.

'And yet you do, without even knowing it. Have you heard about life before the Healthy Living Protocol? When someone was resistant to standard methods of behaviour regulation, more serious steps were taken to ensure compliance.'

The projection swirled and shifted once more, reforming into a different scene. The quality of the image was blurred and grainy, but Silas recognised an old-fashioned health facility. Three blue-robed and masked technicians were leaning over a table. Whatever they were looking at was illuminated by a large circular ceiling light.

'An operating room,' Helen Steele remarked. 'Take a look.'

Silas and Kesiah edged forward warily and peered over the shoulder of the nearest technician. A body lay on the table, covered over except for a vast expanse of exposed abdomen. With a sharp-bladed instrument, one of the health workers had already begun to make a deep incision in the swollen stomach.

'Despite guidelines, education and encouragement, during the peak of the obesity epidemic, there were those who refused to make the correct choices for their health.'

'What are they doing to him?' Kesiah asked.

'The health professionals at the time did the only thing they could to help. It seems brutal now, but this procedure was known as a compulsory gastric bypass. It was effective, though in those who survived. It forced a level of food compliance on the patient, but it saved their life. Similarly, you are both unable to make the correct choices for your personal well-being, and it is my responsibility to help you... so we are left with no other option.'

'What do you mean?' Silas asked, unable to tear his eyes away from the bloody tableau before him.

'Don't be alarmed, Silas. It is nothing as barbaric as our ancestors had to do.' She gestured to the projection and it disappeared. 'Simply a targeted frontal lobe adjustment. It won't even leave a mark,' she said with a smile. 'It will help you to trust your Flawless Leader a little more.

'Advisor Price, place them in holding until Dr Veron makes time in her schedule to arrange a compliance procedure.'

Chapter 37

Silas was locked in. He had tried shouting and beating at the walls, but he was just one more screaming voice among the pitiful cries that seeped through the wall of his cell.

He had passed simple fear now and was careening headlong into terror. He knew what was going to happen. There was no way out. What if the procedure was irreversible? Soulsight could undo Re-education, but Helen Steele was talking about an invasive procedure. Would he no longer care about the fate of his Unseen friends? Would he even remember them when they were gone? Jono and Bubba Gee would not survive the vaccination, Silas was certain of that. There was no space in Helen Steele's world for such imperfection.

He stalked around the small room once more. What was he going to do?

'Dr Veron is ready for you.' A voice filled his small cell. 'Lie face down on your bed and await further instructions.'

Trembling, Silas did as he was told, but angled his head to watch as the door to his cell slid open.

A disruptor was pointed directly at him.

'Your brainstem is acquired. Stand slowly and walk towards the door.'

Unable to see another option, Silas meekly walked ahead of the Advisor, past the long rows of cells and the floor full of Biocubicles, back to the laboratory.

This was the first time Silas had seen Dr Veron without Soulsight. Her dark head was bowed over a data stream as he entered the lab and, if anything, she seemed even more focused on her work than before. Eventually she raised her eyes and glanced at Silas.

The mixture of hollow Re-education and the alarming shard of obsession had been replaced by a short, stocky woman with the same brown skin and dark freckles as her daughter. Even her eyes were like Zoe's, just older and framed with a fine network of papery wrinkles.

Silas eyed her warily. 'Where's Zoe?' he said, trying to look around the room. Maybe she could intervene and prevent her mother from performing the compliance procedure, but it was as if he hadn't spoken.

'Where do you want him?' the Advisor asked.

'Over there, against the wall.' Dr Veron pointed to the other side of the room. 'Is this truly necessary, though?' she said, sounding impatient.

Silas looked hopefully at Dr Veron.

'The Flawless Leader knows what is best, Dr Veron. I hope you do not doubt her wisdom,' the Advisor said, his voice heavy with warning.

'I have had to divert memory units for this procedure, and I require maximum function for my final data analysis,' she said, extinguishing Silas' fragile hope that her concern had been for him.

The Advisor gestured sharply with his disruptor and, with his head lowered, Silas meekly crossed the room.

'Back to the wall,' the Advisor instructed.

'Laboratory. Restraints, table, anaesthesia ready for compliance procedure,' Dr Veron said, and as she spoke, the wall altered around Silas, moulding to his body and fixing him in place. Slowly he was rotated, and the wall extended beneath him to form a ledge. He tried to wriggle free, but smooth restraints had curled over his arms and legs.

'No!' Silas pleaded, feeling the pliable fabric begin to tighten. He started to struggle. 'You don't need to do this. I am compliant. I'll do what I'm told. Please, Dr Veron. It's me, Silas Corelle... I'm a friend of Zoe's... please...'

His desperate cries seemed to have no effect on Dr Veron, and her expression remained fixed.

'Anaesthesia ready,' the lab chimed.

'You are no longer required,' she said dismissively to the Advisor.

'I have been instructed to remain here.'

Silas watched out of the corner of his eye as Dr Veron slowly rounded on the Advisor. 'If you are remaining in here, then you may as well assist the computer with the procedure and I shall return to my far more important work.'

'My role is not to leave the subject while he is a potential threat. I have my orders, Dr Veron.'

'A threat?' she asked with a sneer. 'Lab, administer sedation,' she instructed.

At once, Silas felt a soothing numbness spread from the back of his neck across his jaw and slowly, blissfully, begin to descend to his chest. The restraints no longer seemed to be a hindrance as he felt himself begin to float up to the laboratory ceiling.

Gazing around, he could see beauty in the symmetry of the room, the swirl of information circling towards the centre, like a spiralling cluster of stars.

Where had he seen stars like that? Ah, yes. With Zoe. That had been a happy time, in the Community with Jono and Zoe. But Jono was dead. Or was he alive? Silas couldn't remember.

The twisting vortex of data fed into Dr Veron's workstation, and Silas felt his vision drawn downwards.

'Thash my…' he was looking for the word 'bottle' but it had slipped from his mind.

There was a woman standing over him who seemed familiar. Of course. 'Zoe…' he grinned, 'you're here.'

'He is sedated. You can return for him when I have finished the procedure.' The woman seemed angry, and Silas felt frightened of her.

Suddenly she bent close to his ear. 'Silas,' she said urgently. 'I know what I need to do. I can stop this. Helen Steele must not find out, so when you wake you will need to pretend that you are fully compliant.'

'Need 'tend,' he managed to mumble.

'Don't let her know!'

The woman was insistent, and he tried to give her an encouraging smile before succumbing to overwhelming tiredness.

Silas groaned and rolled on to his side. His mouth flooded with saliva as nausea churned through him.

'I hope you enjoyed your rest. The Flawless Leader awaits you in the health suite.'

The voice reminded him of Reeph, and he slowly opened his eyes, half-expecting the hologram to be leaning over him.

'Where am I?'

He gazed around the luxurious room. Shimmering trains of light spilled from the ceiling to create billowing walls. It was excessively bright and there was far too much movement. Feeling dizzy, he closed his eyes once more.

'You are in the Radiance Suite in the Spire, the honoured guest of the Flawless Leader.'

'The Spire? That's not possible…'

Desperately he tried to order his fragmented memories.

He remembered the laboratory and the restraints around his arms and legs and Dr Veron standing over him. What did she do to me? he thought. A vivid picture of a health worker slicing into an abdomen filled his mind, and instinctively his hands felt for wounds across his own smooth stomach. No. That hadn't been it. His procedure was different. It was something in his head. Compliant… that was the word. The Flawless Leader had wanted him to become compliant – permanently obedient.

Fear and anger mingled in increasing intensity and he curled into a ball, trying to contain his developing rage. Am I altered? Am I no longer myself? he thought. I don't feel any change, but how would I know? She's made me into a mindless puppet. I'll have to do whatever she says.

Then, through the fog of fury, new memories surfaced. Dr Veron had told him something important, and before that he had seen her workstation and his bottle of Soulsight. His *empty* bottle…

A different picture began to form as her words came back to him. *I know what to do… Helen Steele must not find out.*

That could only mean one thing. Dr Veron had broken free of the Re-education. Soulsight had helped her to see the truth. His plan had been to get Dr Veron away from the quarantine facility, but perhaps things could work out far better than any of them had intended. Now she had the perfect opportunity to sabotage the whole vaccination programme from the inside.

'The Flawless Leader would like you to join her in the health suite,' the Spire computer repeated.

Whatever happened, he must not allow suspicion to fall on Dr Veron. *'Pretend to be fully compliant.'* That had been her instruction, and now he understood. He had to make sure Dr Veron had enough time to do whatever she could to stop Helen Steele.

Still a little wobbly from his drug-induced sleep, Silas carefully stood up.

'Spire, is there any way to make the walls stay still?'

'Of course, Silas.'

'And make them a bit less bright?'

The waving, ballooning effect stopped, and the harsh light softened. Experimentally, Silas brushed his hand against the walls, expecting them to give way beneath his fingers, but they had become rigid and unyielding.

'Please follow me.' The lights behind him dimmed further, and the hallway lit up. Intricate whorls and patterns chased around the floor and ceiling, creating a continual stream of light.

Had Silas never seen the Soulsight caverns, he would have been impressed by the clever designs that ran around his feet, moving forward with his every step. However, the Spire's version was mediocre compared with the richness of the colours of the natural wonder that he had witnessed at the crater.

He followed the flow of light until he reached a dead end.

'Spire. Where now?'

'This is an elevator. Please stand still,' came the gentle reply as, with another breezeless billow, a fluid wall fell silently into place and then solidified, boxing him in at the end of the corridor.

The tiniest vibrations ran through the soles of his feet, and seconds later the rigid curtains softened and lifted to reveal a vast health suite.

'Wow!' he breathed. Not even Vitality Clinic could boast such an impressive array of equipment. Everything about it was perfect: the space, the light… it was a room designed to entice you to continue exercising all day.

At the furthest end of the suite was a swimming pool, and beyond that, the inky black of the night sky. The pool water rippled as a sleek head and shoulders broke the still surface and Helen Steele stepped gracefully up and out of the water. Her white suit glistened as the water beaded into hundreds of tiny shining diamonds which rolled down her body to form puddles around her feet.

She smiled at Silas and he immediately smiled back, forgetting that this incredible-looking woman was not to be trusted. Then he remembered he was meant to be different, compliant… so he allowed his smile to linger for a few seconds longer.

'How are you feeling, Silas?' she asked.

'I feel well, thank you, Flawless Leader.'

'I'm glad,' she smiled again. 'How lovely to meet the boy, or should I say the man, behind all those distracting and conflicted ideas. You will be so much happier now that you can trust me. We have an hour or so before dawn, and I thought you might like a chance to enjoy yourself.' She gestured around her.

'Yes, thank you,' Silas said.

'You are a speciality climber. You may like this.' She nodded at something behind him, and he turned to see a climbing wall.

'Like' was an understatement, and Silas stared in amazement. The most magnificent wall arched high in a curling wave up what must have been the side wall of the Spire. The studs and handholds tapered on to the vast domed ceiling. The target point was a swing suspended high above his head.

'No way,' Silas gasped, not needing to pretend to be impressed.

'Try it out,' she said. 'If you can get to the swing seat, you can watch the sunrise from up there.'

'I haven't got my climbing harness, and there aren't any ropes...' Silas hesitated. Would he query her command if he were truly compliant?

'Care for one's self is important; however, the Spire climbing wall comes with special safety features. I would not allow you to be harmed. You can trust me.' Her voice was silken and calm but there was an underlying edge to her insistence. This was something more than an invitation. This was a challenge. A test.

Unable to question her further without giving himself away, Silas approached the wall. His hands were sweaty, but the grips seemed to compensate by becoming rougher and dryer. He began to climb.

He had never truly free-climbed before. Even when he had scaled the waterfall with Jono and Zoe, he'd had the feeble support of a rope, but now he had nothing. He nervously looked down at Helen Steele, who was standing watching, a half-smile lingering on her face. Was she expecting him to fall? Did she already know about Dr Veron's betrayal?

'Keep climbing, Silas. I have said that you can trust me,' she called up to him.

He reached the top of the wall safely, but he now faced the underbelly of the cresting wave that formed the ceiling.

Unwisely, Silas glanced at the floor. It was a long way down.

'Get to the swing, Silas. Do as I say.'

Her command left him in no doubt. This was a test. If he refused, she would know.

'I am your Flawless Leader. You *will* do as I say.'

He must not give Dr Veron away. She was the only person who could save Jono and all the other Unseen. Silas knew what he had to do.

Chapter 38

He wasn't strong enough. The swing was a few holds away, but the muscles in his arms were screaming in agony. Trying to take some of the strain off, he twisted his hips into the wall and forced more pressure into his toes. It didn't help. He had to move. Flexing his right bicep, he pulled upwards and reached forward with his hand.

He got the hold and curled his fingers around it, but the stretch was too great and his foot slipped.

'Help! I can't do it,' he cried out, trying not to think about the damage he would do to his body if he fell. Both legs broken, that would be unavoidable... but his back... his neck...

'That is why you have to build muscle, Silas. You are too weak. You will have to let go.'

'I can't!' he called again.

'Trust me, Silas. Let go now!'

He didn't voluntarily let go but his fingers could no longer hold on. He closed his eyes as they slipped from the shallow handholds.

He fell.

Immediately his back came into contact with something, and his downwards plummet dramatically slowed to a steady descent.

His heart resumed its beating in a frantic catch-up of delight, and a ragged wail escaped his lips.

Something had caught him. He looked to either side but he appeared to be floating down on a layer of air. It must be some kind of transparent net, he thought. It felt cool and soft under his fingers, and as he neared the ground, it altered to become opaque. A thick band of white, springy material.

It was the same strange fabric that had hung in the guest suite, and as Silas stood up and stepped off of it, it slowly began to lift upwards before becoming transparent once more. The adrenaline rush from his fall had receded, and his legs were trembling.

'Good.' The Flawless Leader nodded at Silas, but he knew she wasn't congratulating him; she was impressed by the apparent success of the procedure. 'Such obedience. No one has ever climbed the wall without proof of the net, but you trusted me.'

'Yes, Flawless Leader,' Silas said, trying to stop his voice from shaking.

'Now you will be able to join me at the ceremony this morning, and you will inform Terin Poltz how wrong you were about me.'

'Yes, Flawless Leader,' Silas said again, feeling sick. He didn't know how much longer he could keep up this pretence.

'You may stay here for a while. Have a swim; try the climbing wall again. The Spire will let you know when it is time to join me for the ceremony,' she said, finally walking towards the elevator. The curtain dropped shut. He stared at the alcove, waiting, in case she returned.

After several moments had passed, Silas began to relax a little. She wasn't coming back. He had been tested and had passed. Gazing up at the climbing wall, he shuddered. He had fully believed that he would die; he had been ready to. There was something far more important at stake than his health or even his life.

Silas was drawn to the large glass wall overlooking the dark city. With his hands pressed against the glass, he stood silent and still until a blue-grey tinge stained the horizon, and then a pink hue touched the underbelly of a few sparse clouds. For the first time, Silas felt fear that the night was ending.

'Please return to your rooms for cleansing and nutrition.' The Spire computer interrupted his thoughts, and with a sense of weighty foreboding, he left the health suite.

The strange fabric walls of the guest suite had resumed their billowing movements.

'Spire, please keep the walls still,' Silas said. Anxiety knotted his stomach. There was so much resting on Dr Veron. What if she hadn't had enough time to stop the Flawless Leader's plan and get herself, Zoe, Kes and Jono out of quarantine?

Leaving his exercise kit in a crumpled heap, he showered and dried. Hanging beside the bed was a green suit. With no other clothing option, he pulled on the soft fabric. It fitted perfectly, and on catching sight of himself in the shower room mirror, he was surprised to see that he looked good. The deep green was shot through with silver tones which caused his chest to look broader and his arms stronger.

After a moment of self-admiration, Silas frowned. He knew more than most what true beauty was. Why was he deluding himself into thinking that anything about his external appearance really mattered?

'The ceremony is about to begin. Please follow me,' the Spire instructed. Swallowing nervously, Silas left the temporary safety of the guest suite.

This time the elevator opened on to a room full of people. And not just any people. Health, beauty and strength radiated from the most important and influential Seen from across the nation.

The far less beautiful sight, however, was the array of gleaming Biocubicles, set in ranks and all facing a raised platform on which stood another solitary Biocubicle.

Nervously, Silas stepped out of the elevator and eyed the people in front of him. Despite looking his best in the enhancing clothes, he was clearly the odd one out. He felt as if he had stumbled into the Gold 1 warm-up room at Vitality Clinic. Sticking to the edge of the room, he tried to remain unnoticed.

Helen Steele was nowhere to be seen. However, there were a few faces that Silas recognised. The first was Taylor Price. She was dressed in her Advisor uniform and seemed to be monitoring the crowd. Silas looked away before she saw him watching. He wasn't certain he could sustain a pretence of compliance in front of her.

Manager Gilroy from Vitality Clinic was in one corner talking to Terin Poltz, the presenter from *Prima Life*. A hovering camera was angled unobtrusively between them, recording the interview. Whatever Helen Steele was expecting, Silas was not going to defend her on *Prima Life*.

'Silas?' A hand gripped his shoulder.

'Dad?'

Surprise made his voice louder, drawing curious stares from the other guests.

'The Flawless Leader said that she had found you. Where have you been?' his father said through clenched teeth. 'I heard she was able to help you... so I wanted to check that you aren't going to do anything inappropriate.'

'No, Dad, it's not like that,' Silas said. 'She hasn't helped me; she wants control. You have to believe me. She's manipulating you. Helen Steele isn't what you think she is.'

'Enough!' he hissed angrily, tightening his grip on Silas' shoulder. 'You need to stop this nonsense. The Flawless Leader has been good to me... to us. Her backing and support has allowed Bio-health to develop in ways I could never have imagined. Allow me to have this, Silas, without spoiling it. It's the only good thing that's happened in... well... for many years.'

It was all said in a low voice, but his words cut deep. His father was blind, not only to the bad in Helen Steele, but to the faint possibility that Silas might just be right.

Before he could respond, a hush descended over the gathered guests. His father scowled at him, warning him to stay silent.

The lighting in the room dimmed, apart from one wall which began to change from white to blue and silver, then, starting from the top like the unfreezing of a waterfall, melted into soft folds and glided silently open to reveal Helen Steele.

Dressed in a white gown, she glowed with life. The simplicity of her clothing only served to emphasise her perfection. She truly was flawless.

'Welcome, friends.' She paused to allow her appearance to have the maximum impact, and her guests' murmurs of appreciation increased until they burst into a spontaneous round of applause.

Silas couldn't believe it. She had such power over them all. No one would ever challenge her, not until it was too late.

Helen Steele stepped forward and raised a hand to calm the enthusiasm of her guests.

'This is a new beginning for our nation, a new dawn. You already know that the Future Health programme has provided Biocubicles for every person, Unseen and Seen.'

Another round of applause followed this, and Helen Steele waited for it to settle. 'My dear friend, Anton, founder of Bio-health, has an even bigger vision, and today we will see that come to fruition.'

Everyone's eyes turned from the Flawless Leader to stare in their direction, and Silas felt a sudden tension emanate from his father's body.

'The long-promised vaccine is ready, and today we will walk boldly into the future. Not only will we find ourselves free from the prospect of a contagion, but we will also leap towards the complete eradication of the diseases that have plagued our great nation, and witness an end to the division of Unseen and Seen.'

'It's not ready,' Silas' father muttered through clenched teeth so only Silas could hear him. 'I told her that the vaccine isn't ready.'

It was the first time he had heard his father disagree with anything the Flawless Leader proposed, and it seemed as if Helen Steele must have heard his discontented murmur as well.

'Anton,' she gushed, moving towards him with all the confidence and power of a predator. 'My dear, dear friend, I am eternally grateful to you and the team at Bio-health. Without you, none of this would be possible. You began something that will change the course of our nation, and today, together, we will complete that.'

'But it's not…' Anton tried to explain; however, Helen Steele interrupted again.

'Let's show our appreciation for Anton Corelle, truly the saviour of our nation,' she instructed, leading him into the middle of the room and then standing back to allow him the centre stage.

A burst of applause filled the chamber. Everyone was clapping, and Silas felt he had better join in. The hovering camera floated towards Anton, who straightened his shoulders and puffed out his chest.

Silas felt deeply disappointed in his father. One tiny murmur of rebellion against the Flawless Leader had been completely squashed by his own vanity.

As the applause died down, Helen Steele motioned to the camera and positioned herself in front of the array of Biocubicles. His father hesitantly stepped away and returned to stand next to Silas, but instead of the glassy-eyed adoration that he usually wore after any time spent with Helen Steele, a confused frown wrinkled his brow.

With a chime, the familiar Viva party logo appeared in front of the Flawless Leader as she began her formal address to the nation.

'Dear friends. It is time for us to take a step forward, together, into the future. Today I am privileged to offer you a cure. Not only a cure for the contagion, but a cure for all sickness. We will make illness a dim memory. Unseen, Seen, we are in this together. You are my family, my children, and I will do what is best for you.' She walked elegantly towards the central Biocubicle, which slid open.

'Our Biocubicles are linked so we can share this moment together, as a nation. For health, for life, for a better tomorrow.' She stepped inside, and the door to the Biocubicle closed behind her. Her projection now came from within the cubicle. 'Please join me.'

As one, the crowd hurried to find an empty Biocubicle, not wanting to be left out from the great occasion, until only Silas and his father remained.

'What were you trying to say earlier?' his father asked, a desperate glint in his eye. 'About the Flawless Leader? How can she have the vaccine? Dr Veron took it…'

'Mr Corelle,' Taylor Price courteously interrupted. 'The Flawless Leader insists that all her guests participate. Allow me to escort you to an empty Biocubicle.'

Silas saw his father's frown deepen and knew he was about to argue with Taylor. His eyes fell to the disruptor held loosely in her hand. Silas didn't doubt her role.

'We are not going to keep our Flawless Leader waiting, are we, Dad?' He didn't even glance at Taylor, even though he felt her eyes on him. 'We can talk afterwards.'

His father didn't look convinced, but allowed Taylor to walk them to the last remaining empty Biocubicles. She watched them step inside and, as the door slid closed, Silas heard a faint clink. He reached for the manual override, but it didn't respond. He was locked in.

The Biocubicle com-link sprang to life and the Flawless Leader's face appeared in front of him. It was too close, too intimate, and he backed away until he was pressed against the wall.

Her brown eyes opened and she locked gazes with him. Every single person, young, old, Unseen, Seen, would be experiencing the same seemingly private moment with the Flawless Leader.

'Do not be alarmed if you experience discomfort. That is a normal part of the process. I am with you in this,' she said softly. 'We will journey together.'

'Come on, Dr Veron. Do something. Shut the network down,' Silas said under his breath. This would be the perfect moment for her to sabotage the vaccination programme. Unless… unless something had happened to her. Perhaps the Soulsight had worn off and she had resumed her work.

A feeling of dreadful despair coursed through him as the cubicle began to fill with a barely visible blue glow. Dr Veron had failed. The vaccination was going ahead as planned.

The blue developed into a rich purple haze. Silas braced himself for the painfully icy fingers of light to penetrate his skin, but instead the rays felt pleasantly warm. The flawless Leader had closed her eyes, a beatific smile across her face.

The light turned green, then yellow, and he felt it move beneath the outer layer of skin. But still it didn't hurt. Instead there was a heaviness to his body, as if he were standing in something denser than air. His muscles relaxed, as though all the tension and anxiety were being gently pressed out. The colour intensified, becoming golden, and then oscillating into shades that Silas didn't have words for. He felt wonderful and free. As the light reached his chest, it felt as if some cold part of his core was being slowly ignited, then blissful warmth spread from his heart outwards towards his fingertips and toes.

Gradually the sensation began to fade, but it didn't disappear completely. He closed his eyes to concentrate on the remaining buzzing static that made him feel vibrant and alive. The experience was so far removed from the horror he had witnessed in the laboratory. He had been expecting agony, but had received something that was more like a gift. He felt renewed and refreshed.

The tingling had almost completely subsided and, reluctantly, Silas opened his eyes.

The projection of Helen Steele still filled the front of his Biocubicle, the angelic smile lingering on her lips. However, instead of the rich brown of her irises, all Silas could see was thick, black shadows. Her flawless skin began to wrinkle and pucker, and her smile transformed into a twisted grimace.

Instantly, Silas understood. This was the Flawless Leader's true self... dark and fearful and full of hatred. He was looking into the eyes of a murderer. Choking tentacles of grey smoke bled from her pores, causing her face to writhe and swirl.

The vaccine must have retriggered some residual Soulsight in my system, he thought, shuddering with disgust at the image before him.

Then he heard the first scream. It was muffled by the walls of his Biocubicle, but whoever had screamed was clearly terrified. Suddenly there was more shouting and screaming, accompanied by the pounding of fists on unyielding metal. He could only assume that he wasn't the only person to be seeing the true heart of the Flawless Leader.

The projection of Helen Steele cocked her head as she also became aware of the growing discord. The pits of her eyes were now overflowing with darkness, and her image became monstrously distorted.

'Biocubicle, switch off the projection and open the door,' Silas instructed, trying the manual override again. Helen Steele's hideous form was filling his Biocubicle. He had to get away from her.

Suddenly the projection closed down, to be replaced with a new image.

He blinked and looked closer. How was this possible?

'Zoe?'

The contrast between Zoe and Helen Steele was as stark as light and dark. Silas reached forward to touch her face, but his hand went through the projection.

She seemed nervous, and a tiny flicker of fear dulled her eyes, then a voice that Silas recognised as Dr Veron's prompted her. 'You can speak now. They can hear you.'

The fear shadow was immediately quenched, and when Zoe looked directly into Silas' eyes, all he could see was love. 'Please do not be afraid,' she said, and Silas smiled at her projection.

'I am Zoe Veron, the daughter of Dr Esther Veron. You have been deceived by Helen Steele, but I am going to tell you the truth.'

The shouting and screaming from the other Biocubicles had died down. Everyone was listening to Zoe.

'Bio-health created a vaccine. It was going to transform the health of many Unseen and finally begin to break down some of the barriers between all people in our nation. But what the Flawless Leader failed to tell you was that for many of the Unseen, the vaccine would be deadly. This day, her "new day", would have seen the slaughter of tens of thousands of Unseen, whose only crime was to not fit one woman's idea of perfection. These Unseen would have died this morning standing in their personal Biocubicle, expecting a cure but only receiving pain and death.

'When my mother discovered this, she was left with a choice: to do as the Flawless Leader wanted and allow the vaccine that she had created, which had been intended for life and health, to be used as a weapon, or to show everyone the truth. She chose the truth.

'Helen Steele has lied to us all, about the FGS virus, about the vaccine, about the Biocubicles. We trusted her because we could only see her flawless exterior, but today you have seen past that, you are seeing her heart and her soul.

'The vaccine that you were expecting to receive today has been replaced by a substance called Soulsight. For as long as your Soulsight lasts, use it to see the truth in yourselves and in one another. Do not be afraid. Look for love in each other. Love will drive fear away.'

Chapter 39

With a faint clunk, the Biocubicle doors unlocked.

Silas peered out. The large room was still and unnaturally quiet.

He hurried to his father's Biocubicle. 'Dad,' he whispered, slowly pushing the door wide. His father was sitting on the floor of the cubicle, his head in his hands.

'Dad? It's me, Silas.'

'You knew what she was,' his father muttered through his fingers. 'You tried to tell me, but I wouldn't listen.'

At last his father raised his head. A heartbreaking combination of guilt and remorse gave his healthy skin a papery, sickly look.

'She tricked everyone,' Silas said, squatting down.

'Everyone except you. Look at you,' his father said admiringly. 'You are so… so good…'

'It's the Soulsight,' Silas explained, suddenly finding it difficult to swallow. He had never heard such open praise from his father. 'You can see who I truly am.'

'And me?'

'Yes, I see you too. It's going to be all right.'

A cry of alarm interrupted them, and Silas turned as several more of Helen Steele's guests stumbled from their Biocubicles. They were torn between recoiling from their own pitiful reflections and cowering away in fear from each other.

'The Veron woman has made us into Unseen!' the bloated form of Terin shrieked as she tried to bat away her accompanying camera. 'Stop filming me!'

'Didn't you listen to her?' someone else shouted. 'We are seeing the truth. Helen Steele lied to us. She was going to commit mass murder... and we were going to let her!'

The sound of more arguments broke out around the room. So much for 'looking for love in each other' Silas thought. This lot were going to tear each other to pieces.

'We need to get out of here. I can take you to Dr Veron. She can explain everything to you,' Silas told his father.

'You know where she is?'

'She's at the quarantine facility. Helen Steele was manipulating you both all along.'

Grabbing his father's arm, Silas began to steer him towards the swaying fabric doors of the concealed lift.

'Everyone, stay where you are and listen to me!' Helen Steele's voice filled the room.

The shouting subsided and everyone turned to look at the closed doors of the central Biocubicle.

'I am your Flawless Leader. Do not believe this deception by my enemies. I remain flawless, and only I know what is best for my nation.'

Silas gasped. Even now she couldn't tell the truth.

'Dr Veron has betrayed us. She has replaced the vaccine with a hallucinogenic substance. Return to your Biocubicles and wait until this phase passes. Dr Veron will be held accountable for her violation of our trust in her.'

'It's all a hallucination...' someone muttered. 'Of course, that makes sense.'

'No!' Silas shouted, letting go of his father's arm and moving back into the centre of the room. 'This is your only chance to see the truth. This is Soulsight.' Silas lifted his hands to his eyes. 'Look at me. You can see me, and I can see you. You have the ability to recognise the truth below the surface. Helen Steele is hiding in her Biocubicle because she doesn't want you to see her again for who she truly is. A liar; a killer!'

'You! Silas Corelle!' The hatred filled screech reminded Silas that Helen Steele was not the only monster in the room. Taylor was staring at her own reflection, one hand clawing at her pitted face and the other frantically rubbing the highly polished surface as if to wipe away the twisted image. Suddenly she turned to face Silas, hate and fear billowing from her in a swirling overspill of toxicity.

'I knew you were planning something. You and the girl, the fat one. Look what you have done to me!'

With a fluid and well-practised movement, she reached for her disruptor and aimed it at Silas.

Holding his ground, Silas tried to keep his terror in check. Bubba Gee had said that perfect love would drive fear away, but it was hard to find any shred of love or compassion in his heart towards Taylor.

'I have not done anything to you,' Silas said, trying to keep his voice calm. Her blind eye sockets flickered as she watched him, weighing his appearance more than his words, and some of the writhing hate seemed to settle. Warily, he took a step towards her.

'What you are now is not how you need to stay. You can change. I can show you how, but please, put the disruptor away. I see you, Taylor.'

'Don't,' she cried, her voice cracking as a sudden flare of mistrust clouded her appearance. 'Don't even look at me!'

'Return to your Biocubicles immediately,' Helen Steele's voice commanded again.

'We need to do what the Flawless Leader says.' Taylor looked at the other guests who were hurrying to hide themselves in their Biocubicles.

'She only wants everyone locked in so she can escape from being truly seen.'

'Silas is right.' The unexpected support came from his father. 'Just look at him. If the Flawless Leader has nothing to hide, then let her talk with us face to face.'

Silas' father moved towards the central Biocubicle. 'Basic setting voice recognition. Unlock function Anton Corelle.'

With the now familiar soft clunk, the Flawless Leader's Biocubicle began to open. Silas felt a frisson of terror at what he knew he was going to see, but he forced himself to keep watching.

She had her back to them, but an air of loathing and fear oozed from her undulating skin. A whimper escaped from Taylor as her hands, still holding the disruptor, fell slack to her sides.

'Close your eyes.' The command was given in the calm and soothing manner that the Flawless Leader always used. 'They have tricked you into seeing something that is not me. Listen to my voice. You know that I can protect you, but you cannot trust your eyes. So close them.'

Silas couldn't believe it as Taylor obeyed Helen Steele's command.

'Stop it,' Silas cried. 'Taylor, open your eyes! Look at her. You can see exactly what she is. This is not a trick or a hallucination. This is real. Don't let her tell you otherwise.'

'Shut up, shut up!' Taylor hissed, doubt and confusion mingling with her ever-present fear. Then Silas saw her eyelids flutter open, briefly, for a second, before opening fully.

It was painful as Taylor recognised the awful truth. The traits she had seen in herself were all far more developed in Helen Steele.

With a cry she raised the disruptor once more, but this time it was pointed at Helen Steele. 'You did this,' she cried, as her thumb pressed the Target Acquired button.

'Don't!' Silas shouted, rushing towards Taylor before she could complete the disruption. He knocked the weapon from her hands and he kicked it away. 'Killing her will make you even more like her, not less.' Gripping her shoulders, he looked deep into the pits of her eyes, searching for some goodness. 'If you come with us, I can take you to my friends. They will help you understand what has happened. You can change; you can start again.'

'Silas!' His father shouted a warning.

The Flawless Leader had left the cover of her Biocubicle and grabbed the disruptor. She was pointing it directly at Silas. Rage and loathing boiled from her. 'You could have been part of the future, Silas Corelle, but it seems you have refused my help at every stage. I was going to strengthen our nation, but you have undermined and weakened it. You will be cut away like the dead wood you are.'

'No one will trust you again,' Silas said. 'They know what you are doing now.'

'The nation loves me. My people listen to me. They will believe whatever I tell them to believe.' She gestured at the reflective wall of closed Biocubicle doors behind Silas. Every other guest had obediently returned to their cubicles. Only Silas, his father and Taylor were left to challenge her. 'When this Soulsight trick fades, I will still be here, ready to move us forward. You have merely delayed the inevitable. And as for you, I gave you every chance, but you are deluded. Stuck in a way of thinking that will bring the nation to its knees. If you are not for me, Silas, you are against me.'

With a sudden grimacing leer that split her face like a wound, she pressed the Disrupt button.

Time seemed to slow. His father lunged towards the Flawless Leader as Taylor pushed at Silas, forcing him to the floor. But he knew it was too late. There was no way to dodge the disruptor. Will it hurt? he thought, as screwing his eyes shut, he awaited the sensation of his brain shutting down.

A second passed, bringing the sweet realisation that he was still alive. The disruptor malfunctioned, he thought, as his eyes flew open.

He lay, sprawled across the floor where Taylor had pushed him, and his gaze fell on Helen Steele. She was changing, altering. The dark clouds that surrounded her rolled in, and the distortion of her body settled. For a millisecond she stood, a beautiful, perfect, flawless, yet utterly empty shell. Then her legs buckled and her lifeless body fell to the floor.

Taylor howled and ran to Helen Steele's side.

Silas and his father stared at one another.

'She didn't acquire another brainstem,' Taylor muttered, her voice thick with shock. 'The disruptor was still locked on to her. It hadn't been reset. Even with the weapon pointed away, she was too close...' Grief gripped her. Moved by her sorrow, Silas got up and stepped closer.

'You tried to protect me,' he said, amazed that even Taylor had kindness somewhere inside her.

'I did this!' Taylor's grief turned in on itself, morphing rapidly into a consumptive guilt. Looking sickly and weak, she continued to kneel by the beautiful form of Helen Steele. 'I acquired her, and she... the disruptor beam must have... I killed the Flawless Leader. She was perfect... beautiful. What have I done?!'

Silas frowned. 'It wasn't you. Helen Steele pressed the Disrupt button. This was self-inflicted...'

Anger suddenly coursed through Taylor's body, and Silas backed away. 'You will not label her with that! I did this and I will take the punishment.'

'Silas, leave her.' His father caught hold of his arm.

'But... she didn't do anything.'

'Look.' His father pointed at the globe of the drone camera hovering in the corner of the room. 'The truth will all come out. No one will blame Taylor. Now, I need to find Dr Veron.'

Chapter 40

The streets around the Spire were deserted, and the full impact of what Dr Veron had done started to sink in. For many people, the shock would be extreme. How many of them would believe the lie that the whole experience was merely a hallucination; and would they be able to understand or even care that their temporary alteration had been in order to save the lives of Unseen?

Silas and his father arrived at the quarantine facility to find the door in the wall wide open. Here, at last, there were people, spilling out of the front entrance. Silas assumed they were once Unseen, but with Soulsight it was impossible to tell. All he knew was the intoxicating joy of their new-found freedom that made him want to run and join them as in their ones and twos they headed into the Uninhabited district and away from the threat of quarantine.

'I didn't know,' Silas' father murmured, following Silas past the rows of open and empty Biocubicles. 'Helen Steele was going to use my work at Bio-health as a weapon… and then she was going to lay the blame for the Unseen deaths on me. I was so blind.'

'Everyone was, Dad,' Silas said.

'Hey!'

The shout came from behind them. Remembering the guards and their disruptors, Silas ducked into an open Biocubicle, dragging his father with him.

'"A victory is twice itself when the achiever brings home full numbers." I see you, Silas.' A deep booming laugh echoed down the row.

With an excited yelp, Silas released his father's arm and stepped out from the hiding place.

'Jono! I see you!' he cried out. His friend was striding between the long row of Biocubicles.

With a squeal of delight, Kesiah ducked under Jono's outstretched arm and raced towards Silas.

'We did it!' she said, throwing her arms around him in an extravagant embrace. 'Now everyone knows the truth.'

'I couldn't come back for you, Kes. I was taken to the Spire,' Silas said.

'I know,' she laughed, releasing him only to hug him again even tighter. 'Dr Veron explained when I went for my compliance procedure. She and Zoe then worked all night to reconfigure the Biocubicle network.'

'Er… Kesiah?' Silas' father seemed completely lost for words as he gazed in awe at Kes and then at Jono.

Kes let go of Silas. 'Hi, Mr Corelle,' she grinned.

'Is it just you two here?' Silas asked.

'Most people have gone,' she said.

'Did you find Marc and Bubba Gee?' Silas asked.

'Marc's here too?' Silas' father queried, his confusion growing.

'They've gone to Nana's house with some of the Unseen from the Outerlands. We're just checking that no one's been left behind,' replied Kes.

'What about the Health Advisors? Didn't they try to stop you? And where's Zoe?'

'The Advisors were terrified. They thought they had become Unseen. Most abandoned their posts, although I think a few are still hiding in their Biocubicles. Zoe is in the living quarters with Dr Veron.'

There was something in her tone, a note of caution that made Silas anxious. He rushed towards the stairs, with his friends and his father struggling to keep up.

'Zoe?' Silas called as they entered the deserted laboratory. The door to the living quarters was wedged open.

'Silas, you're here!' Zoe cried, hurrying into the room. She studied him carefully. 'My mother told me what the Flawless Leader had planned for you.'

'It's OK. I'm still me,' he smiled, pulling her into his arms. 'But you... you are brilliant. I couldn't believe it when your projection appeared in the Biocubicle.'

A stain of worry crumpled her appearance, and she drew back from him.

'What is it? What's the matter?'

'Replacing the vaccine was my mother's plan. She wanted everyone to understand the truth. Except she wasn't prepared for her own transformation. The things that the Flawless Leader made her do have left her changed. The human experimentation, the fatalities... she's knotted up with guilt. As soon as she knew the Unseen were safe, she locked herself in the Biocubicle.'

'Maybe I could talk to her? I know what she's going through. I was just as influenced by Helen Steele. Esther might listen to me,' Silas' father said, and his ageing anxiety began to soften as it was replaced by compassion.

Silas and Zoe sat with their backs leaning against the roof-edge wall, waiting for his father. Hesitantly, Silas described Helen Steele's final act of hate that had resulted in her own death.

'So what now?' Zoe asked.

'I don't know,' Silas said. 'It should be a time for celebration. Look at Jono.'

The sun was high in the sky and the roof was bathed in warm light. Jono and Kesiah wandered hand in hand around the perimeter, and Jono angled his head to bask in the bright rays. Silas hoped the rest of the nation's Unseen were also enjoying this window of freedom. It was like a mass initiation. There would be a time of confusion, but as Soulsight diminished, would the lessons last?

'Zoe, your mother would like a word,' Anton said, emerging onto the roof space.

'Is Dr Veron all right?' Silas asked, as Zoe made her way back down to the living quarters.

'She's conflicted,' he said. 'We were all deceived, but she needs time to find peace. She believes she must be held accountable for her involvement and is insisting on going to the Health and Safety courts for judgement.'

Silas frowned. 'But she saved hundreds of Unseen.'

'I know,' his father said. 'But she believes the right thing to do is to be tried and sentenced. She has asked me to go with her. She wants Zoe to return to her grandmother's house. I don't know what the outcome will be, so stay with Zoe until I get back.'

Zoe was subdued as they walked back through the Uninhabited district.

'Mum will be all right, won't she?'

'Everyone has seen the truth, Zoe,' Silas said, holding her hand tightly in his.

It became busier when they approached the Inhabited district, as a few of the braver citizens ventured outside. It was impossible to tell who were Seen and who were Unseen. Just like the Community, Silas thought. External appearance was lost beneath a mixture of wonder and trepidation, bewilderment and joy.

The four friends drew admiring stares as they passed, but it was Jono who received the most attention.

'Why are they looking at me?' he said under his breath.

Silas glanced back at his friend. The self-sacrificial love that had matured during his time in the caverns caring for William was now further embellished by security and deep happiness. It was shocking to believe that Jono's life had been considered worthless by Helen Steele. 'Because you are the best of us,' he said with a huge grin.

Gone was the subterfuge of the secret meetings at Nana's house. Her front door was flung wide open, and the noise of laughter mingled with excited chatter spilled out on to the street. Here was the celebration that Silas had been expecting.

Across the crowded front room, Silas spotted Mags. 'My brother!' she shouted, pointing at the man next to her, whose exuberant happiness perfectly matched his sister's.

Bonnie was sitting on the floor, keeping an eye on the twins as they played with an assortment of Nana's ornaments. Jono immediately pushed past Silas, eager to reach baby William.

'Jono, I see you,' Bonnie cried, as he crouched down. William immediately stretched out his arms, his childish features suffused with trust and love.

Leaving Jono and Kes playing with William; Silas and Zoe headed through the house to the nutrition area. Zoe pushed the door open, and the rich aroma of freshly cooked stew billowed into the hallway.

'Zoe!' Nana cried, abandoning the pot of bubbling stew to embrace her. 'You were spectacular; you've turned Prima upside down. You've turned the nation upside down! Is your mother with you?'

'She's gone to the Health and Safety courts,' Zoe explained. 'There are things that happened at the quarantine that she feels responsible for.'

Nana laughed. 'The whole nation has seen what Esther is responsible for. She has saved so many lives – you both have. My granddaughter and daughter are heroes.'

'This calls for a toast!' Bubba Gee was sitting at the table, proffering drinks from a large glass flask. The man next to him politely declined. Silas didn't recognise him at first. The fully developed soul, brimming with courage and compassion, was remarkable. Then it dawned on him.

'Marc?'

Chapter 41

Bubba Gee dragged a chair up for Silas.

'I see you, Silas,' he said gruffly, sipping his pungent-smelling drink.

'I see you, Bubba Gee. What is that? Waterberry rum?'

'Alas, no,' Bubba Gee smiled wistfully. 'This is rowan rum. Vastly inferior. Would you like to try some?'

'No, thank you,' Silas said, catching Marc's eye and grinning. 'I saw you and Bubba Gee trying to break into the quarantine facility. It was a brave thing to do.'

'And everyone saw you challenging the Flawless Leader. I couldn't let you be the only one to stand up against her.'

'Marc contacted us and offered to help,' Bubba Gee explained, 'and it would have been the perfect plan, if it had worked.'

'What happened at the Spire?' Marc asked Silas. 'We've only heard rumours so far.'

Silas shook his head. 'I'll tell you later,' he replied, glancing to where Nana was still excitedly embracing Zoe.

More people arrived, and the volume increased as someone discovered that the exercise pacemaker system was rigged to play music. The gathering developed into a party, and Nana's stew and Bubba Gee's rowan rum were liberally distributed.

New acquaintances developed into firm friendships as Seen and Unseen segregation was forgotten. Marc and Jono were deep in conversation in one corner. Zoe, Mags and Kes were chatting to a surprisingly content Derry. Bubba Gee and Nana were holding the twins as Bonnie helped Mags' brother perform a slow and clumsy dance in the centre of the room.

Silas had never felt so happy. This was what he had missed – all the love, freedom and honesty of the Community, but this time it was happening right here in Prima.

It was nearing evening when Silas' father arrived with Dr Veron. Guilt still weighed her down, but the volume of love that greeted her began to thaw her self-condemnation.

Bubba Gee began the impromptu initiation by calling out in his deep voice, 'Esther Veron, see as you are fully seen.'

'I see you, Mum,' Zoe cried from across the room, lifting her hand to her eyes and then pointing towards her mother.

The cry was echoed by all Nana's guests, and as tears coursed down Dr Veron's cheeks, it was as if her reproach was being washed away.

Initially the party seemed as if it would continue for as long as the Soulsight lasted, but eventually the guests began to disperse. Pleading exhaustion, Dr Veron excused herself before going upstairs. Zoe was quick to follow her, but first found Silas.

'I need to stay with Mum tonight,' she said, 'but come over first thing tomorrow.'

He held her close. 'First thing,' he echoed, kissing her goodnight.

Bonnie and the twins were next to leave, and Silas and Jono helped carry the sleepy children to a waiting Autocar.

'We're going to head home too,' said Marc, as he and their father joined Silas in waving Bonnie off.

'Do you want to come with us?' Silas asked Jono, as his brother and father walked away. 'We have a spare bed. All Nana can offer is the floor… or she has a cellar.'

'I might stay a bit longer,' Jono grinned.

'Kes?' Silas asked.

'"If thou rememb'rest not the slightest folly That ever love did make thee run into, Thou hast not loved."'

'Sure… as long as you "rememb'rest" that you turned down a comfortable bed for the night. I'll see you in the morning,' Silas cried, running to catch up with his father and Marc.

272

'What happened at the courts?' Silas heard Marc ask as he fell into step beside them.

'They were deserted,' his father shrugged. 'I suggested that Dr Veron should leave a recorded confession. Then we went to Bio-health and disabled the Biocubicle network.'

'But that's your work… that's everything.' Marc was aghast.

'Look at me,' Anton said. 'You can see that I've done the right thing.'

Silas stared at his father. A tranquillity had settled around him.

'The Biocubicles were meant to help us, but in the wrong hands, look at what they became… a weapon. I need to put in new safeguards.'

'But what about the vaccine – that could still be used to protect and cure so many?' Silas protested.

'When people are ready to trust the Biocubicles, to trust me and Dr Veron, then we can offer the vaccine. Tomorrow, when the Soulsight wears off, we will discuss how we can best help the Unseen.'

Silas slept fitfully. His dreams were full of Helen Steele. Her grotesque true form was clutching at him, trying to consume and destroy him. As he tried to escape, he found he was trapped in a doorless Biocubicle.

Waking up in a sweat, he pushed his crumpled bedding away.

'It's a dream,' he muttered as his racing heart began to settle. 'She's gone. House, is it morning?'

'It is 06:13,' the house responded.

Wondering if it was too early to go to Zoe and Nana's, he stared around his room. The newly installed Biocubicle sat waiting in the corner. And there it will stay, waiting, Silas thought. Today there are no levels to achieve, no targets to attain. Nothing but the chance to be with Zoe and Jono and Kes.

Feeling the potential for a whole day begin to unlock, Silas wandered into the bathroom and caught sight of his reflection.

He stopped and stepped closer. Despite his disturbing dreams, an underlying happiness had given him a striking serenity.

'I'm still seeing with Soulsight,' he said with surprise, running his hand over the mirror.

His father was in the health suite, but the equipment remained untouched.

'Dad?' Silas stood alongside him in front of the large mirrored wall.

'Isn't it supposed to have worn off?' Anton answered, gazing at his altered reflection.

'Normally, yes,' Silas agreed. 'Perhaps it's lasting longer this time because…'

'… of the Biocubicles,' his father finished, turning to face him. 'But why would that make a difference? Unless the weighted light acted as an enhancer.'

Silas looked thoughtfully at his father. 'How much more time do you think we will get? An extra day?'

'I don't know, but everyone will be looking to Bio-health for some kind of answer. I'll com Dr Veron. I'll have to meet her at the quarantine facility and run some tests. Will you be all right on your own? Yesterday was unpleasant with Helen Steele. It was a lot to face and… I mean, you look good, at peace, but…'

'I'll be fine,' Silas nodded. 'I was going to go to Nana's, anyway.'

'Silas, I see you,' Nana cried, opening the door. 'Isn't it wonderful? It is like being at the Community but even more so. The Soulsight isn't fading away.'

'I see you.' Silas grinned with shared delight.

'Come in. Zoe's in the nutrition room.'

Jono, Zoe and Kesiah were sitting around the table, discussing the continuing Soulsight.

'At last!' Zoe said happily, as Silas walked in. 'I thought we were going to have to come and find you. We want to show

Jono around Prima, in the daytime, before the Soulsight wears off, and Kes thinks we should take him to the tree.'

They started by going to Vitality Clinic, but their happy chatter and laughter attracted attention. Faces peered from hastily darkened windows, and the less fearful ventured from their homes to shout questions.

'What's happened to us? Why are we still like this?'

'Who are you? Are you Advisors?'

'Where are you going? Can we come with you?'

As Jono stopped to explain once more about the lingering effects of Soulsight, a crowd began to gather.

'Shall we skip the city tour and go straight to the tree?' Zoe suggested, as more people drifted towards them. 'I think this lot seem to be about to make Jono their new Flawless Leader.'

Silas pushed through to where Jono was. 'Tell them to go home. That seeing things as they truly are will free them; that they don't need a leader but they can be led by truth - or something like that,' he said.

'Why me?' Jono asked.

'They will listen to you. Look at them, they trust you,' Kes agreed, squeezing in beside Silas.

'"Some have greatness thrust upon them,"' Jono murmured, looking at the growing numbers of confused and fearful people. 'Friends,' he began, 'lend me your ears.'

Silas rolled his eyes at Jono's dramatic tone, but the crowd seemed ready to listen, and a respectful silence fell.

'Look around you. This is not a time for fear, but for celebration. A time to see the truth, and to enjoy a new freedom. For "we know what we are now, but not what we may become". You have been encouraged to find the love in one another, for that is what will drive fear away. The answers are not to be found out there but in here.' He pressed his hand to his chest. 'And in here.' His hand drifted out to the crowd. 'So now, truly see one another for the first time.'

The fear diminished as the people surrounding Jono obediently began to look at one another. Silas grabbed Jono's elbow and pulled him into a side alley.

'We can go this way,' he said. 'Quick, or they'll all start following.'

'I feel bad for them,' Zoe said looking over her shoulder. 'It's like they don't know how to *be* without someone telling them.'

'They'll work it out, maybe even before the Soulsight wears off,' Silas said. He led them through the maze of back routes and forgotten streets, and soon they were in the heart of the Uninhabited district.

'This is more like it,' Jono said, as they reached the cottage ruins. He took a couple of steps backwards to fully appreciate the height and girth of the tree.

'It looks a bit bare in winter,' Silas said apologetically. 'I've started a platform, but it's not nearly as impressive as your home was in the Community.'

But Jono had already kicked his shoes off and, with a small hop, placed one foot on the trunk and swung his other leg and arm around the lower branch.

A moment later he was shouting down. 'This is good! We can push the walls up higher at the back. See what other wood you can find in that old cottage, because I should be able to get started on a roof!'

The difference made by Jono's expertise and enthusiasm was remarkable. After a couple of hours, there was enough of a shelter so that when the sky suddenly darkened and drops of rain began to fall, they could huddle to the back of the platform and stay dry.

The rain grew heavier until it washed past them in vast opaque sheets.

'It's like a waterfall,' Zoe shouted over the noise as they settled in the hut to watch the ferocity of the cloudburst.

Content and secure, Silas glanced at his friends. He felt so proud of them and of who they truly were. Even when the Soulsight faded, he felt sure he would know the real them. But everyone else would only see the exterior. Kesiah the Gold Standard; Jono the outcast Unseen; and himself and Zoe fitting somewhere in between. If only he could keep this moment forever.

He sighed.

'Are you OK?' Zoe asked, leaning into him.

He nodded, wrapping his arms around her. 'I just don't want this... us... Soulsight... to end.'

'We won't let it,' she said, and, despite his unease, he believed her.

Chapter 42

Eventually, hunger motivated them to abandon the tree and return to Nana's house.

It was nearly dark as they herded through Nana's front door and into the welcoming warmth of the nutrition room. Hoping to see a pot of stew bubbling on the stove, Silas was a little disappointed to see an empty pan.

'You're back,' Nana said, emerging from the lounge. Behind her came Marc and Bubba Gee.

'Hi, Nana. We've been showing Jono around, but we couldn't stay in the Inhabited district because people were following him,' Zoe said.

'We've been catching up on some family history.' Nana smiled at Marc.

'We were talking about Mum, about what she was like,' Marc explained, and Silas heard the emotional catch in his brother's voice.

'I believe she would have been very pleased with both of her sons,' Bubba Gee said warmly.

'Any news from Dad or Dr Veron?' Silas asked.

'They have asked *Prima Life* to air an update. It'll be broadcast soon.'

Nana didn't have a separate Image room, so the quality of the projection was poor. The spinning golden torch emblem flickered in the middle of the nutrition room, and Silas half-expected to see Helen Steele's image step forward. Instead, a voice filled the room.

'Good evening, Prima. This is your reporter, Terin Poltz. We at *Prima Life* are still experiencing certain... technical hitches, and cannot offer a projected image.'

'She doesn't want anyone to see her true self,' Silas muttered.

The disembodied voice continued. 'Following the dramatic events that are still unfolding across the nation, I have been able to secure an exclusive interview with Anton Corelle from Bio-health. Anton, are you there?'

'Good evening, Terin.' Silas' father confidently stepped into the projection, then to their surprise, Dr Veron also walked into the camera eyeline. Although marred by traces of guilt, her courage added a raw strength to her appearance.

'Can you give any more information as to the lingering visual disturbances that we are experiencing? Can we expect things to return to normal?' asked Terin.

Silas' father seemed to weigh the question carefully. 'I am not sure that the "normal" world that Helen Steele was moving us towards is something we should ever want to return to. I would like to start by reminding you that under her control, the Biocubicles had been set to initiate a vaccine that would have killed many of our Unseen brothers and sisters. To protect those innocent lives, Dr Veron made a difficult decision. She replaced the vaccine with Soulsight. It was intended to be an emergency measure, to produce a temporary state where we could recognise the truth behind the lies we had been told. We all saw Helen Steele for who she was.'

An image of the Flawless Leader's transformation sprung into Silas' mind. Her projection had been so close, so terrifying...

Dr Veron began to speak. 'We have investigated the phenomenon. The weighted light in the new Biocubicle appears to have acted as a catalyst and triggered a fusion of Soulsight throughout the cells and synapses of the nervous system. We are unable to exactly determine how long the effects will last. Perhaps a week, a month, but given the disposition of the nervous system, I am inclined to believe that the effects may well be of a more…' she hesitated and glanced at Silas' father before continuing, '…*permanent* nature.

'I can see the real you, and you can see the real me… a somewhat frightening prospect in part. All my faults, my guilt; but most importantly you can see the truth, no more masks or deception,' she continued. 'And I ask you this… Can a nation be changed? Without violence or the shedding of innocent blood? A whole nation be made anew? This is the opportunity, the gift, the second chance we have been given.'

Dr Veron looked again at Silas' father, who nodded in agreement. 'We knew only one way of life,' he took up the theme. 'We were consumed by the importance of physical health and fitness. We believed it was the correct and responsible way to live; and there is truth in that. Physical training is of some value, but character and goodness are of value for all things. I have come to see that now. We naively followed Helen Steele's promise of a future with no more sickness, no more imperfections. But we were blind to both the beauties and the sicknesses of the soul beneath the exterior. Her way was leading us all to death.'

A smaller projection began to run alongside Dr Veron, and Silas gulped as he recognised himself faced by the true form of Helen Steele. Cruel, angry and utterly ruthless, she lifted the disruptor.

'It's the recording from Terin Poltz's camera,' Silas muttered faintly. He felt Zoe's hand reach for his as the scene replayed. Taylor's attempt to push him out of the way, his father moving to intercept and then the moment that the disruptor homed in on Helen Steele's pre-acquired brainstem, and she began to revert to a beautiful, empty shell as her brain shut down.

Silas' father was still talking as the image faded away. 'That was the truth of Helen Steele. The way of death ultimately led her to her own demise. I no longer want to be part of that future. But now we are presented with an alternative. A new way. One that embraces life in all its diversity and richness.'

Hope shone from his father and from Dr Veron. It triggered a response in Silas as certainty kindled in his own heart. He had known what it was like to live with Soulsight, when he had been at the Community. There he had been truly free, and now, here was a chance for everyone to live in that freedom.

'So in answer to your question, Terin, things will not return to normal. The Biocubicle network is disabled. However, for those Unseen who would have benefited from Dr Veron's work and the vaccine, Bio-health will run tailored treatment sessions. Change is upon us, and there will be more changes to come. As a nation we will learn this new way, one that is not built on outward appearance, or on physical strength, or on might, but one that has different foundations. We can be a nation where what is valued is whole hearts and souls.'

Silas looked around the room. Joy and amazement lit every face. Here were his closest friends and family – Kes, Jono, Nana, Bubba Gee, Zoe and Marc. Nothing would keep them apart any more.

'We are no longer Seen and Unseen,' his father continued, confirming Silas' thoughts. 'We have something different. We have Soulsight that doesn't fade. We have Soulvision. Together, as one people, we are changed, and this is just the beginning.'

Jono's Shakespearean quotes in order of appearance:

Twelfth Night, Act 5 scene 1
Twelfth Night, Act 2 scene 2
Henry IV, Part II, Act 2 Scene 1
Romeo and Juliet, Act 2 scene 2
Romeo and Juliet, Act 2 scene 2
Romeo and Juliet, Act 2 scene 2
As You Like It, Act 3 scene 4 (emphasis and alteration, author's own)
The Tempest, Act 3 scene 1
Love's Labour's Lost, Act 4 scene 3
Julius Caesar, Act 4 scene 3
Much Ado About Nothing, Act 1 scene 1
As You Like It, Act 2 scene 4
Twelfth Night, Act 2 scene 5
Julius Caesar, Act 3 scene 2
Hamlet, Act 4 scene 5

Have you read *Soulsight*, the prequel to *Soulvision*?

Fitter… faster… stronger… perfection… success!

This is all Silas knows… until he meets new-girl, Zoe.

What is she hiding beneath the surface, and what does she know about the mysterious Community?

Will he risk everything to uncover the truth… then risk everything to protect it?

Silas' world gets turned upside down as he experiences the terror… and wonder… of SOULSIGHT.